# A STARLESS CLAN

# WARRIORS

## SHADOW

# ERIN
# HUNTER

**HARPER**

*An Imprint of* HarperCollins*Publishers*

ISBN 978-0-06-305021-1 (hardcover)

Typography by Jessie Gang
23 24 25 26 27 LBC 5 4 3 2 1

First Edition

A STARLESS CLAN

# WARRIORS

## SHADOW

# WARRIORS

## A STARLESS CLAN

*Book One: River*
*Book Two: Sky*
*Book Three: Shadow*

*Special thanks to Cherith Baldry*

# ALLEGIANCES

## THUNDERCLAN

**LEADER**    **BRAMBLESTAR**—dark brown tabby tom with amber eyes

**DEPUTY**    **SQUIRRELFLIGHT**—dark ginger she-cat with green eyes and one white paw

**MEDICINE CATS**    **JAYFEATHER**—gray tabby tom with blind blue eyes

**ALDERHEART**—dark ginger tom with amber eyes

**WARRIORS**    (toms and she-cats without kits)

**WHITEWING**—white she-cat with green eyes

**BIRCHFALL**—light brown tabby tom

**MOUSEWHISKER**—gray-and-white tom

**BAYSHINE**—golden tabby tom

**POPPYFROST**—pale tortoiseshell-and-white she-cat

**LILYHEART**—small, dark tabby she-cat with white patches and blue eyes

**NIGHTHEART**—black tom

**BUMBLESTRIPE**—very pale gray tom with black stripes

**CHERRYFALL**—ginger she-cat

**MOLEWHISKER**—brown-and-cream tom

**CINDERHEART**—gray tabby she-cat

**FINCHLIGHT**—tortoiseshell she-cat

**BLOSSOMFALL**—tortoiseshell-and-white she-cat with petal-shaped white patches

**IVYPOOL**—silver-and-white tabby she-cat with dark blue eyes

**EAGLEWING**—ginger she-cat

**MYRTLEBLOOM**—pale brown she-cat

**DEWNOSE**—gray-and-white tom

**THRIFTEAR**—dark gray she-cat

**STORMCLOUD**—gray tabby tom

**HOLLYTUFT**—black she-cat

**FERNSONG**—yellow tabby tom

**HONEYFUR**—white she-cat with yellow splotches

**SPARKPELT**—orange tabby she-cat

**SORRELSTRIPE**—dark brown she-cat

**TWIGBRANCH**—gray she-cat with green eyes

**FINLEAP**—brown tom

**SHELLFUR**—tortoiseshell tom

**FERNSTRIPE**—gray tabby she-cat

**PLUMSTONE**—black-and-ginger she-cat

**FLIPCLAW**—brown tabby tom

**LEAFSHADE**—tortoiseshell she-cat

**LIONBLAZE**—golden tabby tom with amber eyes

**QUEENS**
(she-cats expecting or nursing kits)

**DAISY**—cream long-furred cat from the horseplace

**SPOTFUR**—spotted tabby she-cat (mother to Bristlekit, an orange-and-white tabby she-kit; Stemkit, an orange tabby tom; and Graykit, a white tom with gray spots)

**ELDERS**   (former warriors and queens, now retired)

THORNCLAW—golden-brown tabby tom

CLOUDTAIL—long-haired white tom with blue eyes

BRIGHTHEART—white she-cat with ginger patches

BRACKENFUR—golden-brown tabby tom

# SHADOWCLAN

**LEADER**   TIGERSTAR—dark brown tabby tom

**DEPUTY**   CLOVERFOOT—gray tabby she-cat

**MEDICINE CATS**   PUDDLESHINE—brown tom with white splotches

SHADOWSIGHT—gray tabby tom

**WARRIORS**   TAWNYPELT—tortoiseshell she-cat with green eyes

STONEWING—white tom

SCORCHFUR—dark gray tom with slashed ears

FLAXFOOT—brown tabby tom

SPARROWTAIL—large brown tabby tom

SNOWBIRD—pure white she-cat with green eyes

YARROWLEAF—ginger she-cat with yellow eyes

BERRYHEART—black-and-white she-cat

GRASSHEART—pale brown tabby she-cat

WHORLPELT—gray-and-white tom

HOPWHISKER—calico she-cat

BLAZEFIRE—white-and-ginger tom

**FLOWERSTEM**—silver she-cat

**SNAKETOOTH**—honey-colored tabby she-cat

**SLATEFUR**—sleek gray tom

**POUNCESTEP**—gray tabby she-cat

**LIGHTLEAP**—brown tabby she-cat

**GULLSWOOP**—white she-cat

**SPIRECLAW**—black-and-white tom

**FRINGEWHISKER**—white she-cat with brown splotches

**HOLLOWSPRING**—black tom

**SUNBEAM**—brown-and-white tabby she-cat

QUEENS     **DOVEWING**—pale gray she-cat with green eyes (mother to Birchkit, a light brown tom)

**CINNAMONTAIL**—brown tabby she-cat with white paws (mother to Firkit, a brown tabby tom, Streamkit, a gray tabby she-kit, Bloomkit, a black she-kit, and Whisperkit, a gray tom)

ELDERS     **OAKFUR**—small brown tom

# SKYCLAN

LEADER     **LEAFSTAR**—brown-and-cream tabby she-cat with amber eyes

DEPUTY     **HAWKWING**—dark gray tom with yellow eyes

MEDICINE CATS     **FRECKLEWISH**—mottled light brown tabby she-cat with spotted legs

**FIDGETFLAKE**—black-and-white tom

MEDIATOR     **TREE**—yellow tom with amber eyes

**WARRIORS**

**SPARROWPELT**—dark brown tabby tom

**MACGYVER**—black-and-white tom

**DEWSPRING**—sturdy gray tom

**ROOTSPRING**—yellow tom

**NEEDLECLAW**—black-and-white she-cat

**PLUMWILLOW**—dark gray she-cat

**SAGENOSE**—pale gray tom

**KITESCRATCH**—reddish-brown tom

**HARRYBROOK**—gray tom

**CHERRYTAIL**—fluffy tortoiseshell-and-white she-cat

**CLOUDMIST**—white she-cat with yellow eyes

**TURTLECRAWL**—tortoiseshell she-cat

**RABBITLEAP**—brown tom

**WRENFLIGHT**—golden tabby she-cat

**REEDCLAW**—small pale tabby she-cat
**APPRENTICE, BEETLEPAW** (white-and-black tabby tom)

**MINTFUR**—gray tabby she-cat with blue eyes

**NETTLESPLASH**—pale brown tom

**TINYCLOUD**—small white she-cat

**PALESKY**—black-and-white she-cat

**VIOLETSHINE**—black-and-white she-cat with yellow eyes

**BELLALEAF**—pale orange she-cat with green eyes

**QUAILFEATHER**—white tom with crow-black ears

**PIGEONFOOT**—gray-and-white she-cat

**GRAVELNOSE**—tan tom

**SUNNYPELT**—ginger she-cat
**APPRENTICE, BEEPAW** (white-and-tabby she-cat)

**NECTARSONG**—brown she-cat

QUEENS    **BLOSSOMHEART**—ginger-and-white she-cat (mother to Ridgekit, a reddish she-kit with a white nose, and Duskkit, a white tom with brown paws and ears)

ELDERS    **FALLOWFERN**—pale brown she-cat who has lost her hearing

# WINDCLAN

LEADER    **HARESTAR**—brown-and-white tom

DEPUTY    **CROWFEATHER**—dark gray tom

MEDICINE CATS    **KESTRELFLIGHT**—mottled gray tom with white splotches like kestrel feathers
**APPRENTICE, WHISTLEPAW** (gray tabby she-cat)

WARRIORS    **NIGHTCLOUD**—black she-cat

**BRINDLEWING**—mottled brown she-cat

**APPLESHINE**—yellow tabby she-cat

**LEAFTAIL**—dark tabby tom with amber eyes

**WOODSONG**—brown she-cat

**EMBERFOOT**—gray tom with two dark paws

**BREEZEPELT**—black tom with amber eyes

**HEATHERTAIL**—light brown tabby she-cat with blue eyes

**FEATHERPELT**—gray tabby she-cat

**CROUCHFOOT**—ginger tom

**SONGLEAP**—tortoiseshell she-cat

**SEDGEWHISKER**—light brown tabby she-cat

**FLUTTERFOOT**—brown-and-white tom

**SLIGHTFOOT**—black tom with white flash on his chest

**OATCLAW**—pale brown tabby tom

**HOOTWHISKER**—dark gray tom

**QUEENS**   **LARKWING**—pale brown tabby she-cat (mother to Stripekit, a gray tabby tom, and Brookkit, a black-and-white tom)

**ELDERS**   **WHISKERNOSE**—light brown tom

**GORSETAIL**—very pale gray-and-white she-cat with blue eyes

# RIVERCLAN

**MEDICINE CATS**   **MOTHWING**—dappled golden she-cat
**APPRENTICE, FROSTPAW** (light gray she-cat)

**WARRIORS**   **DUSKFUR**—brown tabby she-cat

**MINNOWTAIL**—dark gray-and-white she-cat

**MALLOWNOSE**—light brown tabby tom

**HAVENPELT**—black-and-white she-cat

**PODLIGHT**—gray-and-white tom

**SHIMMERPELT**—silver she-cat

**LIZARDTAIL**—light brown tom

**SNEEZECLOUD**—gray-and-white tom

**BRACKENPELT**—tortoiseshell she-cat

**SPLASHTAIL**—brown tabby tom

**FOGNOSE**—gray-and-white she-cat

**HARELIGHT**—white tom

**ICEWING**—white she-cat with blue eyes
**APPRENTICE, MISTPAW** (tortoiseshell-and-white tabby she-cat)

**OWLNOSE**—brown tabby tom

**GORSECLAW**—white tom with gray ears

**NIGHTSKY**—dark gray she-cat with blue eyes

**BREEZEHEART**—brown-and-white she-cat
**APPRENTICE, GRAYPAW** (silver tabby tom)

## ELDERS

**MOSSPELT**—tortoiseshell-and-white she-cat

A STARLESS CLAN

WARRIORS

SHADOW

CAT VIEW

GREENLEAF TWOLEGPLACE

TWOLEG NEST

TWOLEG PATH

TWOLEG PATH

CLEARING

SHADOWCLAN CAMP

HALFBRIDGE

SMALL THUNDERPATH

GREENLEAF TWOLEGPLACE

HALFBRIDGE

ISLAND

STREAM

RIVERCLAN CAMP

HORSEPLACE

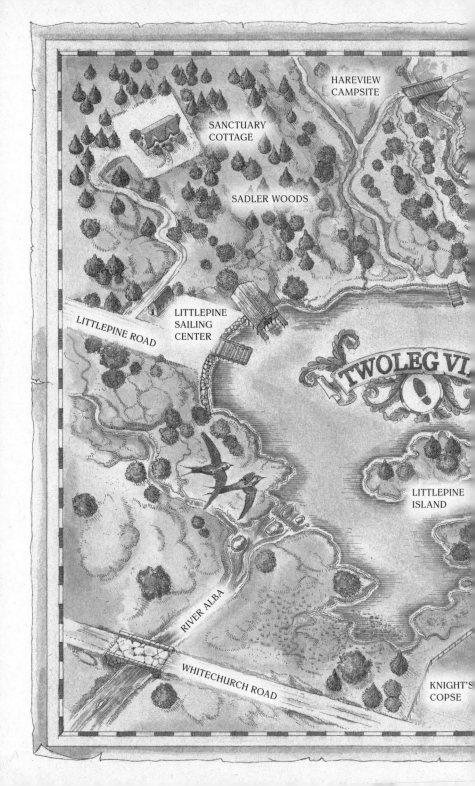

# PROLOGUE

❧

*StarClan help me!*

Berryheart flailed helplessly, struggling to free herself from Darktail's claws. But they dug deep into her shoulders, and she could feel her strength ebbing, swamped by an overwhelming wave of pain. In spite of all her efforts, the water of the lake closed over her head.

*This evil cat has destroyed ShadowClan!* The thought wrapped her mind in a fog of despair. *And I helped him. . . .*

When Darktail had first arrived in the forest, Berryheart remembered how persuasive the rogue had been. He had lured her and several of her Clanmates to abandon Shadow-Clan and join the group he called his Kin. Only later had she realized that he intended to bring the whole forest under his evil claws. Any cat who disagreed with him became the target of his vicious anger.

*Just like me . . . What a flea-brain I was!*

As water filled her nose and ears, Berryheart summoned the last of her courage. She had to live. She had to put right the wrong she had done.

*I have to save my Clan—all the Clans—from this invader!*

Berryheart let herself go limp, as if she had finally succumbed to the smothering water. To her relief she felt Darktail's grip relax; a heartbeat later his powerful hind legs thrust her away, farther into the lake. She let herself float below the surface, the wavering sunlight just above her head, holding her breath for as long as she could.

When the ache in her chest became too much to bear, Berryheart braced herself to start swimming. *Have I drifted far enough?* she wondered anxiously. But she couldn't delay any longer. *This is my last chance!*

She kicked out until her head broke the surface and she could snatch a breath. She kept expecting to hear Darktail's voice behind her, howling curses as she swam out of his reach. While he didn't seem to have spotted her, the fear alone was enough to force every last scrap of strength into her straining muscles.

*I'm no RiverClan cat,* she thought. *But Darktail will never catch me now.*

Her strength was draining away when at last the bank of the far side of the lake loomed in front of her. Gasping with relief, she pulled herself up onto dry ground and gave her pelt a good shake. When she looked around, she saw a thick bank of ferns just ahead that gave way to dense shrubs and forest trees. *This looks like RiverClan territory.*

Tottering on legs that felt ready to give way, Berryheart headed into the undergrowth and collapsed, shivering, on the soft debris beneath an elder bush. All she wanted was to run back to ShadowClan, but there was no ShadowClan left to run to.

As she tried feebly to groom the water out of her fur, Berry-heart promised herself that if ShadowClan could ever be restored, if Rowanstar and her Clanmates ever forgave her for following Darktail and allowed her to come home, she would give every scrap of her strength to make her beloved Clan as powerful as before. She would be the most loyal ShadowClan cat who had ever lived in the forest.

And she would *never* let an outsider trick her into trusting them again.

# CHAPTER 1

*Frostpaw's pelt prickled with tension; the* air of the RiverClan camp was filled with it, as if a storm were about to break. Everywhere she looked, she could see injured warriors. Some were lying down and licking their wounds, total defeat in their eyes and the droop of their heads. Others crouched close together, muttering furiously and casting hostile glances at Tigerstar and the victorious cats of ShadowClan.

Not long ago, RiverClan had been thriving. But the death of the Clan leader, Mistystar, followed almost at once by the death of her deputy, Reedwhisker, had thrown the Clan into confusion.

Guilt and regret swept over Frostpaw. As the only medicine cat with a connection to StarClan, she had been responsible for finding a new leader. *And I failed,* she thought miserably. *I failed twice.*

Once the other Clans had realized RiverClan's desperate need, Tigerstar had attacked. He believed that only his leadership could rescue the leaderless Clan from chaos, and the weakened RiverClan had been unable to prevent him from taking over.

Now Tigerstar jumped to the top of the Highstump. *Just as if he were Clan leader!* Frostpaw thought resentfully. *My mother should have been standing there. I had a sign from StarClan that she was to be our next leader.* Inwardly she shuddered at the horrific memory of Curlfeather torn apart by dogs on her way to the Moonpool. *She would have been great.*

She turned her back on Tigerstar as he began to address her Clan, instead padding up to Mallownose and beginning to lick the tear in his ear, where blood had trickled down into his pale tabby fur.

"I can't believe any of our Clanmates would just do what another Clan tells them. It should at least be Owlnose giving the orders, right?" he mewed, fiercely indignant on his son's behalf.

Frostpaw went on busily licking, her excuse for not replying. *After Curlfeather, I thought Owlnose was destined to lead us. How could I have been so wrong?* Owlnose had admitted to Tigerstar that he hadn't received his nine lives, but only Frostpaw, Owlnose himself, Mothwing, and Fidgetflake knew the real reason why: He didn't believe that he was the right cat to lead his Clan.

"We need hunting patrols," Tigerstar announced. "I want volunteers. Not all of you are badly hurt."

Not many cats were listening to him, and those who were didn't respond, only gazing up at the ShadowClan leader with sullen expressions. Mallownose looked around with a satisfied gleam in his eye, pleased that none of his Clanmates were letting Tigerstar order them around.

"Come on!" Tigerstar growled, with an irritated lash of his tail. "Do you expect the prey to jump into your mouths?"

As he finished speaking, Splashtail tottered to his paws, his shoulder fur bristling. "Why should we do what *you* tell us?" he demanded, glaring at Tigerstar. "Why *isn't* Owlnose in charge? I know StarClan hasn't given him his lives yet, but at least he was chosen by a RiverClan cat!"

Many of Frostpaw's Clanmates were nodding at Splashtail's words, letting out murmurs of assent. Frostpaw was worried that the young tom had made Tigerstar angry, but when the ShadowClan leader spoke again, his voice was calm and measured.

"Perhaps if some cat could explain what happened at the Moonpool," he began, "and exactly *why* Owlnose is not Owlstar right now, then we would all be better informed, and we could move on."

There was an edge to his tone, and he stared pointedly at Owlnose as he spoke. Frostpaw fought down a rush of panic, convinced that Tigerstar had realized something had gone wrong—convinced that he had figured it out faster than the RiverClan cats, who were beginning to gather around Owlnose.

"Owlnose, what happened?" Havenpelt asked.

Podlight's eyes were full of confusion. "Yeah, why *didn't* you get your nine lives?"

Owlnose's expression was miserable; he was staring at his paws, obviously reluctant to answer. Frostpaw was aware that the RiverClan cats were looking at her and Mothwing, too, but Mothwing ignored their questioning glances, her jaws firmly clamped shut.

*What should I say if Tigerstar starts interrogating me? Should I tell him about the doubts I've been having?* Frostpaw stared at her paws. She hadn't even shared her doubts about her connection to StarClan with her own Clanmates. Surely she couldn't tell Tigerstar first!

Frostpaw didn't know what to do. Mothwing had wanted to keep RiverClan's problems a secret from the very beginning; surely she would be furious if Frostpaw revealed what had happened at the Moonpool. She was acutely aware of Tigerstar's piercing amber gaze, until Owlnose at last took a deep breath, straightened up, and raised his head.

"I didn't become your leader," he explained, his voice carrying clearly across the camp, "and I never will—by my own choice. I know that I wouldn't make a good leader, and so I didn't go through with the ceremony."

Furious yowls broke out across the camp as Owlnose made his confession.

"Why would you refuse StarClan's call?" Splashtail asked, his eyes wide with shock.

"And why are you telling us this *now*?" Lizardtail added.

Even though she was relieved that the truth had come out without her needing to speak, Frostpaw flinched inwardly as Tigerstar let his scathing gaze travel across the camp. "Are you suggesting Owlnose should have lied to us?" he meowed. "Like you lied at the Gathering? This is exactly your problem," he continued, his claws working into the top of the Highstump.

"Every time you hide what's really going on, you dig yourselves into a deeper hole. Owlnose"—he dipped his head respectfully to the brown tabby tom—"I thank you for your honesty. It's clear that RiverClan has no leader, StarClan-approved or not, which is why I am here." His gaze swept across the RiverClan cats again, domineering now. "So, yes, for now you will take orders from me, to keep this Clan from falling apart until you can find a real leader."

More yowls of outrage greeted his words, but Tigerstar remained unmoved, standing tall upon the Highstump as several of the RiverClan cats advanced on him, their fur bristling and their claws extended.

Frostpaw's belly lurched at the thought of more bloodshed, especially as her Clanmates stood no chance of winning. Some of Tigerstar's warriors moved closer to the stump, but before the RiverClan cats could attack, Harelight stepped forward, intercepting them.

"Have you got bees in your brain?" he demanded. "If you're hurt, go and see Mothwing, and if you're not, go and hunt something. Can't you see there's nothing we can do?"

Duskfur let out a snort of disapproval. "Why do we have to listen to Harelight?" she muttered. "He spent so much time in ShadowClan, he's practically one of them!"

Frostpaw could see one or two of the other RiverClan cats nodding agreement. When Ashfur had usurped the leadership of ThunderClan, he had persuaded Mistystar to send Mothwing into exile. After the Clans fought against the impostor, Mistystar had exiled Icewing and Harelight, too, for disobeying her orders and fighting to defeat Ashfur, even though the rest of RiverClan had been fighting on his side. Tigerstar had welcomed them into ShadowClan, where they'd lived until the Lights in the Mist defeated Ashfur in the Dark Forest and Mistystar allowed them to return. Frostpaw could understand why her Clanmates might be suspicious, but she realized that at the same time they didn't want to reject orders from one of their own Clanmates in front of ShadowClan.

Harelight opened his jaws to defend himself, but before he could speak, Duskfur swung around to confront Owlnose, her tail lashing with rage.

"This is all your fault," she growled. "If you had done your duty at the Moonpool, we would have a leader by now, and we could tell Tigerstar and his mange-ridden warriors to get their tails off our territory!"

"That's not fair," Icewing protested, slipping between the two cats and laying a calming tail on Owlnose's shoulder. "Sure, we need a leader, but we *don't* want one who knows in his heart that it's wrong for him to lead. Owlnose has done something very brave and good for the Clan by choosing to step down."

Duskfur's only response was an angry hiss.

Stepping closer to her, Icewing continued in a lower voice. "We have to go along with this for now. Perhaps the time will come for us to fight again and win, but this is not that time."

Frostpaw watched Duskfur choke back her anger as she listened to Icewing's wise words. Owlnose, too, though he still looked ashamed, was clearly encouraged by what the white she-cat had said.

*Is this the right time for me to confess?* Frostpaw wondered. The messy scene at the Moonpool had convinced her that she wasn't a medicine cat. The more she thought about her visions, the more she felt that they had to be a product of her own imagination. Unlike the other medicine cats, she'd never seen herself among StarClan in their hunting grounds. Instead, the cat images she'd seen had been blurred, appearing out of a shimmering mist. But if she told that to her Clan, what would happen to her? She could become a healer like Mothwing, without a connection to StarClan, but she knew that wasn't what RiverClan needed right now.

*RiverClan needs a medicine cat who can receive signs and prophecies from StarClan. How else will we ever find a new leader? My Clanmates have been relying on me—they'll be so disappointed!*

If she told the truth, Frostpaw wondered, would she have to retrain as a warrior? She felt a pang of regret, because she loved helping her mentor to heal, but being a warrior seemed much more fun than living under the intense pressure she had felt since Mistystar died. *I'm ready to change . . . I think.*

Straightening up, Frostpaw cleared her throat, but before she could speak, she felt the touch of a tail on her shoulder and turned to see Mothwing at her side.

"Look at Shimmerpelt over there," her mentor meowed. "She has a bad shoulder wound. Go to the den and fetch some horsetail." As Frostpaw obediently brushed past her, Mothwing added in a whisper, "This isn't the time. The whole Clan has enough on its paws right now. Besides, I need help with the herbs, and you know them."

*It's like she can read my mind!* Frostpaw thought, the tension in her chest easing at the thought that she could put off the decision for a little while.

As she headed toward the medicine-cat den, she spotted Icewing staring at her, as if the white she-cat wanted to ask her something. But at that moment Mallownose sprang up and began hissing insults at a ShadowClan warrior who had stepped on his tail. Icewing turned away with a scowl and went to break up the argument.

When Frostpaw returned with the horsetail for Shimmerpelt's shoulder and began to chew it to a pulp, she realized that the arguments had died down and a fragile peace lay over the camp. But she was still startled when Tigerstar let out a yowl from the top of the Highstump, calling RiverClan to attention.

"I am going back to ShadowClan for now," he announced. "You are not my Clan, and this is not a conquest." Frostpaw felt slightly encouraged by his words, though she wondered how much trust to place in them as the ShadowClan leader continued: "Some ShadowClan cats will remain behind—my deputy, Cloverfoot, and two other warriors."

Howls of protest rose from the RiverClan cats around him, and even though Tigerstar raised his tail for silence, it was some moments before he could make himself heard again.

"My warriors are here to help you, not just to tell you what to do," he assured the angry cats.

"Yeah, and hedgehogs fly," Duskfur growled.

"Like we'd believe a ShadowClan cat," Splashtail added.

Several other cats were murmuring agreement, flexing their claws as they glared up at Tigerstar.

Icewing let out a long sigh. "Don't be such mouse-brains," she told her Clanmates. "Tigerstar was always going to want a presence in RiverClan. And if we want to convince Shadow-Clan that we can cope on our own, and find our leader quickly, we should all want that too. Otherwise Tigerstar will just continue to be convinced that we can't manage our own Clan."

"Thank you, Icewing," Tigerstar meowed. "I'm glad there's one cat here with enough sense to accept the inevitable. You and Cloverfoot should share the leader's duties for now, and bring any concerns or news from RiverClan to me directly."

Frostpaw could see that few of her Clanmates were happy with this idea. The muttering and resentful glances continued until Duskfur rose to her paws.

"What a surprise—you've chosen Icewing," Duskfur sneered. "There's another cat who spent too long with ShadowClan. She even trained with you in the Dark Forest, didn't she? Why didn't you choose Splashtail?" she added, turning toward the brown tabby tom. "He's young, but he's still our deputy."

"That's right," Splashtail growled.

Several cats yowled in support of Splashtail. Frostpaw wanted to support her friend too, but she couldn't help remembering that he had been appointed by Owlnose. *If Owlnose was never our leader, he couldn't appoint a deputy,* she realized.

Tigerstar gazed thoughtfully at Splashtail, pausing for a few heartbeats. "I appreciate your passion for your Clan," he responded at last. "But you're very young, and your Clan will benefit from the guidance of an experienced warrior like Icewing."

Frostpaw could tell that this wasn't Tigerstar's only reason, and she guessed that most of her Clanmates realized it too. The ShadowClan leader must have known that Splashtail would never cooperate with him; he was too angry about losing the battle.

"The best way to remove ShadowClan from your camp is to find your real leader," Tigerstar continued. "I suggest that you focus on your connection with StarClan."

Every cat turned their gaze toward Frostpaw. She concentrated on chewing up the horsetail, as if she could hide from her Clan's expectations, which felt like a heavy weight on her shoulders. It had been bad enough feeling responsible for the Clan's fate when she'd thought StarClan was with her. Now that she was sure they never had been, it was almost too much to bear.

When she had finished patting the horsetail pulp into Shimmerpelt's shoulder, Frostpaw hurried back to the medicine cats' den. She was grateful that she had something practical to do, using a skill she knew was real, while her mind was still full of her fears for the future.

*What will happen now?* she wondered. *Will RiverClan ever be free again? Will we find a real medicine cat, or a real leader, or will StarClan leave us to be swallowed up by ShadowClan?*

As she left the den with a mouthful of herbs, Frostpaw almost collided with a barrier of white fur—Icewing's chest. Icewing stood aside to let her pass, but as Frostpaw did so, the older cat leaned over to murmur into her ear.

"Come find me later. We need to talk."

# CHAPTER 2
❧

*Sunbeam padded along the lakeshore on* her way back to Shadow-Clan. Her limbs ached from the battle with RiverClan, but she had escaped any serious wounds. Inwardly she felt torn: She was glad that Tigerstar had managed to convince at least some of the RiverClan cats that ShadowClan only wanted to help, but her heart was heavy about the fighting. She wished it hadn't come to a battle.

Berryheart was padding alongside her. Sunbeam had been feeling awkward with her mother since she'd realized how Berryheart's hatred of outsiders had overcome her, and how she was prepared to do anything to keep intruders out. But now she could see her own uneasiness reflected in her mother's eyes.

Glancing around for Tigerstar, Sunbeam spotted him so far ahead that she felt safe enough to talk to Berryheart in a low voice. "I'm worried that some of the RiverClan cats will spend all their energy fighting us," she murmured, "instead of looking for their new leader."

Berryheart let out a snort. "Never mind them!" she meowed scornfully. "What about us? If Tigerstar is focusing on another Clan as well as his own, what will that mean? Leaf-bare is coming. Our leader won't have time to care for us, and our Clan will end up suffering for the problems of outsiders!"

Sunbeam rolled her eyes. *Of course Berryheart isn't thinking of anything outside ShadowClan!* Even so, she had to admit that her mother had a point. Tigerstar was making a risky move. But she still couldn't help thinking about the RiverClan warriors, lying injured and defeated in their camp. *What kind of night will they have?* And what would the other Clans say when they heard what Tigerstar had done?

By the time she and her Clanmates made it back to camp, Sunbeam was exhausted. She wanted nothing more than to head for her nest in the warriors' den and go to sleep. But as she pushed her way through the thorns that surrounded the camp, she saw Blazefire running to meet Tigerstar.

The two cats stood for a moment with their heads close together and briefly exchanged words. It looked as though Blazefire had something urgent to tell his Clan leader. But no matter how hard Sunbeam strained, she couldn't hear what they were saying.

Then Tigerstar turned to stare at Sunbeam, a quizzical look on his face. Sunbeam felt every hair on her pelt begin to prickle, as if ants were crawling through her fur. *What is going on?*

Blazefire bounded over to her, his eyes glowing. "Well, that was a surprise!" he announced. "But I'm so happy for you. Congratulations!"

As they padded side by side down the slope into the camp,

Sunbeam was about to tell him that she had no idea what he was meowing about. But as soon as they reached the center of the camp, she guessed: Nightheart was standing beside the fresh-kill pile, talking to a small cluster of ShadowClan warriors.

*I'm the only ShadowClan cat he knows,* she reasoned. *He must be here for me. But . . . really?*

Sunbeam knew the ThunderClan tom liked her, but they'd never discussed becoming mates, and they'd *definitely* never discussed switching Clans for each other. She froze for one appalled moment, then forced her paws to move and carry her over to the ThunderClan cat.

"You wouldn't believe how close Sunbeam and I are!" he was telling Gullswoop as Sunbeam came into earshot. "I want to spend the rest of my life in ShadowClan so I can be with her."

"Really?" Gullswoop looked as if she were contemplating the juiciest piece of prey on the fresh-kill pile. "I had no idea!"

"Yes, we fell in love when we went on the mission to find herbs to fight the greencough." Nightheart's voice was loud enough to carry right across the camp.

Sunbeam felt her whole head begin to throb. She was flattered by Nightheart's bubbling enthusiasm, the way he loved her and wanted to be with her forever . . .

*But if that's how he feels, he should have told* me *before he told Gullswoop!*

As Sunbeam approached, determined to get to the bottom of whatever Nightheart thought he was doing, Gullswoop spotted her and touched the tip of her tail to the ThunderClan cat's shoulder, angling her ears in her direction. Nightheart spun around, gazing at Sunbeam with ears and whiskers twitching nervously. She had known that he liked her; now she could see how much he loved her. In his eyes she could see how vulnerable he felt, terrified that she might send him away.

*Okay,* Sunbeam thought. *At least he seems to realize that I didn't see this coming.* "I need to talk to you," she mewed as gently as she could as Nightheart bounded up to her. She glanced uneasily at Gullswoop. "Alone."

But it wasn't as easy as Sunbeam had thought to manage a few moments with the cat who was, apparently, supposed to be her future mate. Her Clanmates kept coming up to congratulate them, crowding around so they could hardly shift their paws a mouse-length.

Sunbeam's brother Spireclaw was one of the first, with his mate, Fringewhisker, who had come from SkyClan to be with him. "I'm so pleased you've found the right cat," Spireclaw told his sister. "I want you to be happy."

"I know how hard it is to leave your Clan," Fringewhisker told Nightheart. "But I don't think you'll regret it. Sunbeam's a great cat."

Sunbeam was grateful for their encouragement, but less impressed with the many cats who only wanted to say how surprised they were. *Or cats like Gullswoop, who will gossip about this for moons!* No cat seemed to realize that *she* was surprised, too, and desperately impatient to talk alone with Nightheart.

At last the crowd of her Clanmates melted away as Tigerstar

approached, and stood for a moment looking thoughtfully from Nightheart to Sunbeam and back again. Sunbeam's belly lurched, anxious about what the Clan leader's reaction would be; his expression was giving nothing away.

"Nightheart, I hear that you're asking to join Shadow-Clan." When he began to speak, Tigerstar's voice was calm and measured; it reminded Sunbeam of how he had sounded when he was talking to the RiverClan cats. "You'll be allowed to stay in our camp for now, and according to the new addition to the warrior code, you will be able to try proving your loyalty to ShadowClan and to Sunbeam. If you—"

"I can't wait to get started!" Nightheart interrupted.

Sunbeam winced, while Tigerstar went on as though the ThunderClan cat hadn't spoken.

"If you succeed, you will be part of the Clan. Until then, you are a visitor who will have duties, but hold no rank within the Clan. Is that understood?"

Nightheart dipped his head respectfully. "Yes, of course, Tigerstar."

Tigerstar gave a brisk nod and stalked away.

Finally Sunbeam was able to lead Nightheart out of the camp. Her gaze darted around to find a spot with a good chance of privacy, and alighted on the shade of a low-growing pine tree a few fox-lengths away.

"Nightheart, *what* in the name of StarClan are you doing?" she began when they were settled in the shelter of the pine. "We barely know each other—how can we be mates? I don't even know if I want a mate!"

Nightheart blinked at her, looking startled, as if he had

expected her to welcome him and declare her undying love. "I'm sorry . . . ," he muttered, his head drooping dejectedly.

Instantly Sunbeam felt sorry, too, for pouncing on him as if he were a piece of fresh-kill. "I shouldn't have snapped at you," she meowed. "I'm flattered, sort of. But honestly, Nightheart, couldn't you have told me how you felt, instead of just showing up in my Clan with no warning?"

"I suppose you're right," Nightheart mewed after a moment. "I admit I rushed it, and I'm really sorry. But I do really like you, Sunbeam, and I want to get to know you better. How could I do that while I was trapped in ThunderClan?"

"You could still have talked to me first," Sunbeam pointed out.

"I know," Nightheart sighed, his gaze fixed on her face. There was love and longing in his eyes, but a hint of anxiety, too, as if he was worried about what he would do if she rejected him. "Please forgive me, and give me a chance to prove myself, to you and your Clan."

Now that the shock of his declaration was wearing off, Sunbeam remembered everything he had told her about not feeling that he belonged in ThunderClan. She wondered if his leaving his birth Clan was really about her at all. At the same time, she liked his earnest demeanor, and she was surprised to feel herself softening toward him. *He doesn't do things by halves, does he?*

"I forgive you, Nightheart," she began. "But I need time to think about what I want. What will you do if my answer is no?"

"The choice will be yours," Nightheart promised, sincerity

shining in his eyes. "If you really don't want me around, I'll leave. But I hope that if we don't end up being mates, you'll be okay if I stay so we can still be friends and Clanmates."

For a heartbeat Sunbeam thought of Blazefire, then pushed his image away as if she were saying good-bye to the life they might have had together. Leaning forward, she murmured assent, touching noses with Nightheart. She did like him, she realized, and maybe that feeling could grow into something more. *I may as well give him a chance,* she decided.

As soon as she and Nightheart returned to the camp, Sunbeam spotted her mother bearing down on her. She felt her heart begin to thump as she saw the ominous look on Berryheart's face.

"I want to talk to you," Berryheart snapped, with a glare at Nightheart. "Alone."

"And I would love to chat with Nightheart, my kin," a softer voice added from behind Berryheart. Sunbeam looked up to see Tawnypelt, Tigerstar's mother and the former Clan deputy, watching Nightheart with warmth in her eyes. Sunbeam had momentarily forgotten that she and Nightheart were related; she was Bramblestar's littermate.

Nightheart looked delighted to be greeted with kindness by at least one cat. "Tawnypelt! I'd love to talk to you."

*Why do I suspect your conversation will go better than mine?* Sunbeam nodded at her mother, suppressing a sigh. "Okay," she responded. "Nightheart, you can have some time alone with Tawnypelt, and I'll join you soon."

Nightheart dipped his head, a flash of relief in his eyes at escaping the hostile she-cat, and padded off with the more relaxed-looking senior warrior.

"What are you *thinking?*" Berryheart demanded, not even waiting for Nightheart to move out of earshot. "Inviting an outsider—a ThunderClan cat—into our Clan, without telling any cat! How could you betray your Clan like this?"

"But I didn't—"

Berryheart swept on, ignoring Sunbeam's attempt to interrupt. "I once gave up on my Clan, and it was the worst mistake of my life. I'll spend the rest of my days trying to be worthy of the forgiveness my Clan showed me. How can Nightheart ever be loyal to you if he can't be loyal to ThunderClan?"

As she listened, Sunbeam felt her shoulder fur beginning to bristle. *Berryheart joined Darktail's Kin! That was completely different!*

"Nightheart isn't a traitor, or an outsider," she protested. "He's a good cat. And what about Fringewhisker? She hasn't given any cat reason to doubt her since she became Spireclaw's mate."

Berryheart gave her a sour look, her eyes narrowed, but was visibly trying to control her anger. "All I'm worried about is your happiness," she told Sunbeam. "And you won't be happy if Nightheart fails the test, or if he decides to go back to his real Clan—*or* if he goes back and tells them all of Shadow-Clan's secrets."

When Nightheart had first arrived in the camp, Sunbeam had been startled and uncertain. But now her mother's invective made her feel like defending him. He might rush into things, and even be a bit self-centered, but she was completely certain that he wasn't a traitor.

"You can't be all that concerned about my happiness," she snapped, "or Spireclaw's, if you talk about our mates that way. Nightheart deserves the chance to follow the code and become a ShadowClan cat. What you did in the past is your problem. This is now."

Whirling around, Sunbeam stalked away from her mother with her tail bushed out. She felt that she had won the argument, but she wasn't happy about it. It still hurt to fight with Berryheart, even though she was certain that her mother was wrong.

# CHAPTER 3

❧

*It felt strange to Nightheart, approaching* the Gathering island from ShadowClan territory, and even stranger that there was no full moon. Tonight he and his new Clanmates were on their way to an emergency Gathering, called by Tigerstar to discuss the situation in RiverClan. Where Nightheart was used to seeing the forest and the lake bathed in silver light, now, although the sky was clear, only a claw-scratch of moon appeared among the stars.

Nightheart had been shocked to the tips of his claws when Sunbeam had explained to him what was happening in River-Clan, and how Tigerstar had led the ShadowClan cats in a battle to gain control. Sunbeam's account of Tigerstar's reasoning sounded sensible enough, in a way, but he shuddered at the thought that warriors could have been hurt, or even killed. He had heard stories of battles in the past, against the evil rogue cat Darktail, or further back still, against the first Tigerstar, who had tried to take over the whole forest. Surely no cat would risk that happening again! He wondered why the present Tigerstar had ever imagined he could make River-Clan's choices for them.

*I never thought he was a power-hungry cat, but what if I'm wrong?* A chill pricked at his pelt. *Have I made a mistake by joining his Clan to be with Sunbeam?*

He watched Tigerstar striding ahead, leading the way, with Cloverfoot padding at his shoulder; she had just returned from her stay in RiverClan to make her report.

Nightheart pricked up his ears and increased his pace a little so that he could overhear what the Clan deputy had to say.

"Of course, things are still very tense over there," Cloverfoot meowed. "But at least no cat has tried to drive us out."

Tigerstar acknowledged her news with a brusque nod. "Has there been any word from StarClan?" he asked.

"Not yet," Cloverfoot replied. "Their young medicine cat is doing her best, but I'm not sure she's even tried to contact StarClan since the battle. I'm worried that her best might not be good enough."

"You could be right," Tigerstar grunted. "Mothwing is a great healer, but how does she expect to train an apprentice when she never speaks to StarClan?"

Cloverfoot let out a sigh. "True enough. And we have to remember that if RiverClan doesn't sort its problems out soon, the other Clans won't tolerate us occupying their territory for long."

"I know." Tigerstar echoed his deputy's sigh. "The other leaders won't like what I'm going to tell them. I just hope they won't be willing to fight over it."

Nightheart hoped that, too, but when he glanced at Sunbeam, he saw his own apprehension reflected in her gaze.

\* \* \*

In the clearing beneath the branches of the Great Oak, the air was thick with tension. All the other Clans were already there by the time the ShadowClan cats arrived; Nightheart was aware of curious stares and murmuring as Tigerstar leaped up to take his place in the tree.

He was aware too that cats were staring at him, seeing him arriving with ShadowClan and not with ThunderClan, where he ought to have been. He remembered how he had stormed out of the stone hollow, not even telling his Clanmates where he meant to go. Speaking with Tawnypelt, who was supportive of his move, had helped him feel a bit more at home in his new Clan. But it didn't erase the fact that all the *rest* of his kin was likely furious with him.

Lilyheart padded over to him, with Bayshine close behind her. "Nightheart, what's going on?" his former mentor asked. "Where have you been? We were worried about you."

"Yeah, why are you with *them*?" Bayshine added, angling his ears toward the ShadowClan cats.

"We can't talk now," Nightheart muttered. Even though both cats seemed worried about him rather than annoyed, explaining himself was the last thing he wanted to do.

Glancing across the clearing at the other ThunderClan warriors, he felt a pang of sadness pierce his heart when he saw that his mother, Sparkpelt, wasn't there. But the pang was followed by a wash of relief. *Sooner or later I'll have to face her, but thank StarClan I don't have to do it now!*

The representatives from RiverClan were clustered

together at the far side of the clearing near the line of bushes. Icewing and Owlnose were there, with Splashtail and a few others. Even Mothwing had remained with her Clan instead of taking up her position near the Great Oak with the other medicine cats. They sat with heads raised and shoulders straight in a proud kind of silence.

Nightheart could see cobweb plastered along Splashtail's side, holding a poultice in place. He remembered what Sunbeam had told him about the scene after the battle. No cat had leaped into the Great Oak to represent RiverClan. He guessed the cats must have argued about who would represent their Clan, or even whether they would come at all.

"Cats of all Clans." Tigerstar's voice rang out across the clearing from his place in the Great Oak. "We are here to—"

"I'm surprised you dare show your face!" The interruption came from Leafstar, who was crouched on a branch a tail-length above the ShadowClan leader. "How can you excuse yourself for taking over RiverClan?"

Nightheart heard gasps of shock coming from the Wind-Clan cats; Harestar was staring at Tigerstar with a look of disbelief on his face. *WindClan didn't know that part,* he realized. *Though some cat obviously told Leafstar.*

"This was a foolish act," Leafstar continued, leaning down to hiss in Tigerstar's face. "It will never benefit you or Shadow-Clan! I've heard the stories of what happened when the first Tigerstar took over RiverClan, and I'm sure *you* haven't forgotten them. You should be ashamed to follow in the paw steps of your *famous* ancestor! Don't imagine that any cat here would *ever* let that happen again."

Tigerstar stretched up on his branch to face her. "I'm not the first Tigerstar!" he snarled. "I would never make the same mistakes. And I'm not taking over RiverClan. I'm *helping* RiverClan sort out their problems."

"Oh, really?" Leafstar's voice was icy. "And hedgehogs fly. What *actually* happened," she continued, addressing the assembled cats, "is that ShadowClan invaded RiverClan's camp and forced them to fight. I'm sure that the warrior code would never permit that. So what's your excuse, Tigerstar?"

Tigerstar turned away from the SkyClan leader to look out across the cats in the clearing. Nightheart could see that he was making a massive effort to control his anger, his paws quivering as he dug his claws into the branch.

"Look, it was like this," he began. "RiverClan was in chaos. As you heard at the last Gathering, Owlnose was chosen to lead them." He paused, and Nightheart felt that every cat was holding their breath for what was to come next. "But Owlnose did not become their leader," Tigerstar continued. "He refused to set his paws on the path into StarClan's territory, and he has not been given his nine lives."

At his words, an outcry broke out among the assembled cats.

"What? Owlnose *refused*?"

"Really?"

"I don't believe it!"

As the clamor went on, Nightheart saw Leafstar give a contemptuous sniff. Her comment was clearly not meant to be shared with the whole Gathering, but he was close enough to hear her response. "I can't say that I'm terribly surprised. He wasn't behaving much like a Clan leader at the last Gathering."

Across the clearing, Owlnose seemed embarrassed by the outcry. He gave an awkward flick of his tail, then sat with his head bowed, contemplating his paws. Icewing, who was sitting next to him, rested her tail on his shoulder.

Tigerstar raised his tail for silence. "I went to RiverClan to help and advise them," he went on once he could make himself heard. "They attacked my warriors—which I admit was their right—but we defeated them, and that proves they can't defend themselves, and they need our help."

Nightheart felt his pelt grow warm with embarrassment on behalf of the RiverClan cats. He could see the hurt in their eyes at Tigerstar's harsh assessment, though they remained silent.

"I swear on the spirits of my warrior ancestors," Tigerstar continued, "that I have no designs on RiverClan's territory, and no intention of keeping a ShadowClan presence in River-Clan for any longer than I have to. But until they sort out their leadership problems, RiverClan needs our help."

When Tigerstar had finished speaking, every cat seemed frozen into silence for a few moments. Nightheart could see cats exchanging uneasy glances, as if they were beginning to realize that the ShadowClan leader might have had a good reason for what he had done.

"And you, Bramblestar?" Leafstar asked, turning to gaze

down at the ThunderClan leader, who was crouched in a fork of the tree trunk a little way below her. "What do you think? Surely ThunderClan must have something to say about the way Tigerstar has overreached himself."

Bramblestar did not reply at once, instead turning his head to gaze at Tigerstar and blinking thoughtfully. "Tigerstar," he began at last, "surely you understand that when the first Tigerstar, your—no, *our*—kin, took over RiverClan in the old forest . . . that was wrong?"

"Of course!" Tigerstar snapped back, his fur beginning to bristle. "As I already *explained*, my aims are nothing like his! I don't want to lead RiverClan! But I don't want chaos, either. If one Clan is falling apart, all the rest are in danger."

Bramblestar nodded slowly, as if he was taking all that in. "Haven't we had enough fighting among cats who should be allies?" he meowed. "Tigerstar, I believe your heart is in the right place. But I think . . ."

Nightheart had known Bramblestar for his whole life, and listening to him now, he could tell that the dark tabby tom didn't know what he thought. It was awkward, and Nightheart did not dare to meet any other cat's gaze, because the ThunderClan leader was letting himself sound so uncertain, and at a Gathering, too.

While Bramblestar was still hesitating, Squirrelflight looked up from her place with the other deputies on the roots of the Great Oak. "ThunderClan understands the need for strong and reliable leadership," she asserted, "but I personally agree with Leafstar. Tigerstar has gone too far."

A murmur of agreement broke out at Squirrelflight's confident and decisive words. Nightheart wondered how Bramblestar felt about his deputy speaking up and offering such a strong opinion, but the ThunderClan leader hardly seemed to have heard her.

All this while, Harestar had been listening quietly; now he dipped his head to the other leaders and gathered himself to speak. "I can see Tigerstar's point of view," he admitted, giving the group of RiverClan cats a long, meaningful stare. "RiverClan is a strong, proud Clan with a great history, but they have been suffering lately, and they shouldn't be too proud to accept help from another Clan. *But*," he added, "I might change my mind about how helpful Tigerstar is being if RiverClan doesn't find another leader soon, or if Shadow-Clan encroaches on them any further."

"That's enough talking *about* RiverClan," Leafstar growled with an irritated twitch of her tail. She turned to the cluster of RiverClan cats. "Why aren't we hearing anything from *you*? What is life like for you now? Do you feel that Tigerstar should leave you to deal with your own problems?"

No RiverClan cat responded until Nightheart saw Tigerstar give a nod to Icewing, who rose to her paws and stepped forward.

"I admit things have been difficult in RiverClan," she meowed in a measured tone. She was clearly trying to calm the anger among the assembled cats. "Tigerstar's arrival in our camp wasn't welcome, as you will all understand, and no RiverClan cat wants to be controlled by him. However, we have to admit that we have all been more comfortable and better fed since the ShadowClan cats took over the running of our Clan."

Nightheart saw Splashtail's eye twitch at his Clanmate's words; for a moment he looked as if he was about to spring to his paws and disagree. But before he could move, several of the SkyClan and ThunderClan cats erupted into yowls of protest. Thornclaw let out a snarl, his eyes flaring with suspicion at the way Icewing had accepted ShadowClan's presence in the RiverClan camp, while Dewspring leaped to his paws, sliding his claws out as if he was ready to fight.

Lionblaze was whispering to Mousewhisker; the two toms were so close behind him that Nightheart could hear the low-voiced comments beneath the general clamor.

"Icewing spent a long time living with ShadowClan. I wonder how much her time there might have changed her."

Glancing back, Nightheart saw several other cats leaning closer and nodding agreement.

"Yeah." Mintfur from SkyClan butted in. "Can her Clanmates really trust her?"

"I'd bet a moon of dawn patrols that they don't," Mousewhisker responded. "Every cat in RiverClan must feel the same way."

"Cats of all Clans, listen!" Squirrelflight's voice rang out across the clearing; she had sprung to her paws and was standing very tall and straight on her oak root.

*She looks more like a leader than Bramblestar,* Nightheart thought.

Her forceful command had reached the protesting cats,

and their yowls gradually died away.

"Even beyond the first Tigerstar," Squirrelflight went on, "meddling in another Clan's business has never ended well. Good intentions aren't the only thing that matters. Your words are friendly, Tigerstar, but they're not worth a couple of mousetails if they still end in bloodshed. In the end, invading another Clan makes you no better than Darktail or the first Tigerstar."

Silence fell as she finished speaking, and Icewing stepped forward again, with a respectful dip of her head toward the ThunderClan deputy.

"I admit that RiverClan has not always told you the truth," she meowed, letting her gaze travel around the clearing. "Mistystar died of old age, and before we could find Reed-whisker to give him the news and arrange for him to go to the Moonpool, he was killed in an accident." She paused, swallowing, as if the next part of what she had to say was even harder. "We made up the excuse that we had greencough in the camp, partly because we were so confused we had no idea what to do, and partly because we didn't want the other Clans looking into our affairs."

*And how did that work out for you?* Nightheart thought.

No cat commented out loud, and Icewing continued, describing how RiverClan had been cut adrift from their warrior ancestors, with only a half-trained apprentice to make the connection and find them the leader they so desperately needed.

Nightheart cast a glance at Frostpaw and saw her flinch

WARRIORS: A STARLESS CLAN: SHADOW          33

at Icewing's assessment of her skills. *That's not fair,* he thought sympathetically. *No apprentice should be under that kind of pressure.*

Some of Icewing's story was new to Nightheart, and listening to her made him nervous. He wondered what ThunderClan would have done if Bramblestar and Squirrelflight had never made it back from the Dark Forest. Part of him thought they might not have coped as well; at least none of the RiverClan cats were fighting to make themselves leader. Remembering the arguments over who should lead in Bramblestar's absence, and the many challenges to Squirrelflight's leadership, even though she was the Clan deputy, Nightheart knew that he couldn't say the same of his former Clan.

*We would still have had our medicine cats, though,* he comforted himself, sympathy welling up for the RiverClan cats, who seemed to be losing almost everything that made them a Clan.

When Icewing had finished speaking, Leafstar still seemed dissatisfied, her whiskers twitching as she worked her claws into the branch of the Great Oak.

Squirrelflight too, Nightheart noticed, was still unhappy. "It's impossible for a Clan to function without a trained medicine cat who can speak with StarClan," she insisted. "Another medicine cat needs to go to help Mothwing and Frostpaw. Alderheart, will you—"

At once Alderheart sprang to his paws, but before he could speak, Tigerstar cut off what the ThunderClan deputy was about to say.

"Thank you, Squirrelflight, but that won't be necessary. Puddleshine and Shadowsight will help out as much as they can." He paused, looking slightly awkward, then turned to Icewing. "Do you agree?" he asked her.

Icewing responded with a nod.

Leafstar let out a hiss of irritation. It was clear that without Bramblestar's or Harestar's support, she was outnumbered. "I admit that your intentions *seem* honorable," she told Tigerstar, "and so I will not commit SkyClan to driving you out of RiverClan territory. Not yet. But if this drags on," she warned him, "and if we don't see any progress by the next Gathering, I hope my fellow leaders"—she broke off to glare at Bramblestar—"will reconsider whether this is really the right solution for RiverClan."

For a moment Nightheart was still unsettled by Leafstar's willingness to lead her warriors into battle. From what he knew of her, she had always seemed to be a peaceable cat. But then he remembered the stories the elders had told him: how before Darktail ever came to the lakeside territories, he had invaded SkyClan's gorge and driven them out to wander, homeless. It was no wonder Leafstar was sensitive about one Clan assuming command over another, and taking over their camp to do it.

"That is reasonable." Bramblestar roused himself out of his indecision and responded to Leafstar with a nod. Giving Tigerstar a long, thoughtful look, he added, "You have made yourself responsible for a whole second Clan. No cat has ever done that without it ending badly. Now is your chance to prove you can—but to do that, you must let the power and responsibility go when it's done."

"And make sure you're out of RiverClan before the other Clans feel we have to *make* you leave," Squirrelflight added.

"That won't be necessary," Tigerstar retorted coldly.

There was a stir in the clearing, as if the assembled cats expected the ShadowClan leader to declare the Gathering at an end. Instead, Tigerstar stepped forward on his branch.

"I've one more announcement to make," he meowed; Nightheart felt shock like a heavy paw slamming down on his chest as he realized the ShadowClan leader was looking at him. Tigerstar gestured with his tail for him to step forward. "The ThunderClan warrior Nightheart has left his Clan and seeks to join ShadowClan to be with my warrior Sunbeam."

Once again Nightheart felt as though the gaze of every cat in the clearing were trained on him. Murmurs of surprise rose up around him, with a few cats offering their congratulations, but the ThunderClan cats remained in stony silence. Nightheart could feel their reproachful glances scorching him as if his pelt had caught fire.

"I have something to say." The voice came from among the ShadowClan cats; Nightheart turned to see that the speaker was Berryheart.

His belly lurched, and he felt the taste of vomit in his mouth. It had been obvious that Sunbeam's mother wasn't very keen on his joining ShadowClan, and he had been afraid that she would turn Sunbeam against him. But he hadn't thought that she'd challenge him at a Gathering, in front of his old Clanmates.

"It's too easy to switch Clans," Berryheart announced,

stepping forward to stand at the foot of the Great Oak. "Any cat can declare that they're in love with another, and then pass one easy test! Surely this is an invitation to cats who want to cause trouble, or who haven't *really* left their old Clan behind."

"Are you saying we should go back to the old way?" Tigerstar asked, heavily disapproving.

*Of course he wouldn't want that. His mate, Dovewing, was originally ThunderClan,* Nightheart thought. *He knows how cats suffered—he suffered himself.*

"No, I'm not saying that," Berryheart retorted, though Nightheart was fairly sure she would like that better. "I just think we need a safeguard against cats who are doing it for frivolous reasons, or maybe to spy on their new Clan."

More murmuring broke out among the cats in the clearing; Nightheart could see that several of them—including Yarrowleaf and Whorlpelt from his new Clan—were nodding agreement with Berryheart, while Spireclaw and Fringewhisker let their pelts bush out with anger.

"It's tough enough leaving your kin and the only home you've known." The protest came from Crowfeather, the WindClan deputy. "No cat would do that just for a whim!"

"But it's worth making absolutely sure that a cat is loyal to their new Clan," Mousewhisker pointed out. "That's the only way they should be accepted as members."

"I agree," Birchfall meowed, supporting his Clanmate. "It shouldn't be too easy."

"I think we all remember Graystripe, or we've heard the story," Mothwing put in. "No cat will ever forget his time in

RiverClan. He wanted to do the right thing, to be with his kits, but in the end his heart lay in ThunderClan."

A restless silence fell over the clearing until Finchlight rose to her paws with a respectful dip of her head to the Clan leaders. "I have an idea," she announced. "Why don't we make it three tasks, instead of one?"

Nightheart couldn't suppress a gasp at his sister's words. *She really wants to make it hard for me!*

The Clan leaders glanced at each other, while a stir of assent rippled through the clearing. Finchlight sat down again, obviously pleased that her suggestion was being taken seriously.

"That sounds sensible," Harestar mewed after a few moments.

Bramblestar and Leafstar added their agreement, and all the leaders turned to gaze at Tigerstar. The ShadowClan leader hesitated for a heartbeat, then gave a brusque nod. "Fine, we'll do that," he meowed.

"And they'd better be *tough* tasks," Berryheart growled.

A shiver went through Nightheart. *Berryheart* really *doesn't want me in her Clan.*

Tigerstar finally spoke the words that brought the Gathering to an end, and the cats began to head through the bushes and toward the shore of the island. Nightheart spotted his sister and caught up with her as she was about to leave the clearing.

"Why did you say that?" he asked her, unable to hide his anger. "It's not like you want me to come back, is it?"

Finchlight glared at him, stung by his tone. "Of course I

do! And so does Sparkpelt. She's very upset that you left, and now that you're not there, the younger warriors have to work harder because there still aren't any apprentices. Every cat wants you to come back."

For a few moments Nightheart had begun to believe that his family was really missing him. Then he realized that Finchlight didn't care about him at all.

"So you just want me back so you'll have some other cat to do all the annoying apprentice jobs. Now you know how I felt when I had to do them by myself!"

Finchlight looked taken aback. "That's not what I meant! If you come home, we'll share the work out more fairly."

Nightheart didn't want to believe her. "Why didn't Sparkpelt come to talk to me herself, if she misses me so much?" he demanded.

"Well, she's just . . . she doesn't . . . ," Finchlight began, then broke off awkwardly, as if she didn't know what to say.

"She doesn't *want* to," Nightheart finished. "She probably doesn't miss me at all. More likely she's just angry with me." He turned away and began to push his way through the bushes.

Behind him, he heard Finchlight call out, "Nightheart, come on!" but he didn't stop. Bounding down to the lakeshore, he joined the group of ShadowClan cats who were waiting their turn to cross the tree-bridge.

He would do however many tasks or tests Berryheart wanted to set for him, if it meant he would never have to return to ThunderClan.

# CHAPTER 4

*Leaving the marshes behind, Frostpaw headed* for the RiverClan camp, a massive bunch of horsetail clamped in her jaws. She had just crossed the stream and was climbing the slope that led to the entrance when she heard some cat calling her name.

"Frostpaw! Hey, Frostpaw!"

Frostpaw halted and turned to see her littermates, Graypaw and Mistpaw, following her up the slope, with their mentors, Breezeheart and Icewing, a few paw steps behind. Frostpaw took a step back at the sight of Icewing. She hadn't forgotten how the white she-cat had told her they must have a talk. But she'd managed to avoid the senior warrior for days now, because that was the last thing Frostpaw wanted.

*The longer I can put off talking to Icewing, the longer I can pretend that nothing's wrong . . . and that I don't have a huge choice to make.*

She turned back to Graypaw and Mistpaw. The apprentices' pelts were clumped with debris clinging to their fur, but their eyes were bright, and they both looked pleased with themselves.

"We've been battle training!" Mistpaw exclaimed, bounding up to Frostpaw. "I killed Graypaw!"

"Did not!" Graypaw retorted as he joined his littermates. "I was just pretending, so I could grab you and *shred* you!"

"You both did very well," Icewing meowed as she padded up. "You can take a break now, and help yourselves to fresh-kill. And after that," she continued, "give yourselves a good grooming. You look as if a fox dragged you across the territory."

"Thanks, Icewing!" Mistpaw exclaimed.

Graypaw stood up straight as he gazed at Breezeheart. "I promise we'll clean up." Breezeheart gave his apprentice a fond nod before walking into the camp.

Frostpaw's pelt bristled as she desperately tried to think of a way to excuse herself before Icewing pulled her aside. *She's bound to ask me if StarClan has spoken to me about our new leader. And what will I tell her?*

"Frostpaw," Icewing meowed. "Just the cat I was hoping to meet. Is this a good time for us to have our talk?"

Frostpaw dropped her huge bunch of herbs. "Sorry, Icewing," she responded, pleased that she had a reason to get away. "I have to get this horsetail back to camp."

Icewing narrowed her blue eyes, as if she was well aware that Frostpaw was making an excuse. "Later, then." She gave a curt nod and headed down toward the stream.

Breathing a sigh of relief, Frostpaw gathered up the scattered stems, then continued toward the camp with her littermates. She felt a little wistful; it sounded as if their training had been fun—much more fun than sloshing around in the marshes gathering horsetail.

"Come and eat with us," Mistpaw invited when they reached the camp. "Mothwing won't mind—not when you've collected all that horsetail."

Frostpaw hesitated, then decided that her sister was right. There was nothing urgent going on in the medicine cats' den, and the few moments she would take to eat a piece of prey wouldn't make any difference.

"Okay," she mumbled around the horsetail stems, and followed her littermates to the fresh-kill pile.

When Frostpaw had set down the horsetail stems to put away later, she chose a vole and crouched down to eat it. She noticed the ShadowClan deputy, Cloverfoot, sitting nearby with a ShadowClan warrior she didn't recognize. She wished she could overhear their low-voiced conversation, but she was too far away.

"It's weird being without a leader, and having ShadowClan in our camp," Graypaw began between bites of the squirrel he was sharing with Mistpaw. "And Tigerstar having a paw in all our decisions."

"We really need a new leader," Mistpaw agreed. "Frostpaw, are you sure that Owlnose wasn't the right cat?"

"I'm sure," Frostpaw replied, feeling ashamed all over again. "I made the wrong choice, and Owlnose was sensible enough to see that."

"Well, what about Duskfur?" Mistpaw suggested. "Or Icewing? They would make great leaders."

Frostpaw shook her head. "StarClan told me to look for an unlikely cat," she meowed. Privately, she accepted that she had imagined all the messages she'd once believed came from StarClan. She wouldn't be the cat who chose RiverClan's new leader.

*But that's what every cat expects me to do.* Her belly roiled with the pressure of her Clanmates' expectations. *What am I going to tell them?*

"How are you enjoying your training?" she asked her littermates. She was eager to change the subject, but also collecting information. Soon, if she told the truth, she would have to choose between becoming a medicine cat like Mothwing, unable to communicate with StarClan, or starting over with an apprenticeship as a warrior. Until now she'd been so busy with her medicine-cat apprentice duties that she'd barely noticed what her littermates had been up to.

"It's great," Graypaw replied. "I know we have to do all the duties like clearing out the soiled bedding from all the dens, and treating the elders' ticks with mouse bile—"

"Yuck!" Mistpaw put in.

"But the battle training and hunting are really fun, and we're learning how to defend and feed our Clan."

"That sounds great," Frostpaw mewed, trying to keep the jealousy out of her voice. "I know Curlfeather would have been proud of you."

"She'd have been proud of you, too, Frostpaw," Mistpaw assured her. "She knew how important your visions were."

Frostpaw acknowledged her sister's words with a nod, wondering how their mother would have reacted to the discovery that her visions weren't real at all. A pang of grief shook her at the thought that she had only imagined talking to her mother's spirit in StarClan.

"We were always a little jealous of you," Graypaw went on.

Frostpaw flicked her ears up in surprise. "Of *me*?"

"Yeah, because you're going to be such a vital member of the Clan," Mistpaw meowed. "But now we see how much pressure you're under, trying to find our new leader and dealing with ShadowClan—I'm definitely happier training to be a warrior."

"And we're learning so much," Graypaw added. "Mistpaw, let's show Frostpaw the move we learned this morning."

"Okay," Mistpaw mewed, swallowing a mouthful of squirrel. "You be a ShadowClan warrior coming to attack me."

As Graypaw scampered back a few paces, Frostpaw hoped that the ShadowClan warriors hadn't overheard her sister's remark. Any sensible cat wouldn't take an apprentice seriously, but the situation in RiverClan could so easily erupt into violence again. But Cloverfoot was peacefully grooming herself, and the other ShadowClan warrior looked half-asleep, his eyes half-closed and his tail wrapped around his paws.

Graypaw let out a fierce growl and charged toward his sister. Just before he reached her, Mistpaw reared up on her hind legs and fell forward on top of him, dealing him two sharp blows over his ears.

"Ow!" Graypaw shoved her off and got to his paws, shaking his head.

"That was brilliant, Mistpaw," Frostpaw meowed. "If I were attacking our camp, you would scare me."

"Hey, Frostpaw, why don't you try it?" Graypaw suggested. "Even a medicine cat might have to defend herself someday."

Embarrassed, Frostpaw drew back. "Oh, I couldn't. . . ."

"Of course you could." Mistpaw gave her a friendly nudge. "Go on, try. I'll be the ShadowClan cat this time."

Reluctantly Frostpaw rose to her paws. "Okay."

Mistpaw dashed away, then spun around and hurled herself forward. Frostpaw tried to remember how her sister had timed her leap, but waited just a heartbeat too long. As she reared up on her hind legs, Mistpaw barreled into her, bearing her to the ground, though Frostpaw still managed to get in a couple of swipes before her sister landed on top of her.

"I messed up," she mewed ruefully as she scrambled to her paws.

"No, you didn't," Graypaw insisted. "That was great for a first try."

"Yeah, you would have really hurt me if you hadn't had your claws sheathed," Mistpaw added.

Frostpaw stood blinking, warmed by their praise. She realized how much she loved her littermates, and how much she had missed them since they'd become warrior apprentices. They had been apprenticed before her, while Mistystar and Mothwing decided whether StarClan had chosen her to be a medicine cat.

*Maybe I could be a warrior after all,* she thought. And if she gave up being a medicine cat, she could at least spend more time with Mistpaw and Graypaw.

Inside the medicine cats' den, Frostpaw was gently easing off the poultice she had placed on the tear in Mallownose's ear. As she licked away the last of the horsetail, she could see that the wound had closed up nicely, the scar a healthy pink.

"How does it feel?" she asked Mallownose.

"It's fine," the brown tabby tom replied. "It hardly hurts at all."

"Good. I don't think you need any more horsetail. We'll let the air get to it, but come and see me again tomorrow, so I can check it out."

"Sure thing." Mallownose dipped his head. "Thanks, Frostpaw."

As she watched him leave the den, Frostpaw took a few deep breaths. She knew she should feel pleased that the warriors wounded in the battle with ShadowClan were getting better, but she couldn't relax. Icewing had to know something was up with her, or she wouldn't keep asking to speak privately. And the longer Frostpaw kept the secret of her imagined visions, the more miserable she felt. Mothwing was wise, and she was right that there was a lot going on within the Clan, but Frostpaw worried that her Clanmates would be furious if they thought she had lied to them. RiverClan's situation was dire, but hiding the truth and pretending she was just a vision away from solving their problems wasn't helping any cat.

*Mothwing hasn't had much experience with StarClan, and she doesn't trust them. What if she wants me to keep this secret because she thinks we don't need a connection to StarClan?* Frostpaw respected her mentor, but she knew that wasn't true. *We need a leader—and we need*

*StarClan to help us find that leader.*

She had almost finished tidying up the scraps of horsetail from Mallownose's poultice when she heard movement at the entrance to the den and looked up to see Splashtail. Her pleasure at seeing him calmed some of her anxiety; he had been very busy the last few days, hunting or patrolling, and she had scarcely spoken to him.

Now she noticed that he was limping as he crossed the den and gave her an affectionate lick on her nose. Chunks of the poultice on his flank had fallen off; Frostpaw could see that the wound had opened up and blood was oozing from it.

"Splashtail, that looks awful!" she exclaimed.

The young tom twisted his head around to get a good look at his injured side. "Oh, it's healing fine," he mewed. "Though I guess it could be better."

"No, it is *not* fine," Frostpaw scolded him. "Mothwing told you to rest, didn't she? And I can see you haven't been doing that. You do know you can't solve all of RiverClan's problems by yourself, right?"

Splashtail shrugged, wincing. "Okay, but we all have to do everything we can to show ShadowClan that we RiverClan cats can take care of ourselves. You're doing your bit—every cat comes out of your den feeling much better. I just want to do mine."

Frostpaw sighed. "Sit down and let me clean that up."

As she washed Splashtail's wound with strong, rhythmic licks, Frostpaw wanted more than anything to tell him her secret. But something held her back from just coming out with it. "Well," she mewed instead, pausing in her licking, "my job was supposed to be to listen to StarClan and pick out our new leader, and I chose wrong when I picked Owlnose, so I'm not exactly doing my bit to get rid of Tigerstar."

"Cheer up!" Splashtail told her. "I'm sure StarClan will help you, and even if they don't, RiverClan will be okay. Owlnose was a good guess, since StarClan told you that the new leader was an unlikely cat. That could have meant any cat."

Frostpaw nodded, remembering once more that the message from StarClan hadn't been real; she had imagined it.

*And the sign . . .* Her belly lurched with a sickening pang. *The sign that led me to my mother.* The curled feather she had found beside the path that led down to the Moonpool had prompted her to choose Curlfeather for leader after Reedwhisker was found dead. *That has to have been a coincidence, too.*

While she was putting a fresh poultice on Splashtail's shoulder, she was distracted by a cough from the entrance to the den. Turning her head, she saw Shadowsight, the Shadow-Clan medicine cat. With a wave of her tail, she invited him to come inside.

"Greetings," Shadowsight mewed, dipping his head to the two RiverClan cats. "You're hard at work, Frostpaw."

"Yes, treating a warrior who doesn't know what *rest* means," Frostpaw responded. She plastered the last bit of cobweb along Splashtail's side. "There, you're all done."

"Thanks, Frostpaw. I promise I'll take more care this time." Splashtail headed out of the den, giving Shadowsight a coldly polite nod as he passed him.

"It's good to see you, Shadowsight," Frostpaw meowed, slightly embarrassed that Splashtail hadn't been friendlier. Shadowsight had nothing to do with his father taking over RiverClan. *And he's always been kind to me.*

"I'm glad to see you, too, Frostpaw. How are you all coping in RiverClan?"

Frostpaw tilted her head. "Things could be better," she replied. "But you know that, of course. At least our warriors are recovering from the battle. I don't think we'll lose any of them."

"Good. You know, Frostpaw, if you can find your new leader, all this could be over quite quickly."

Frostpaw knew that Shadowsight meant to be encouraging, but his words sent a shiver of apprehension through her. She wondered how long Mothwing would go on forbidding her to confess. *If she waits much longer, maybe I should name the cat I think would make the best leader. If I choose wrong, StarClan will just refuse to give them their nine lives.*

Then she realized that she had a sympathetic medicine cat here in her den, with no other cats listening to them. Besides, Shadowsight had experienced something like her own problem. He had received visions that led to Bramblestar's death, and he had realized too late that they were not sent by StarClan.

*He's the perfect cat to help me. I mustn't waste this chance!*

"Shadowsight," she began cautiously, "can I ask you a question about StarClan?"

"Of course," Shadowsight responded, sounding faintly

surprised. "I'll try to answer—though you are aware they haven't spoken to me since I came back from the Dark Forest, right?"

"Yes," Frostpaw mewed. "That's sort of what I want to know about. What did it feel like, to realize that the messages you got from StarClan weren't real?"

Shadowsight flinched. "You don't mince words, do you?"

"I'm sorry—" Frostpaw at once felt guilty for delving so deeply into Shadowsight's secrets. She didn't know him well enough to expect him to confide in her.

"No, it's fine, I don't mind telling you," Shadowsight reassured her. "It was . . . painful. I still feel guilty about what I did to Bramblestar—to all the Clans—by blindly following Ashfur's instructions. I thought they were real messages from my ancestors, but it was Ashfur, not StarClan, sending them." He paused for a moment, his eyes fixed on something Frostpaw couldn't see. "I had other visions, when I was younger," he went on at last. "They were true visions from StarClan, but I wasn't strong enough, and I used to have seizures. I only lost the ability to contact StarClan at all after it was all over."

"Do you miss it?" Frostpaw asked.

Shadowsight shook his head. "Honestly, I don't. If I can spend the rest of my life simply healing sick and injured cats, that will be enough for me. And I'll see my friends in StarClan when I die, just like any other cat."

Frostpaw thought that over, feeling slightly reassured. The mistake Shadowsight had made had almost destroyed the Clans, yet even he was at peace now. Her own situation wasn't nearly as bad. It was comforting to know that she too could find peace in being a medicine cat who believed in StarClan but couldn't contact them.

Shadowsight remained quiet for a moment, turning his head aside to give his tabby shoulder fur a lick. Frostpaw wondered if he was reflecting that not every cat made it to StarClan; perhaps he was thinking about Bristlefrost. She had heard the stories about the ThunderClan warrior who had died in the Dark Forest, her spirit never reaching StarClan.

Then Shadowsight licked one paw and drew it thoughtfully over his ear. "Why do you want to know all this?" he asked. "Are you all right? Are your Clanmates asking too much of you?"

Frostpaw was tempted to tell him everything, but then reminded herself that this was one of the ShadowClan invaders. She could hear Splashtail's voice inside her head, telling her not to make their Clan seem weak. *I can't tell Shadowsight the truth!*

"It's just that my Clanmates think I can just drop in on StarClan whenever I want," she explained, "and come back with the answer to all our problems, but I'm not sure it's going to be that easy. I'm under a lot of pressure."

"You can always come to me, if you need to talk," Shadowsight mewed. "And that reminds me—when I was on my way here, Icewing gave me a message for you. She wants to talk to you. She's helping out in the elders' den right now, if you don't have any other cats to look after."

Frostpaw's heart sank. *I suppose I can't put her off any longer—I've got to face her,*

She thanked Shadowsight, and checked that no other cats

were waiting outside her den. Then she said good-bye and headed into the camp to find Icewing.

The white she-cat was standing outside the elders' den, helping Mistpaw and Graypaw to roll up a bundle of soiled bedding and carry it out of camp. "There, that's done," she mewed, sitting down and dusting her forepaws. "Now you can collect some fresh moss and make a comfortable new nest."

"Yes, and make sure there aren't any thorns," the elder Mosspelt added, raising one hind paw to scratch vigorously behind her ear.

Frostpaw padded up with a mew of greeting for her littermates. She was surprised to see Icewing helping with a task that was far below her status as a senior warrior. "Why are you doing that?" she asked.

Icewing turned toward her. "Oh, there you are, Frostpaw. As for that . . ." She waved a paw toward the departing apprentices. "The job needed doing, so I helped. This will be my den soon enough, so I'd better make sure it's nice and cozy."

Some of Frostpaw's reluctance faded in admiration of the white she-cat. She let out a *mrrow* of amusement. "You might be an older cat, Icewing, but you're certainly not an elder yet!"

Icewing gave Frostpaw a searching look, then asked, "Do you want to take a walk?"

Frostpaw took in a deep breath, her pads prickling nervously. *I guess this is happening—I have to just see what she has to say and use my best judgment.* Mothwing couldn't be mad at her if Icewing guessed that there was something wrong, could she? *I can't lie to her.* A tiny part of Frostpaw was almost excited. If Icewing guessed the truth, then this could be her chance to confide in some cat who might be able to tell her what to do.

"Okay," she mewed.

Icewing led the way out of the camp and along the shore of the lake. Frostpaw felt soothed by the gentle lapping of waves on the shore, and the rustle of wind through the reeds.

"How are you doing, Frostpaw?" Icewing asked.

The question surprised Frostpaw. She had expected Icewing to either demand a leader or the truth—not to worry about Frostpaw's feelings. She shrugged. "I—I'm not sure."

"I'm sorry there's so much pressure on you right now," Icewing continued, "especially as it's been barely a moon since you lost your mother. I know you were very close to Curlfeather, and she trusted you completely."

A lump like tough fresh-kill lodged itself in Frostpaw's throat. She remembered her time in the nursery, feeling so safe and protected in the curve of her mother's body. She couldn't speak.

"Puddleshine, Shadowsight, and Mothwing have all talked about your talent as a medicine cat," Icewing went on after a moment. "I'm very proud of you."

Frostpaw hadn't expected that, either. She felt she'd messed up in her role as medicine cat so completely, Icewing's praise hit her where she least expected it, and for a moment she had trouble speaking. The compliment felt like a massive paw, gripping her tighter and tighter until she couldn't bear it anymore. *I don't deserve it—I've never deserved it!*

"I'm not sure I'm a good medicine cat," she confessed. "I don't think I'm a medicine cat at all."

Icewing fixed her with a concerned gaze. "What do you mean?" she asked.

"I *thought* I was hearing from StarClan!" Frostpaw had struggled against this confession for so long, it was a relief to let the words spill out. "But Puddleshine described his visions to me, and they sound completely different from anything I've seen. Curlfeather died before she could become leader, and Owlnose was obviously the wrong choice. The more I think about it, the more I'm sure I never had any real visions at all. I just imagined things so I could tell every cat what they wanted to hear."

For a moment Icewing was silent, her eyes wide with shock. "You're sure?" she asked.

Frostpaw nodded emphatically. "The way Puddleshine described his visions—they were so much more detailed. He said he's been to StarClan's hunting grounds, that he's talked to them face-to-face. I just saw . . . shapes. Shadows. And I thought I heard voices, but I don't think they were ever real."

Icewing took a deep breath and gave her pelt a shake. "That must have been hard for you to realize," she mewed calmly. "You're right to say something. The first thing we should do is tell Mothwing, and Tigerstar, too. He needs to know that the situation is more complicated than he thought at first."

"Mothwing already knows," Frostpaw responded, with a pang of guilt that she was betraying her mentor, "and she advised me not to tell Tigerstar."

Icewing blinked in surprise. "Well. Perhaps we should both go and talk to Mothwing."

She turned and strode off in the direction of the medicine cats' den.

*What—right now?* Frostpaw froze in dismay for a heartbeat, then scurried after her. What would Mothwing say when she realized that Frostpaw had gone against her advice and told Icewing the truth? Frostpaw felt sure it was the right thing to do, but she'd never disobeyed her mentor so completely. She dreaded this confrontation with every hair on her pelt.

When Frostpaw and Icewing reached the medicine cats' den, they found Mothwing in the shelter of the twisted thorn tree that overhung the entrance, sorting a bundle of fresh herbs.

"Mothwing, we need to talk," Icewing announced as they approached, a sharp edge to her voice. "I know about Frostpaw's visions. Or should I say her lack of visions?"

A shiver of guilt and anxiety went right through Frostpaw as Mothwing turned a deep amber gaze on her.

"You shouldn't have told Icewing," she meowed. "Not yet."

"This isn't Frostpaw's fault," Icewing retorted, not giving Frostpaw the chance to respond. "What were you thinking, Mothwing, letting us all lie to Tigerstar about how we're going to find our new leader?" Mothwing opened her jaws to reply, but Icewing swept on. "Without a link to StarClan, it's going to take much more time, which means ShadowClan will be hanging around in our camp for much longer. What did you think would happen? I thought you didn't believe in miracles!"

Mothwing let out an annoyed hiss. "I can see your point,

Icewing, but think what will happen if we *do* tell Tigerstar we have no connection to StarClan. ShadowClan will dig their claws in here, maybe for good! The best thing that could happen then would be that the other Clans would come and fight them off, but how likely is that? It's only Leafstar who is keen for battle. And do we really want more blood to be spilled? No more cats should be hurt over this if we can avoid it." Taking a breath and deliberately calming herself, she turned to Frostpaw. "You're young," she meowed, "and you've been through a lot. It's only natural you should have doubts—and maybe all you need is time."

Frostpaw couldn't remain silent any longer. "No, I don't need time," she asserted. "If anything, I've already taken too much time. I'm *certain* that I'm not having visions, and how do you think I feel, Mothwing, when you don't listen to me when I tell you that?"

"I'm sorry," Mothwing responded with an irritated twitch of her tail, "but I still don't see the point in telling Tigerstar what's happening, and throwing the Clan into chaos while ShadowClan is right here in our camp."

Icewing heaved a deep sigh. "I can agree with that, at least," she stated. "We should all sleep on this. But in the morning, we'll have to tell Tigerstar *something*."

Noise in the camp woke Frostpaw. Mothwing had already left the den, and though her nest was still shadowed, Frostpaw could see pale sunlight shining down on the stream outside.

Stifling a yawn, she struggled to her paws. She had scarcely slept the night before, roused by fearful dreams and then lying awake worrying about the future of her Clan—and her own future. Mothwing and Shadowsight both served their Clans as healers without a connection to StarClan. But when Frostpaw thought about it, she knew that wasn't what she truly wanted. *I'm sure that wasn't what Curlfeather wanted for me, either. Could I really train to be a warrior. . . ?*

Now every paw step was an effort as she tottered out of her den and gave her pelt a perfunctory grooming to get rid of the scraps of bedding that clung to it.

Sounds of movement and cats' voices were coming from the camp. Forcing herself to shake off her weariness, Frostpaw scrambled up the bank and headed in the direction of the noise.

When she reached the center of camp, Frostpaw saw that Tigerstar had returned. Hopwhisker and Slatefur were with him; she supposed they were meant to take over from the ShadowClan warriors who had been staying in the camp.

Frostpaw watched as Icewing padded up to meet the ShadowClan leader, with Mothwing at her shoulder. Splashtail followed them, and more RiverClan cats crowded behind.

*This is it!* Frostpaw thought; she wasn't sure what Icewing had decided, but she still felt an unpleasant fluttering in her belly, as if a bird were trying to escape.

She didn't want any cat talking about her when she wasn't there, so she bounded across the camp and wriggled through the crowd until she could stand at Icewing's side.

Icewing saw her there and gave her a nod. Then she braced

herself as if she was coming to a decision. "Tigerstar," she meowed, "there's something you should know." The Shadow-Clan leader twitched one ear but said nothing. "Something not every cat in our Clan knows yet, but they should know it, too," Icewing continued. "Frostpaw has realized that she is not able to talk to StarClan."

Shocked silence followed her words for a couple of heart-beats. Then a clamor broke out as the RiverClan cats pressed closer to Frostpaw, battering her with questions and growls of protest.

"What do you mean, you can't talk to StarClan?" Gorse-claw demanded. "What happened?"

"I thought you were supposed to be a medicine cat!" Havenpelt added.

Duskfur pushed forward until she stood nose to nose with Frostpaw. "Have you tried recently?" she asked. "Have you been back to the Moonpool since you went there with Owlnose?"

Overwhelmed, Frostpaw couldn't find the words to answer. Glancing at Splashtail, she thought that he looked almost frightened, and when he noticed her gaze resting on him, he looked away.

*Is he upset with me for not telling him first?* Frostpaw wondered.

She wanted to tell her Clanmates how sorry she was, but the questions were still coming one after another; she felt as if she were standing underneath the waterfall that cascaded into the Moonpool.

"Quiet!" At last Icewing's voice rose above the outcry.

"Leave Frostpaw alone. It's not her fault, but you should believe her. She knows best whether she has visions or she doesn't."

Frostpaw took a deep breath as the noise began to die down. "I *never* had visions," she announced, forcing her voice to be steady though her legs were trembling. "Curlfeather thought I had talent, but it was all imagination."

Now that the words were out, she felt a sudden relief. *They can yowl at me all they like. It can't get any worse than this.*

But though several cats let out gasps of shock, and there was an angry hiss from Duskfur, no cat attacked her with any more questions. Most of them turned to Tigerstar; Frostpaw could see they were wondering what his reaction would be. *I'd like to know that, too!* she thought, every hair on her pelt prickling with nervousness.

At first Tigerstar did not respond. Frostpaw remembered that Shadowsight was his son, and Tigerstar must have found it a struggle to cope with *his* changing relationship with StarClan.

For a moment the ShadowClan leader just looked tired, his head drooping, and Frostpaw asked herself whether he had bitten off more than he could chew. She reflected that maybe RiverClan had been wrong to try so hard to prove they were all fine. *We should pile all our problems on him until he gives up!*

"This just proves that I was right to come here," Tigerstar began with a sigh. "This is exactly RiverClan's problem, and has been since Mistystar died. You're all lying and keeping secrets, not just from me, but from each other! It has to stop, or I'll never be able to trust that you can run your own Clan."

His gaze raked over the crowd of cats, but when he came to look at Frostpaw, he softened slightly. "I'm not angry with you, Frostpaw. It's hard to speak up when something goes wrong, especially when every cat is depending on you. But from now on, you all need to tell me straight away when you aren't sure what you should do."

Soft but furious growls rose from the crowd of cats around him.

"You're not our leader!" Podlight snarled.

"Yeah," Duskfur agreed. "We don't have to tell you anything!"

For a few heartbeats Frostpaw was afraid that fighting was going to break out again. Duskfur was facing Cloverfoot, stretching her neck out and hissing, even though she was still having difficulty breathing from the last battle.

"Calm down!" Icewing exclaimed, touching Duskfur's shoulder with her tail-tip while her gaze took in the rest of her Clanmates. "We all have the same problem here: no leader, no StarClan. What do we do about it?"

"It seems obvious to me," Tigerstar responded, recovering his air of command. "You will have to train Frostpaw as a warrior, and wait for another cat to have a real vision. StarClan won't abandon you for long. Meanwhile, as you're all temporarily ShadowClan cats, you will tell me if you're having issues, and I will deal with it."

"ShadowClan cats!" Even Icewing stared at Tigerstar, outraged, while clamor broke out again all around her. "No way are we ShadowClan cats!"

"We're *RiverClan*!" Harelight growled. "And I'll rip the fur off any cat who says we aren't."

Tigerstar seemed to realize that he had gone too far. "I said *temporarily*," he protested. "No cat is trying to take your Clan away from you. But you need to treat me like your leader until you have a real one of your own."

His words didn't have much effect. The argument raged on, all the while threatening to descend into fighting. Hopwhisker and Slatefur stood on either side of their leader, their claws out and their muscles bunched, ready to leap into battle.

In the midst of it, Mothwing glanced across at Frostpaw and met her eyes. She didn't look angry, but Frostpaw thought she seemed as if she would like to say, *I told you so.*

Even with conflict surging around her, Frostpaw felt a heavy weight lifted off her, as if she had just climbed out of the lake and scattered all the water out of her fur in one vigorous shake.

*I'm going to be a warrior!* RiverClan's leadership problems were no longer her concern. And it would be great to learn how to hunt and fight without the crushing weight of every cat counting on her to save her Clan. *I'm free!*

# CHAPTER 5

♣

*"You're looking upset,"* Sunbeam meowed. "Is something the matter?"

She and Nightheart had settled together in a sheltered spot at the edge of the ShadowClan camp. Even as Sunbeam asked the question, she had some idea of what the answer would be. Nightheart had seemed restless, uneasy, ever since the Gathering. Sunbeam was sure that his sister, Finchlight, had said something to bother him when they spoke privately at the end, though Nightheart hadn't told her what that was.

*His kin must be angry that he left ThunderClan for ShadowClan.*

"Are you sure about this?" she asked when Nightheart didn't respond. In her own mind, she wasn't sure at all, but she couldn't tell him that.

Nightheart turned toward her, looking deep into her eyes. "I've made my choice," he insisted. "And I'll do whatever it takes to become a ShadowClan cat."

"Let all cats old enough to catch their own prey join here in the middle of the camp for a Clan meeting!"

Sunbeam sat upright, startled, then exchanged a confused look with Nightheart. The voice was her mother's. "She's not the leader or the deputy," Sunbeam mewed. "What could she

61

possibly be calling a Clan meeting about?"

Cautiously, she and Nightheart padded down into the center of the camp to join her Clanmates around Berryheart. Sunbeam spotted Gullswoop giving her a look of approval at seeing her walking beside Nightheart, and her brother Spireclaw looking as confused as Sunbeam herself felt.

Berryheart waited until all the cats had gathered around her before starting to speak. "Cats of ShadowClan," she announced. "Tigerstar has chosen me to take charge of the tasks for cats who want to change their Clan."

Sunbeam felt a stab of panic and exchanged a glance with Nightheart. He looked disconcerted, but at the same time there was a flicker of amusement in his eyes.

"Well, *that* can't be good," he murmured, half joking.

Sunbeam leaned toward him and spoke softly into his ear. "If you knew my mother better, you wouldn't find this funny," she told him. "You don't understand how bad it could be."

As Berryheart continued, Sunbeam wasn't surprised to find out that she had been right.

"I've spoken to Tigerstar," Berryheart told her Clanmates, "and we've agreed on what was suggested at the Gathering. The rules have changed. Instead of having to perform only one task, cats who want to change their Clan will need to perform three. And that will include Fringewhisker."

As murmured comments broke out among the Clan, Spireclaw raised his voice in protest. "That isn't fair! Fringewhisker is already a member of the Clan! She completed the task she was given."

Berryheart met her son's gaze calmly. "The rule is now

three tasks," she informed him. "If Fringewhisker thinks she's too good to do what every other newcomer to ShadowClan will have to do, perhaps she doesn't want to be in ShadowClan that badly. Perhaps she should leave."

Spireclaw opened his jaws to retort, but Fringewhisker cut him off by laying her tail on his shoulder. "I'll do the two extra tasks," she mewed with a sigh. "Of course I will. I'll be happy to."

"Then your second task will take place at sunhigh," Berryheart told her.

Fringewhisker nodded. "I'll be ready."

Sunbeam flexed her claws in frustration at Berryheart's attitude. Her mother was determined to put difficulties in the path of every cat who came to ShadowClan for the sake of love. She felt the touch of Nightheart's nose against her ear as he whispered, "Fringewhisker is taking this well."

"She has no choice," Sunbeam responded. "Berryheart has Tigerstar behind her. Besides, if she let Fringewhisker get away with just one task, cats could always raise doubts about whether she was *really* a ShadowClan cat. Do you think Fringewhisker doesn't know that?"

Nightheart was looking particularly dejected. "Berryheart is making me more nervous about my tasks," he admitted. "She's clearly planning something! I know she'll try to think up impossible tasks for me and Fringewhisker, just to make sure we fail. Finchlight would *love* that."

"Ah, but there's one thing your sister doesn't know," Sunbeam purred.

Nightheart gave her a puzzled look. "What's that?"

Sunbeam butted his shoulder with her nose. "You've got me." She felt a *mrrow* of laughter rising in her throat as she added, "Come on, it's high time you had a tour around the territory."

She climbed the slope up to the barrier of brambles that surrounded the camp, with Nightheart padding in her paw steps. "It's easier if you keep low as you push your way through," she explained, leading the way. "You're much less likely to snag your fur on the thorns."

Leaving the camp behind, Sunbeam led the way into the forest until she halted beside a tall pine tree that was blackened and burned from its roots to its tip.

"This must have been struck by lightning seasons ago," she told Nightheart. "Long before the Clans came to the forest. Now it's where we bring the apprentices to train them for night hunting."

As they headed through the pine trees toward the lake, Sunbeam couldn't stop thinking about Nightheart's sister, Finchlight. She hoped they could settle their differences if Nightheart succeeded in his tasks and stayed in ShadowClan.

"Do you think Finchlight really wants you to fail?" she asked gently.

Nightheart shrugged uneasily. "It's more like she expects me to fail," he responded. "Or maybe she does want me to, because she resents that I left."

"Maybe she doesn't resent you," Sunbeam suggested. "She might just miss you. I know I—" Abruptly she broke off. She had only just stopped herself from saying, *I know I'd miss you if you left ShadowClan.* She sympathized with the way he felt estranged from his family, and admired his courage in facing the prospect of life in an unfamiliar Clan. For the first time she felt that perhaps it could work out with him.

*But I'm not ready to tell him all of that!*

Nightheart turned to her, a warm look in his eyes, as if he understood what was going through her mind. "I think you're giving Finchlight more credit than she deserves," he meowed. "But it's nice to think that she might care more than I realize."

Sunbeam led the way closer to the lake, wondering what else she might show Nightheart that would help him with his challenges. When she could see the lake water shining through the trees, she stopped beside one of the outlying pines.

"There's a bees' nest up there," she told Nightheart, pointing with her tail to a gap about halfway up the trunk. "They're best left undisturbed."

"I don't see any bees," Nightheart meowed, peering up at the gap.

Sunbeam looked more closely and realized that he was right. Usually she could see bees flying in and out, but today there was no movement. "Maybe they've abandoned it," she mused. "We ought to check it out. Puddleshine would be really grateful for some honey. It's good for soothing wounds and binding poultices together."

"Okay, let's do it," Nightheart agreed.

He sprang into the tree and began clambering from branch to branch. Sunbeam felt her heart beating harder as she followed him. *What if he falls?*

Just below the gap a thin branch stuck out from the trunk. It was the obvious way to get into the nest, but right before Nightheart reached it, Sunbeam remembered that he wasn't ShadowClan. *This is something I can teach him!*

"That branch will never bear your weight!" she called out anxiously. "It's better to stand on the branch below and reach up from there."

Nightheart turned his head to look at her, laughter in his eyes. "Who do you think you're teaching?" he asked. "Do you think ThunderClan doesn't have any trees?"

Sunbeam felt her pelt grow hot with embarrassment. "Sorry," she mumbled.

"Don't worry," Nightheart responded. "I know my way around a tree."

He climbed the last couple of tail-lengths, and instead of trusting himself to the weak branch, he clawed his way up the trunk and vanished into the abandoned nest, just his tail waving around in the open.

"It's empty!" he called out to Sunbeam. "No bees, but plenty of honey."

Sunbeam heard scrabbling sounds, and within heartbeats scraps of honeycomb began raining down around her. Seeing that Nightheart didn't need her help, she scrambled down to the ground and began collecting the scraps together.

"That's enough!" she yowled after a few moments. "It's all we can carry!"

Nightheart emerged from the nest, a last lump of honeycomb clasped in his jaws. Jumping nimbly from branch to branch, he joined Sunbeam on the ground.

"That was a brilliant idea of yours," he meowed.

Sunbeam felt hot with embarrassment all over again. "It's the ShadowClan way, looking out for things that might be useful," she murmured. "Soon it will be yours, too."

As she was searching the undergrowth for large leaves to wrap around the pieces of honeycomb, Sunbeam noticed that the shadows of the trees had grown short. "It's almost sunhigh!" she gasped. "Nightheart, we have to hurry back to camp. I want to be there to support Fringewhisker when she performs her second task."

Side by side, the two cats raced back through the trees, carrying their leaf wraps. As they pushed their way through the brambles, Sunbeam saw her mother already in the center of the camp, Fringewhisker standing beside her. Spireclaw and several of the other warriors were looking on.

"I'll take the honey to Puddleshine," Nightheart mumbled around his leaf wrap. "You get down there. I'll join you in a heartbeat."

After dropping her own wrap at Nightheart's paws, Sunbeam raced down to join her Clanmates. Berryheart had already begun to explain the second task to Fringewhisker and the others.

". . . an obstacle course," she was meowing as Sunbeam bounded up, panting. "You'll need to leap over a bramble thicket, crawl under a fallen tree, climb up one tree and down another one three trees away, and then make your way to the other side of a ravine."

"That's too hard!" Spireclaw protested.

"Yes," Lightleap agreed. "It's much harder than the log-rolling task."

Berryheart swung around to face the objectors. "It *should* be hard to join another Clan," she snapped. "We only want dedicated Clanmates!"

"Berryheart is right," Fringewhisker mewed. Sunbeam hadn't expected that, and there were murmurs of surprise from the other bystanders. "I'll do whatever it takes to prove my worthiness as a ShadowClan cat," she added with a loving look at Spireclaw.

Berryheart led the way out of the camp and across the territory to the place she had chosen for the challenge. As they headed out, Nightheart caught up to pad along beside Sunbeam.

"Puddleshine was pleased with the honey," he told her. "He said we did a good job—but great StarClan, I'm sticky!"

Sunbeam let out a snort of laughter. "Then stay away from me!"

Eventually Berryheart halted beside a bramble thicket. "This is where you start," she told Fringewhisker. "And keep going in that direction. You'll soon come to the ravine."

Fringewhisker nodded. "Okay."

She took a good long run up to the thicket and sailed over it as if she were a bird. Yowls of admiration came from the watchers.

"Of course. She's a SkyClan cat," Sunbeam murmured to Nightheart. "They're great at leaping—and climbing trees.

I wonder if this challenge isn't as hard as Berryheart thinks it is."

"Don't tell her that," Nightheart responded. "Or she'll think up something worse for the next one."

Hurrying around the thicket, they were in time to see Fringewhisker scramble out from underneath the fallen tree and leap up into the branches of the nearest pine.

"She's making it look so easy!" Sunbeam mewed admiringly.

Berryheart obviously felt the same; she had a thunderous expression as she stalked over to a more distant tree and called out, "You have to come down this one!"

"On my way!" Fringewhisker sounded as if she was enjoying herself.

"I'm surprised she even remembers what she has to do," Sunbeam remarked to Nightheart. "It's so complicated!"

Fringewhisker moved from tree to tree as confidently as if she were strolling along the ground in her own familiar territory. Soon she jumped down to stand beside Berryheart, who simply angled her ears in the direction Fringewhisker needed to go.

"Oh, no!" Sunbeam exclaimed as she and her Clanmates followed Fringewhisker through the trees. "I've just realized where Berryheart is taking her. This ravine is near the Sky-Clan border, and we don't come this way often. We certainly don't have any reason to cross it. Spireclaw," she went on, turning to her brother, "have you ever shown Fringewhisker this part of the territory?"

Spireclaw shook his head, looking worried.

By this time Fringewhisker had reached the edge of the ravine, and was looking around uncertainly, as if she wasn't sure what to do.

"Come on," Berryheart urged her. "All you have to do is get to the other side."

More comments came from the ShadowClan watchers as Fringewhisker still hesitated.

"It's not fair!" Lightleap exclaimed.

"Yeah," Slatefur grumbled. "It's too dangerous."

Sunbeam felt anger swelling up inside her, making her fur begin to spike out. "It's a trick!" she snarled, tearing at the grass with her foreclaws.

"What do you mean?" Nightheart asked.

"You see that tree over there?" Sunbeam began. "The pine that's leaning over the ravine? That looks as if it would be a good way to cross, but if you look carefully, the branches don't stretch quite far enough."

"And they're too thin," Nightheart added, remembering the pine branch by the bees' nest. "You could end up clinging on above the rocks, swinging in the wind!"

"So that would be a bad choice," Sunbeam agreed. "The best way would be to pick your way down this side, cross that stream at the bottom, and then climb up the other side."

Nightheart looked doubtfully down the steep sides of the ravine. Apart from one or two places where twisted thorn trees clung to the sides, there seemed to be very few paw holds. "It's far too dangerous. You could fall and break your neck," he objected with a shiver. "What's wrong with that?" He pointed with his tail at a tree that had fallen from the side nearest Sky-Clan; the branches stretched all the way to the ShadowClan side, spanning the ravine like the tree-bridge that led to the Gathering island.

"A good question," Sunbeam responded grimly. "It looks like the best choice, but only if you don't know that it's crawling with snakes. Back in greenleaf, Gullswoop got a nasty bite when she tangled with a snake there, and now every Shadow-Clan cat knows to avoid it." She hesitated for a moment, then started forward. "I'm going to warn Fringewhisker."

"No!" Nightheart leaped in front of her. "If you interfere, Berryheart might think it's cheating, and she'll fail her."

Sunbeam dug her claws into the ground, knowing that Nightheart was right. "She would, too," she growled.

A mixture of fury and frustration scorched through Sunbeam as she saw Fringewhisker approach the fallen tree. Confidently she scrambled through the branches and set out to pad along the trunk.

But just as Fringewhisker reached the point over the deepest part of the ravine, a long, sinuous body reared up from a hole in the tree trunk. Even at a distance Sunbeam could see the cold, malignant eyes and the spiny teeth as the snake opened its jaws and aimed for Fringewhisker's leg.

Fringewhisker let out a startled cry. She jumped back, and although the snake missed, she was left tottering at the edge of the trunk, struggling to recover her balance. Sunbeam's breath came short with the fear that her friend would plummet down to be smashed on the rocks below.

Instead, Fringewhisker seemed to be clinging on with her claws sunk deep into the tree bark, and managed to pull herself away from the edge. The snake was poised, waiting, but before it could strike, Fringewhisker swiped at it with one paw. It reared back, then darted forward again and wrapped itself around Fringewhisker's foreleg, its fangs aimed at her throat. Fringewhisker tucked in her chin and dug the claws of her other foreleg deep into the snake's body. The snake released her, and before it could recover, Fringewhisker raced across the rest of the trunk, leaped across the roots, and landed safely on the other side. She looked nervous as she checked herself for snakebites, then straightened up, apparently unhurt.

A yowl of congratulation rose from the watching Shadow-Clan cats. Weak with relief, Sunbeam noticed that the only cat who looked displeased was her mother.

Nightheart cheered with the rest, though he was looking shaken. "What should she have done?" he asked Sunbeam.

There was no need for Sunbeam to answer. At that moment Spireclaw began picking his way down the side of the ravine, darted across the bottom, and climbed the other side to join his mate.

"The ravine *looks* steep and dangerous," Sunbeam pointed out, "but it's actually pretty easy to cross safely, provided you take your time."

Nightheart let out a groan. "If that had been my task, how could I possibly have known?"

"That's right." Gullswoop, who was standing close by, gave

Nightheart a nod. "You couldn't. That task was totally unfair."

"No, it wasn't," Yarrowleaf objected. "Yes, the task was hard, but it should be. How else will we know if a cat has what it takes to be a ShadowClan warrior?"

While Gullswoop and Yarrowleaf continued to bicker, Berryheart sauntered up to Nightheart. "We'll hold *your* first task tomorrow," she informed him. "Good luck," she added with a smirk as she padded away.

Nightheart looked after her with a confident gaze, determined not to let her sneering comment bother him. "I'm not worried," he declared. "Whatever it is, I'll make it look easy."

Sunbeam liked his air of assurance—it was sort of attractive—but she wished she could feel as certain. *This is Berryheart we're talking about.* What would her mother have in store for Nightheart?

# CHAPTER 6

❧

"*Let's think about Fringewhisker's first two* tasks," Sunbeam meowed. "There's a lot you can learn from the way she tackled them."

Nightheart was sitting beside her outside the warriors' den as the sun rose over the ShadowClan camp. The air was crisp and frosty, and he felt full of energy, ready to face whatever challenge Berryheart could throw at him.

"Go on," he murmured.

"Well, her first task was to push a huge branch out of the camp. And she was clever enough to break off all the twigs and smaller branches first, so that the branch rolled more easily when she started to push it."

"That was good thinking," Nightheart commented. "So I should think first, instead of just throwing myself into my task." He paused, then added ruefully, "I'm a throwing-myself-into-it sort of cat."

Sunbeam let out a *mrrow* of amusement. "I noticed. Anyway," she went on more seriously, "when Fringewhisker was surprised by that snake, she had the good sense to flee once she'd injured it enough to get it off her. She didn't stick around trying to kill it."

Nightheart nodded thoughtfully. "Her task was to get across

the ravine, not to kill the snake. That's an idea I can use."

"Let all cats old enough to catch their own prey join here in the center of the camp for a Clan meeting!"

This time it was Tigerstar who summoned the Clan, as Berryheart had done the day before. But Berryheart stood by his side, the two cats waiting while the rest of the Clan gathered around them.

"Okay, this is it," Sunbeam mewed. "Good luck, Nightheart. You'll be fine."

Nightheart's stomach clenched as he headed into the center of the camp, but he managed to keep his confident demeanor, his head raised boldly. *I won't let Berryheart see that I'm nervous.*

Once all the Clan was assembled, Berryheart stepped forward to face Nightheart. "You're a warrior," she announced, "so you must be able to hunt. Let's see if you can catch enough prey to feed every cat in the Clan. You'll have the whole day to get it done."

Nightheart was surprised that the task was so easy. *Perhaps Berryheart isn't as tough as she pretends.* Glancing around, he got a rough idea of how many cats he had to feed. *It's going to be hard work, but a few squirrels, a good plump rabbit if I can find one, maybe five or six voles . . . If I start now, it won't be a problem.*

"Okay," he meowed. "I can do that."

He was turning to leave the camp when Berryheart called him back.

"Just a moment. There's something I haven't told you yet. The prey must all be frogs."

Nightheart felt as if a rock had fallen from the sky and hit him. He had never been so completely taken aback. "What?"

he exclaimed. "*Frogs?* I've never caught a frog in my life. Why would I? ThunderClan cats don't eat frogs."

Berryheart looked ready with a sarcastic comment, but Sunbeam forestalled her. "Frogs are special prey, just for ShadowClan," she explained. "There are plenty of them on our territory, and they taste pretty good. But they're hard to catch. You need to—"

"Stop right there," Berryheart interrupted. "If you help Nightheart, I'll have to fail him. He needs to do this alone."

Sunbeam stepped back, flexing her claws in frustration.

"It's okay," Nightheart meowed. "If I'm meant to be a ShadowClan cat, I'll figure it out." *Besides, how hard can it be?*

"Get on with it, then," Berryheart ordered.

Nightheart took a pace toward the edge of the camp, then halted, confused. "Actually . . . where *are* the frogs?" he wondered aloud.

The cats around him let out *mrrows* of amusement; Nightheart felt his fur grow hot with embarrassment. Knowing he couldn't stand around dithering, he raced out of the camp and into the forest.

Once he was on the move, Nightheart remembered his walk with Sunbeam the day before. He had spotted a frog when they were near the lake. *Where there's one, there are bound to be more.*

When Nightheart reached the lake, he padded along until he came to a marshy area where mud, reeds, and long grasses stretched right down to the water's edge. At first he thought he had gotten it wrong, and there were no frogs here, until movement caught his eye and he spotted a frog crawling out of the water onto a tuft of grass.

*Stay right there . . .*

Nightheart dropped into a hunter's crouch, rocking his haunches from side to side, judged the distance, and pounced. But as soon as his outstretched paws touched the frog, they slid off again. *Yuck! It's slimy!* The frog jumped away; Nightheart landed awkwardly and splashed down into the mud. He rose to his paws, hissing with annoyance; his belly fur was dripping, and—worse than that—his pride was bruised.

*I'm glad Sunbeam didn't see that.*

Wading back to drier ground, Nightheart looked for another frog. He found that their greenish-brown skin blended into the colors of the mud and grass, making them hard to spot. They jumped quickly, too, and in unexpected directions, so his stalking skills were useless.

Eventually Nightheart spotted another frog at the edge of the marsh, within his reach if he could manage an especially long pounce. Determined, he pushed off with his powerful hind legs, but while he was still in the air, the frog leaped straight at him and landed with a sucking sound in the middle of his face.

Nightheart wanted to let out a yowl of shock, but the frog was clamping his jaws shut. He couldn't see anything, or smell anything except the reek of frog, and the slimy feel of its skin against his face made him want to vomit.

Panic coursed through him, and he shook his head from side to side, trying to dislodge the creature. But the frog wasn't going anywhere. Finally he tried clawing at it, thinking that at least he might be able to kill it, but at the first touch of his paw the frog leaped off and vanished with a plop into the marshy water.

Nightheart gagged as he licked a paw and cleaned the traces of the disgusting prey off his face. Sunhigh was approaching, and so far he hadn't managed to catch a single frog. At this rate the day would end before he could feed a single Shadow-Clan cat, let alone the whole Clan.

Then he remembered his talk with Sunbeam that morning, and what he had learned from Fringewhisker's tasks. *I'll have to work smarter, not harder.*

At the risk of running out of time, Nightheart sat for a while, frozen in place, and just watched the frogs. A crowd of them had gathered in one part of the marsh, and he realized that they must have been attracted by a swarm of flies that hovered above the swampy water. Every so often, a frog would dart out its tongue, and a fly would disappear.

*Flies must be their favorite prey,* Nightheart thought, the beginning of a plan forming in his mind. *And nothing attracts flies like fresh prey left out in the sun.*

"My main challenge will be patience," he muttered to himself.

Nightheart withdrew a little way along the lakeshore and set himself to hunting voles. It was a massive relief to use his familiar skills, and soon he had caught several. He clawed them open to expose their insides, and placed them several tail-lengths apart, leading from the marsh to a deep abandoned burrow that he had discovered while hunting them. He covered the entrance to the burrow with long ivy tendrils, and placed the juiciest vole at the edge, just at the right spot so that it wouldn't fall in.

Then he settled down to wait. He had set aside one vole for himself, and devoured it in hungry bites, all the while keeping close watch on the prey he had arranged.

As the sun climbed higher in the sky, the heat on the dead voles' bodies called out to the flies. First one landed on the exposed flesh, then another, until they were swarming over the fresh-kill. Nightheart flexed his claws impatiently. *Come on, frogs! Can't you see the juicy treat I've made for you?*

Finally one venturesome frog hopped up to the first vole and began snatching flies out of the air. Another joined it, and then another. As they clustered around, one frog spotted the next vole and jumped over to it. Nightheart couldn't stop himself shaking with relief as the frogs began to follow the trail he had laid.

*It's going to work!*

Finally a frog spotted the last piece of prey balanced on the edge on the burrow, with flies clustered over it. The frog leaped right onto the prey, the prey gave way, and the frog fell into the hole.

*Yes!*

Nightheart peered down at his catch, and thought he could see frustration in the frog's bulging eyes. The burrow was so deep that not even a frog could jump out. "Stay there," Nightheart mewed, stretching down precariously to retrieve the piece of prey. "Some friends will be joining you shortly."

Over and over Nightheart reset his trap, until the burrow was bubbling with frogs. Finally, as the sun was going down, casting scarlet light over the lake, he ran back to the Shadow-Clan camp and burst through the barrier of brambles.

"Tigerstar! Berryheart!" he yowled. "I have your prey! Come and see!"

Tigerstar emerged from his den and Berryheart appeared from the warriors' den, looking surprised and not at all pleased. She was followed by several of her Clanmates; Sunbeam was one of the first. She raced across the camp to join Nightheart.

"Have you done it?" she asked excitedly.

Nightheart nodded, but before he could explain, Berryheart stalked up and stood looking at him with a disgruntled expression.

"You said you had the prey," she snapped. "Where is it?"

"Oh, you have to come and collect it," Nightheart explained, beginning to enjoy himself. Dipping his head to Tigerstar, he added, "Follow me."

Sunbeam padded at his shoulder, with Tigerstar and Berryheart just behind as Nightheart led the way toward the lake. Most of the Clan streamed after them, eager to see how he had fared in his challenge.

Eventually they reached the burrow; Nightheart waved at it with his tail. "In there."

Tigerstar and Berryheart peered down into the burrow for a long time without speaking. Finally Tigerstar looked up. "I wasn't expecting that," he meowed. To Nightheart's relief, he sounded impressed, and there was a spark of laughter in his amber gaze. "The frogs aren't dead, though," he commented. "You haven't killed any of the prey."

"But I wasn't asked to *kill* the frogs," Nightheart pointed out. "Only to *catch* them."

Nightheart heard a snarl coming from Berryheart, while Tigerstar was staring at him as if he wasn't sure what to say. A few heartbeats passed like seasons, until the ShadowClan leader relaxed.

"That's true." He stretched down into the burrow to grab a frog and killed it expertly with one bite. "They're very tasty, too," he added with an amused twitch of his whiskers.

"Yuck!" Nightheart muttered, gagging.

"You'll develop a taste for them eventually," Tigerstar promised, "if you become a true ShadowClan cat. I think we can say that you've passed your first test."

A wave of relief surged through Nightheart as Sunbeam rushed up to him and rubbed her muzzle against his. "Congratulations!" she mewed. "I knew you could do it!"

Her touch made Nightheart feel that he was floating above the forest. But he was brought down to earth soon enough as his gaze locked with Berryheart's.

The black-and-white she-cat stalked up to him. "I see how you managed to wriggle out of killing all those frogs," she hissed. "I'll just have to make your next task even harder."

As she flounced off, Nightheart felt a weight gather in his belly. He realized that while he had won this battle, the war was far from over.

# CHAPTER 7

*Shadows stretched across the RiverClan camp* as the sun went down. Frostpaw could feel her Clan's growing tension as they gathered around the Highstump for a Clan meeting. She knew how deeply some of her Clanmates resented that the meeting would not be led by a RiverClan cat, but by the ShadowClan leader, Tigerstar.

*He sent a message saying he would be here by sunset,* Frostpaw thought. *So where is he?*

The sun was gone, the streaks of scarlet in the sky already fading, by the time Tigerstar rushed into the camp. "Sorry, sorry," he panted as he leaped onto the Highstump. "Which cat put the RiverClan camp so far away from ShadowClan!"

His attempt at a joke was met with icy silence.

Tigerstar paused for a moment, as if he was waiting for a response that never came, then gave a tiny shrug and continued. "I've called you together because I have a few announcements to make."

Some muttering broke out at his words, and Frostpaw heard some cat meow, "We would never have guessed!" But most of the Clan was listening, even if they didn't look happy about it.

"I first want to speak to Mistpaw and Graypaw," Tigerstar went on.

Frostpaw saw her two littermates exchange a glance; their whiskers twitched with surprise, and there was apprehension in their eyes. *Have they done something wrong?* she wondered.

"It is time to be thinking about your warrior assessments," the ShadowClan leader told them. "And yet I know that you must hope to be made warriors by the leader of your own Clan. So for the time being, I think you will have to wait. Perhaps RiverClan will have a new leader before long. If not, I will consider this again, but I want you to know that you haven't been forgotten."

"Thank you, Tigerstar!" the two apprentices chorused, ducking their heads. Their eyes were shining; Frostpaw guessed that they were pleased that the ShadowClan leader had realized how they must be feeling, with no RiverClan leader to give them their warrior names.

*That was really tactful of Tigerstar!*

"And now it's time to make Frostpaw a warrior apprentice," the ShadowClan leader continued.

While Frostpaw felt her heart leap nervously, she was happy that Tigerstar didn't believe *she* had to wait for a new RiverClan leader before she could set her paws on the path she had chosen.

But Duskfur glared up at the ShadowClan leader, fury in her face. "Correct me if I'm wrong," she mewed, her tone sharp with sarcasm, "but I thought that was Icewing's decision to make."

Tigerstar ignored her completely. "I've come here to hold Frostpaw's ceremony," he announced.

Grumbling broke out among the RiverClan cats, while some of them yowled louder protests at the ShadowClan leader.

"It's bad enough that you've taken over our everyday lives," Mallownose growled. "Now you want to take over our sacred ceremonies, too?"

"Yeah, it's unheard of!" Podlight added. "This has to be the job of the RiverClan leader."

Frostpaw thought that was unfair, after what Tigerstar had said to Graypaw and Mistpaw, but more voices were raised in agreement until Icewing pushed her way to the front of the crowd and lifted her tail for silence. Gradually the yowling died away into ragged muttering.

"Do I need to remind you that we don't *have* a RiverClan leader?" Icewing pointed out when she could make herself heard.

"And we never will," Duskfur murmured, "now that we don't have a medicine cat with a connection to StarClan."

Even Mothwing looked annoyed at the older she-cat's words. Frostpaw could feel the mood of the Clan growing still darker, just as night was gathering around the camp.

She hated being the reason for the argument, and wished that she could just disappear. She would have liked to slip away into her den—except that it couldn't be her den anymore, now that she was no longer a medicine cat.

She stood with her gaze fixed on her paws, trying to pretend that none of this was happening, until she felt some cat's fur brush her side, and felt warm breath on her ear. She turned her head to see Splashtail.

"Are you sure about this?" he whispered. "You weren't a medicine cat for very long. Maybe you just need longer to learn what a real vision feels like?"

Frostpaw was taken aback by Splashtail's question—or rather because it was Splashtail who had asked it. Even though she had sometimes wondered if the brown tabby tom might be more to her than just a friend, she had always pushed aside the hope that they might be mates, because she was destined to be a medicine cat.

*But I'm not a medicine cat now,* she told herself. *I'll be a warrior like him. And if he's not happy about it, does that mean he doesn't feel the same?*

Frostpaw shook her head decisively. "I've had plenty of time to think," she responded to Splashtail. "They may not have said so to my face, but I know my Clanmates have doubted my abilities as a medicine cat ever since I chose Owlnose to be leader and he backed out. What difference will it make if they start doubting my ability to be a warrior?"

"I'm sure you'll make a great warrior," Splashtail assured her. "You'd be good at anything you put your mind to. It's just that this is such a hard time for the Clan." He paused thoughtfully, then added, "I know you want to do the right thing—but maybe you *should* give it more time. You shouldn't let pressure from them"—he glanced over his shoulder at his still-wrangling Clanmates—"get to you."

"Thank you, Splashtail," Frostpaw mewed. She felt

comforted by the way her friend was trying to help her, although she couldn't stop herself from asking why. *If he loves me, he should* want *me to be a warrior,* she thought. Then hope tingled through her as she added to herself, *Maybe it's* because *he likes me that he wants me to be sure.* "But this isn't me giving in to pressure," she continued. "If I did, I would have gone along with what Mothwing wants, and stayed a medicine cat. But I know that isn't my path."

"Frostpaw!" Havenpelt's voice cut off anything Splashtail might have said in reply. "Is Tigerstar making you do this?" she demanded. "Did he make you doubt yourself, or convince you that your visions weren't real? You know you don't have to listen to him!"

"Yes, he's not *your* leader," Brackenpelt agreed.

"Tell him to keep his paws out of your business," Shimmerpelt added.

Frostpaw was tempted to agree, and blame Tigerstar for her leaving the calling of a medicine cat. If she did, her Clanmates' anger would be aimed at him instead of her. *I could have a moment's peace!* But Frostpaw knew she couldn't do that, because it wouldn't be true.

"This decision was mine, and only mine," she declared. "And it's not one I took lightly. I'm quite sure—my connection to StarClan was never real."

Frostpaw forced herself not to flinch under the angry gazes of her Clanmates. *I wish they understood, I'd do more damage to the Clan if I went on pretending to be a medicine cat.*

"But what about Curlfeather?" her littermate Graypaw

asked. "She was so sure you were meant to be a medicine cat, even when we were kits. What would she think about all this?"

Frostpaw locked her gaze with his and her chest felt heavy as she remembered the time when they were all kits together in the nursery. She had felt so secure, protected by her mother's overwhelming love.

If Frostpaw admitted the truth, Curlfeather's insistence that her visions made her special was the thing that confused her most of all. *Was my mother exaggerating?* she wondered. *Or was she just wrong? Why did Curlfeather want me to be a medicine cat so badly?*

Desperately needing Splashtail's support, she turned toward him, but now he avoided her gaze, and she was sure that he was a few paw steps farther away from her than he had been a moment before.

"Come here, Frostpaw," Tigerstar meowed, jumping down from the Highstump.

The crowd moved back to make a path for her, and Frostpaw padded along it until she stood in front of the ShadowClan leader.

"You already have your apprentice name, Frostpaw," Tigerstar continued. "So to become a warrior apprentice all you need is a mentor."

"I'll do it," Owlnose offered immediately. "I'd be happy to."

"So would I," Nightsky added.

Frostpaw was grateful that at least some of her Clanmates were supporting her decision by offering to mentor her, though she was disappointed that Splashtail hadn't been one of them. *I thought he liked me. If he were my mentor, we could be together almost all the time. That would have been so great!*

"No, I already have a mentor in mind," Tigerstar responded, dipping his head to Owlnose and Nightsky. "But I thank you for your support of Frostpaw." He paused before continuing, "Harelight, you will be mentor for Frostpaw. You are a loyal and intelligent cat, and I know you will pass on these qualities to your apprentice."

Harelight stepped forward out of the crowd, looking surprised to be chosen, but pleased, too. Frostpaw bounded over to him and stretched up to touch noses with him.

"You have a light-colored pelt, just like me," Harelight mewed in a friendly tone. "I'll show you ways to conceal yourself while you're hunting."

Frostpaw murmured thanks. She liked her new mentor already; he was a respected RiverClan warrior, and surely no cat would be able to find fault with Tigerstar's choice.

But just then she heard Duskfur speaking, low-voiced, just behind her. "Tigerstar calls Harelight loyal, but who is he loyal to? We might have known that Tigerstar would choose a cat who spent time as an exile in ShadowClan."

Frostpaw cringed at the words, hoping that Harelight hadn't heard Duskfur's insult. But the white tom's ears were sharp. He whipped around to face Duskfur, an offended look on his face and his shoulder fur bristling.

"What are you trying to say?" he demanded. "That I'm less loyal because I was forced out of my Clan over an impostor that the rest of you chose to obey? One who wasn't even a RiverClan cat?"

Duskfur didn't seem able to find words to reply. She glared at Harelight for a couple of heartbeats, then turned her back and pushed her way out of the crowd.

"Well, Frostpaw," Tigerstar meowed, "it's clear that some of your Clanmates have doubts about your new path, and Harelight's loyalty. But I'm sure the two of you will work hard to prove them all wrong."

Harelight looked down at Frostpaw. "Are you ready to listen and learn?" he asked.

"Of course," Frostpaw replied, new confidence flooding into her.

"Then we'll make an excellent pair," her mentor purred. "And won't all your Clanmates feel mouse-brained when you turn out to be the strongest warrior of all of them?"

Frostpaw ducked her head shyly, a warmth growing inside her that made her feel that Harelight was the perfect mentor for her. *Unlike so many of my Clanmates, he'll see me as I truly am.*

Frostpaw dashed up to Harelight and at the last moment reared up on her hind paws to give her mentor two swift blows on his ears, then sprang back and darted away again.

"Was that okay?" she panted.

"Excellent," her mentor responded. "Your timing is pretty well perfect. Try it one more time, just to be sure you've got it."

A few days had passed since Frostpaw had become Harelight's apprentice, and now he was teaching her a new battle move on a stretch of level ground not far from the RiverClan camp. She was becoming used to the tough training sessions;

to begin with, she had been almost too exhausted to eat at the end of every day. Now she felt stronger and more agile. Besides, it felt good to be praised, instead of doubting herself all the time.

She was padding away to give herself space to run up, when she noticed Duskfur and Splashtail standing in the shadow of an elder bush. It looked as if they were on a hunting patrol; Duskfur had a vole at her paws.

*How long have they been watching me?* Frostpaw wondered.

"I don't think you've quite got it yet," Duskfur remarked loudly. "Mind you, I don't blame you. Not every cat is meant to be a warrior, after all."

Frostpaw's fur began to bush up at Duskfur's dismissive words. "I'm only just starting to learn," she meowed, defending herself.

"I can see that you hesitate to strike as hard as you could," Splashtail added; his voice was infuriatingly kind. "Your instinct is to heal, not to harm."

Frostpaw thought he might have meant to give her a compliment, but it wasn't one she wanted to hear. "I can—" she began.

"Duskfur? Splashtail?" Harelight interrupted; Frostpaw hadn't heard him come padding up behind her. "Are you Frostpaw's mentors, or am I?" When neither cat responded, he added, "Get back on your patrol, and stop interfering."

Duskfur picked up her vole, and both warriors slunk off into the undergrowth without another word.

"Mouse-brains!" Harelight snorted.

"But do you think they were right?" Frostpaw asked, her newfound confidence wavering. "Do you think I'll ever have the instincts to be a proper warrior?"

Harelight gazed down at her, his eyes warm. "I've never mentored any cat before," he told her, "but you're picking up the training faster than any apprentice I've ever seen. If you keep going at this pace, you'll be one of RiverClan's greatest warriors."

Frostpaw's heart gave an enormous jolt. "Do you really think so?"

"I wouldn't say so if I didn't," Harelight purred.

Returning to camp with a bounce in her step, Frostpaw felt reassured and proud. She couldn't remember the last time she had felt so capable and sure of herself, in spite of what Duskfur and Splashtail—and any other of her Clanmates—might think.

Harelight told her to help herself to some prey, and she found her sister, Mistpaw, beside the fresh-kill pile, finishing off a perch. Frostpaw chose a small trout for herself and sat beside her sister to eat it.

"I had a great lesson with Harelight," she meowed. "He taught me a new battle move, and he said I'm picking up the training faster than any apprentice he's ever seen!"

"That's wonderful!" Mistpaw responded, her eyes wide with excitement. "Maybe you'll catch up with me and Graypaw, and we can all be made warriors together!"

But Frostpaw knew her sister very well. She could tell that something was nagging at Mistpaw beneath her happiness.

"What's the matter?" she asked.

"Nothing," Mistpaw replied. "I'm absolutely fine. I'm really pleased for you."

Frostpaw wasn't going to accept that. "Come on," she mewed. "I can tell there's something. Spit it out!"

Mistpaw let out a sigh and gulped down the last bit of her perch. "It's true I'm pleased for you," she declared at last. "But I'm confused, too. Our mother seemed so sure that you were meant to be a medicine cat. She went on and on about your dreams. . . . It all seemed so certain."

"Well, she must have been wrong," Frostpaw commented.

"That's what's worrying me," Mistpaw confessed, her ears twitching anxiously. "Because it was you, Frostpaw, who said StarClan told you Curlfeather was to be our new leader. But if you were never really a medicine cat, if the visions weren't real, then does that mean that our mother wasn't destined to be our leader after all? Because if she wasn't, then she didn't have to die."

A massive surge of guilt struck Frostpaw at her sister's words. She couldn't think of a response, and an awkward silence settled between her and Mistpaw. She gulped down her trout quickly and rose to her paws.

"I'd better check if Harelight has any duties for me," she meowed, and headed off before her sister could reply.

Frostpaw didn't make much of an effort to find her mentor. What she really needed was time to think over Mistpaw's words while they remained fresh in her mind. She remembered the sign that had convinced her to name her mother as the next leader: the curled feather she had found on the ground beside the spiral path leading down to the Moonpool. She had already decided that it must have been a coincidence she had found the feather there, just when she needed to name the new RiverClan leader.

But had that coincidence cost Curlfeather her life? If she and Frostpaw hadn't been on the way to the Moonpool for Curlfeather to get her nine lives, they would never have encountered the dogs that killed her.

Frostpaw felt bile rise in her throat. *Did I lead my mother to her death? For nothing?*

Besides that, if she hadn't known then that she was making poor decisions, how could she be sure that she was making wise ones now?

What if her becoming a warrior led to something disastrous, too?

# CHAPTER 8

*Sunbeam padded alongside Lightleap as the* two she-cats made their way toward RiverClan. Recently Tigerstar had taken to pairing them up for patrols and other duties, and Sunbeam tried hard not to look for reasons behind it. But it felt as though their leader was trying to force them to be friends again.

*Or maybe he couldn't care less about our petty squabbles, and it's all in my mind.*

Together she and Lightleap crossed the stretch of Thunderpath stuff and plunged into RiverClan territory. Before they had padded on for more than a few fox-lengths, Lightleap halted and announced, "I'm hungry."

"Then maybe we should cross back over the border," Sunbeam meowed. "Are we allowed to hunt on RiverClan territory?"

Lightleap rolled her eyes. "Don't be so mouse-brained! RiverClan *is* ShadowClan, at least for now. Besides, you and I are on our way over there to help them. Surely we shouldn't be expected to starve to death while we do that!"

Sunbeam puzzled over that for a moment. Before she could decide whether she agreed or not, her Clanmate announced,

"I smell rabbit—I'm going for it!"

"Okay," Sunbeam agreed with a sigh. *At least hunting will give us something to do.* "Let's split up, then," she continued. "And we'll meet back here when we're done."

Lightleap nodded. "Fine." Her whiskers drooped a little, as if she was sad that Sunbeam didn't want to hunt with her.

When her Clanmate had disappeared into the bushes, Sunbeam tasted the air for the traces of prey. She picked up the rabbit, but that was Lightleap's. And the rich scents of the soft, marshy ground near the lake made it hard to distinguish any others.

Finally Sunbeam spotted a vole among the vegetation at the water's edge. Flattening herself to the ground, she crept up on it, finding it easy to prowl silently on the soft earth. Pretty soon she was within pouncing distance; pushing forward, she leaped on the vole, trapped it between her forepaws, and killed it with a bite to its throat.

"Thank you, StarClan, for this prey," she mewed.

Glad that her hunt hadn't taken long, she picked up the vole in her jaws and headed back to the meeting place she had agreed on with Lightleap. The prey juices flowed into her mouth and she realized how hungry she was.

But as she climbed the slope from the lake, a patrol of RiverClan cats suddenly emerged from the undergrowth and surrounded her before she could react. Duskfur was in the lead; her eyes were cold and unfriendly.

"That vole you're carrying belongs to us," she informed Sunbeam in a harsh voice.

Sunbeam set the vole down carefully underneath her belly. She felt surprised and alarmed by the patrol's appearance, but she tried not to let it show, holding her head high as she responded. "How do you work that out?"

"Because you're on RiverClan territory—as if you don't know that," Fognose replied. "That means the vole is River-Clan prey."

"Cloverfoot might have something to say about that," Sunbeam retorted swiftly.

Duskfur let out a furious hiss. "If you won't give up the prey, we'll just have to take it from you," she growled.

The patrol began to close in. Badly outnumbered, Sunbeam slid out her claws and let her shoulder fur bristle up, but she knew that a show of courage wasn't going to help her. She had a difficult choice: either meekly give up her prey, or have her fur ripped off.

But before the RiverClan cats could attack, Lightleap appeared around a clump of fern with the limp body of a rabbit in her jaws. She dropped the prey between her forepaws and fixed Duskfur's patrol with a hard stare. "Is there a problem here?" she asked.

Sunbeam had never felt more relieved in her life. "They don't think I'm entitled to this prey," she explained, struggling to keep her voice steady.

"Really?" Lightleap padded forward until she was nose to nose with Duskfur. "Maybe you've forgotten," she meowed, her tone as silky as a newborn kit's fur. "Tigerstar is your temporary leader, which means the prey here is as much

ShadowClan's as it is RiverClan's."

The RiverClan cats exchanged uncertain glances, though they didn't sheathe their claws.

"Just because Tigerstar thinks he can throw his weight around here," Duskfur snarled, "doesn't mean that *you* can."

Sunbeam puffed out her chest, feeling stronger with Lightleap at her side. "If you have a problem, you can take it up with Cloverfoot and Icewing," she meowed.

"Don't think we won't." Duskfur's tone was threatening. "Cloverfoot's word has no meaning to us. And *you* are coming to camp with us, right now!"

Retrieving their prey, Sunbeam and Lightleap headed for the RiverClan camp, flanked by the patrol on both sides. When they arrived, they saw Cloverfoot and Icewing in the center of the camp, with a few cats clustered around them.

"Try hunting closer to the horseplace," Icewing was directing as they approached. "No cat has been that way for a few days."

The group of cats dashed off. Duskfur led the way across the camp; Sunbeam spotted her Clanmates Hopwhisker and Stonewing standing nearby. Their shoulders were slumped with boredom, though they straightened up, their eyes narrowing, at the sight of Sunbeam and Lightleap with their escort.

"What's going on?" Icewing asked.

"My patrol caught these two intruders hunting on our territory," Duskfur blurted out. "I know things are confused in RiverClan right now, but ShadowClan cats need to show a bit of respect. This is still RiverClan territory, and that means that the prey belongs to *us*."

Sunbeam didn't give Icewing the chance to reply. "With Tigerstar running RiverClan, there isn't much difference between our two Clans at present," she pointed out. "Besides, we were only hunting on your territory because we're on our way to relieve Stonewing and Hopwhisker. For StarClan's sake, we're all here to *help* you!"

"No cat asked for your help!" Duskfur spat.

"And where would you be if we weren't helping?" Hopwhisker demanded with a lash of her tail.

Suddenly every cat within earshot had to add their voices. Sunbeam and Lightleap stood looking at each other as the argument raged on, with more RiverClan cats emerging from their dens to find out what was going on. Sunbeam thought that the screeching must have been heard as far away as the ShadowClan camp.

Finally Icewing leaped up onto the Highstump and yowled, "Silence!"

As the noise died away, she jumped down again; Sunbeam suspected she didn't want any cat to think that she was trying to take the position of the Clan leader.

"I can see the problem," she began when she had every cat's attention. "We're all in a situation we've never been in before, and the rules are unclear. While it's true that for the time being ShadowClan is leading RiverClan, it's unusual for ShadowClan cats to hunt on RiverClan territory."

"Unusual? It's forbidden!" Duskfur growled.

Icewing ignored the interruption. "Still, it's unrealistic to expect cats to be in RiverClan for long periods of time without eating."

"We've been eating while we've been here," Stonewing pointed out.

"Yes, and the cats who guarded Ashfur while he was a prisoner in ShadowClan were allowed to eat," Hopwhisker added. "Even though they weren't ShadowClan cats."

"Yes, but none of those cats *hunted*." Mothwing had appeared from the medicine cat's den, and now stood beside Icewing. "That's like treating the territory as your own. You should wait to eat what we give you—and we will give you all you need."

"Wise words," Icewing commented. She thought for a moment, then added, "Let me suggest a compromise. While ShadowClan is here, they can hunt. But for each piece of prey they catch for themselves, they must catch another for RiverClan."

Lightleap let out a sigh. "Does that mean . . . ?"

"It does," Icewing confirmed. "Put your rabbit on the fresh-kill pile. You and Sunbeam may share the vole."

Her paw steps dragging, Lightleap did as she was told. Sunbeam thought that was a fair compromise.

Splashtail padded up to the fresh-kill pile, gave the rabbit a good sniff, then stepped away, drawing his lips back as if he had smelled crow-food. "Yuck! It stinks of ShadowClan!"

"We're all starting to stink of ShadowClan now, since their cats are spending so much time here," Mallownose muttered.

Sunbeam bit back an irritated hiss. *Turning his nose up at perfectly good prey!*

Before she could overhear anything else that would make her angrier, Icewing announced, "It's settled. Let's have no more argument."

"Hopwhisker, Stonewing, you can go home," Cloverfoot added; so far she had remained tactfully silent, letting Icewing deal with RiverClan's problems. "Sunbeam and Lightleap, come with me into the leader's den."

The two ShadowClan she-cats exchanged a glance, then followed the ShadowClan deputy along with Icewing. Sunbeam remembered to pick up her vole. *Maybe sometime we'll get to eat it.*

"Thank you, Icewing," Cloverfoot meowed when all four cats were inside the den, "for coming up with such a sensible solution. You've been a huge help."

"You're welcome, Cloverfoot," Icewing responded. "But to be honest, we both know that arguments like that will happen more often, the longer ShadowClan is here. Your presence is still a sore spot for RiverClan cats."

*That's totally obvious!* Sunbeam thought.

Even so, Lightleap's eyes widened in surprise. "We're only here to help!" she exclaimed. "Great StarClan, what is your problem?"

"Come on, Lightleap." Sunbeam gave her Clanmate a nudge. "I get it, even if you don't. Just imagine if it were the other way around, and ShadowClan was in RiverClan's position. We'd be prickly about it, too!"

"That would never happen," Lightleap retorted. "Tigerstar is too strong a leader!"

"Mistystar was a strong leader, too," Icewing mewed quietly. "Her death has been hard on all of us, and any Clan could find themselves in the same position. You would do well to remember that, Lightleap."

Ducking her head, looking ashamed of herself, Lightleap had no more to say.

Sunbeam was relieved when her two days of duty in the RiverClan camp were over and she and Lightleap could go home. Her spirits rose with every paw step that took her closer to the ShadowClan camp.

"I can't believe that Frostpaw has decided she isn't a medicine cat," she meowed to Lightleap as they headed for the border. "How do you make a mistake about something like that?"

Lightleap shrugged. "It's not our problem."

"But that means RiverClan doesn't have a connection to StarClan," Sunbeam protested. "Mothwing has never been able to reach them."

"It's still not ShadowClan's problem," Lightleap insisted. "If StarClan wants RiverClan to have a medicine cat, they'll send them one."

Sunbeam couldn't dismiss RiverClan's troubles so easily. The thought of a Clan cut off from the spirits of their warrior ancestors sent a shiver of horror and disbelief right through her. *What was Frostpaw thinking? Did she have visions, or didn't she?*

Besides, the lack of a medicine cat wasn't RiverClan's only difficulty. Sunbeam's short stay in their camp had convinced her that ShadowClan shouldn't be trying to control them. The RiverClan cats seemed to be fighting the whole time, among themselves as well as with the visiting warriors, and Cloverfoot's attempts to mediate were only making it worse.

While Sunbeam and Lightleap had been there, Owlnose and Lizardtail had fought bitterly over who would patch up a hole in the brambles sheltering the warriors' den. When Cloverfoot had tried to solve the problem, suggesting that they work on the task together, the two toms had been so furious that they attacked each other.

Cloverfoot had called Sunbeam and Lightleap to pull the battling cats apart, and for a moment Sunbeam had thought that she would feel their claws, too.

At the last moment, Lizardtail seemed to think better of fighting. "None of this would be happening if it weren't for you!" he spat at Owlnose before stalking off.

Cloverfoot had been sleeping in the leader's den because she didn't feel safe with the warriors in their den. "Mistystar decorated the walls with shells and feathers," she explained to Sunbeam and Lightleap, "and now the RiverClan cats keep accusing me of moving or changing them. And I haven't touched a single one!"

"That's really unfair!" Sunbeam exclaimed.

"And that's not all," Cloverfoot went on. "I often go into the den and find my bedding strewn across the floor, or a piece of crow-food left in my nest. I can't prove it, but I'm sure RiverClan warriors are behind it."

"Well, it's certainly not ShadowClan," Lightleap meowed.

Icewing had been having trouble, too, struggling to get her own Clanmates to maintain the camp properly. When she tried to assign them tasks, some of the more senior warriors refused, saying they wouldn't keep the camp comfortable for invaders. So far Icewing and Cloverfoot, working together, had managed to convince them to do their duties, but only after a lot of grumbling and anger.

Even though Sunbeam knew that RiverClan was in serious trouble, after what she had witnessed, she thought they would be better off sorting themselves out. Tigerstar was only making matters worse by insisting that ShadowClan should lead them.

But as Sunbeam traveled home with Lightleap, she knew she couldn't say any of that to her. Lightleap was Tigerstar's daughter, and she would support him whatever he might do.

*I can't criticize him at all,* Sunbeam reflected. *Things are awkward enough between me and Lightleap, without me telling her that her father has bees in his brain.*

Instead, just to fill the silence, she started to talk about the other reason she was eager to get home. "I can't wait to see Nightheart."

The moment the words were out, Sunbeam realized that it felt good to talk to Lightleap about the ThunderClan tom. It seemed as if they were friends again, the way they used to be.

Lightleap turned to her, eyes shining eagerly, as if she was excited to have Sunbeam confide in her. "I'm so happy you've found some cat," she told her. "I'm sorry that I came between you and Blazefire. I hope you know I didn't intend to—well, I didn't mean to hurt you."

"I know that now," Sunbeam assured her. "But there's something I'd like to ask you. . . . How did you know that Blazefire was the cat for you?"

Lightleap didn't speak for a few heartbeats, padding along with her gaze fixed on her paws. At last she began hesitantly. "I knew my feelings must have been real, because of what they cost me. It hurt to lose you as a friend—more than you'll ever know. But I couldn't deny my feelings for Blazefire any longer. We made the choice to be together, and every day we make the same choice all over again. That way we know that we aren't together for any reason other than that we want to be."

Sunbeam didn't find Lightleap's answer as comforting as she had hoped. She could admit to herself that she wasn't ready to commit to Nightheart. And yet he was already going through so much because he had committed himself to her by leaving his Clan.

"What if Nightheart completes his three tasks and I change my mind about him?" she asked Lightleap. "The same way Blazefire changed his mind about me?"

"No cat can answer that for you," Lightleap mewed sympathetically. "You'll just have to listen to your heart."

# CHAPTER 9

*The bright beams of the rising* sun struck through the trees, patterning the forest floor with alternating stripes of light and shadow. There was little warmth in the sunlight, but the air was crisp and fresh as Nightheart padded through the pines on his way back to the ShadowClan camp.

He hadn't felt entirely comfortable among the ShadowClan warriors while Sunbeam was away on duty in RiverClan, but he was doing his best to fit in. He was pleased that he had been chosen for an early hunting patrol with Gullswoop and Pouncestep; the squirrel and the mouse dangling from his jaws were proof enough that he could be an asset to his new Clan.

*Maybe it will all work out,* he thought. *I'm not scared of Berryheart and her tasks.*

But when he reached the camp, the first cat he spotted was Berryheart, sitting beside the fresh-kill pile. Yarrowleaf was with her, and when Nightheart headed for the pile to deposit his prey, Berryheart's ears flicked up and she leaned over to mutter something into Yarrowleaf's ear.

"I want a word with you," she announced, as soon as Nightheart was in earshot.

*What about "Well done" or "Great catch"?* Nightheart did his best to stifle the stirring of resentment. The last thing he wanted was to get into an argument with Berryheart. His relationship with Sunbeam's mother was bad enough as it was.

"Sure, Berryheart," he meowed, dropping his prey and dipping his head politely. "Whatever you want."

"Not here." Berryheart rose to her paws. "Follow me."

She led the way across the camp to a quiet spot near the nursery, in the shelter of a thornbush. Yarrowleaf trailed after them; Nightheart felt almost like a prisoner, with the two she-cats as his guards.

Berryheart sat down and angled her ears to show Nightheart that he should sit next to her; reluctantly, he obeyed. Yarrowleaf sat a fox-length away, between them and the rest of the camp. Nightheart felt his shoulders cramping with tension, but he did his best to show Berryheart a calm expression.

"Sunbeam is my daughter," Berryheart began, "and obviously I care a lot about her happiness."

"So do I!" Nightheart declared.

Berryheart gave him a narrow-eyed glare; clearly it hadn't been his turn to speak yet. "I always thought she would mate with a ShadowClan tom," she continued, "and I still don't see any reason why she wouldn't. Where did the two of you meet, anyway?"

"We started talking at a Gathering," Nightheart replied. He had no intention of telling Berryheart how he and Sunbeam, for different reasons, had felt unhappy in their Clans, and had been able to confide in each other when they couldn't confide in their Clanmates.

Berryheart gave a disdainful sniff. "There's too much mingling at Gatherings, if you ask me."

Nightheart could understand why Berryheart might feel that way. That must also have been how her son, Spireclaw, had met Fringewhisker.

"You must care a lot for Sunbeam to have left your Clan for her," Berryheart went on. "You obviously think she's the right cat for you. But what makes you think that *you're* the right cat for *her*?"

For a moment Nightheart wasn't sure how to answer. He couldn't possibly make Berryheart understand the delight, the sense of belonging together, that he felt when he was with Sunbeam.

"Well . . . ," he began awkwardly. "We get along—we like the same sort of things, and we have the same sense of humor."

Berryheart let out a snort, as if she wasn't impressed; in a way Nightheart couldn't blame her.

"I'll do everything I possibly can to make her happy," he declared.

"I'm sure you *mean* to," Berryheart meowed. "But can you really promise to be loyal to her?"

Offended, Nightheart let his fur bristle up. "Of course I can!"

"Oh, of course . . ." Berryheart's tone was derisive. "Are we forgetting that you betrayed your Clan and your kin to come here and try to join ShadowClan? And at a time when ThunderClan is still trying to recover from all the damage

Ashfur did? How can I believe that you'll be loyal to any cat?"

"I can't *make* you believe it," Nightheart admitted. His pads prickled with guilt; Berryheart wasn't wrong in her accusations, even though she didn't know his reasons for leaving ThunderClan. "But if I pass my tasks and become a Shadow-Clan cat, I'll show you how loyal I can be."

"And hedgehogs fly!" Yarrowleaf snapped.

"Well, maybe you can be loyal." Berryheart didn't sound any more convinced than her Clanmate. "I don't suppose Sunbeam has told you about Blazefire?" she added.

"Yes, she did!" Nightheart couldn't keep a hint of triumph out of his voice. "If you mean that she once thought that she would be mates with him. She told me everything."

"Everything?" Berryheart repeated. "How she loved him ever since she was a kit? How she trusted him and imagined having kits with him? And how heartbroken she was when he betrayed her with Lightleap?"

"I know about all that," Nightheart asserted, though that wasn't entirely true. A cold trickle of doubt stirred around his heart; he hadn't known how committed Sunbeam had been to the idea of a life with Blazefire, or for how long. *Can I really take the place of a cat she loved so deeply?*

"I can understand how Sunbeam feels," Berryheart went on. "After losing Blazefire, she could easily fall for the first tom who started padding after her. But what if she changes her mind? You'll make her life much harder if you stay. Look how hard Spireclaw and Fringewhisker have had it so far."

*Yes, they've had it hard because of the way you've behaved,* Nightheart mused, but he had the sense not to speak the thought out loud. Sunbeam's mother was hostile enough without him trying to make it worse.

"I'll stay as long as Sunbeam wants me," he responded.

Berryheart gave a shrug. "I can see I'm not going to change your mind," she meowed. "But I warn you, you'll never be truly accepted as a *real* ShadowClan cat, even if you do pass your tasks."

"Yeah, no cat wants you here," Yarrowleaf put in.

For a heartbeat Nightheart wanted to unsheathe his claws and tear the smug expressions off both she-cats. But he knew how stupid that would be. If Yarrowleaf didn't like him, it wasn't important, but Berryheart was Sunbeam's mother, and if he was to stay in ShadowClan, he somehow had to make himself get along with her. Life would be much more difficult for him *and* for Sunbeam if he couldn't do that.

Taking a deep breath, Nightheart rose to his paws and dipped his head respectfully to Berryheart. "I'm sorry you feel this way about me," he meowed. "There's nothing I can do now to convince you that I'm the right cat for Sunbeam. I just hope you'll give me the chance to show you how faithful I can be."

Without waiting for a reply, he turned, brushed past Yarrowleaf, and headed toward the warriors' den.

Rising to his paws, Nightheart tried hard not to shake in his pelt as he joined the ShadowClan cats in the center of the camp. Instead he did his best to look bold and unconcerned, his chin lifted and his tail in the air. It was hard, because he knew that Tigerstar was about to announce his second task.

Nightheart wouldn't have felt nearly as nervous if Sunbeam had been there, but she was still on duty in RiverClan. This was the day she was supposed to come home; he had looked out for her ever since dawn, but she hadn't arrived yet.

*Whatever I have to face, I'll have to do it alone.*

As Nightheart padded up to Tigerstar's side, the Shadow-Clan leader gave him a curt nod. "I know you were expecting the announcement of your second task," he meowed. "But my mate, Dovewing, has a better idea."

He glanced affectionately at the gray she-cat who stood beside him, waving his tail for her to speak. Nightheart felt his belly begin to churn with apprehension as she turned her green gaze on him.

"Completing the three tasks is important," Dovewing began, "and it's also important for a cat to find closure with their former Clan. I used to be a ThunderClan cat, and I remember how difficult it was to leave my Clan and my kin behind to be with the cat I love. So, Nightheart," she continued, "I'll be taking you to ThunderClan, so you can say good-bye and be ready to move on."

"Is this my second task?" Nightheart asked.

"No," Tigerstar replied, in a voice that didn't encourage Nightheart to argue. "But it's something we feel you need to do."

This was even worse than Nightheart had feared. He had braced himself for the most difficult task Berryheart could think up, but instead he would have to face his kin and his Clanmates, who would all blame him for the decision he had made. From what Finchlight had said at the Gathering, it sounded as if his mother, Sparkpelt, was furious with him, and they both expected him to fail.

Besides, he was still struggling with doubts after his earlier conversation with Berryheart. Some of the things she had said had struck him too close for comfort: the way he had betrayed ThunderClan and his kin; the deep, long-lasting love Sunbeam had felt for Blazefire. *But there's nothing I can do, except live through it.*

"Do I really have to do that?" he asked Dovewing. *I'd rather fight a fox and kill a whole nest of snakes!*

"I think it will be good for you, to make things right with your Clan and your kin," Dovewing responded. "It will be good for ShadowClan, too. We don't want a new Clanmate who brings us unresolved problems with another Clan. How would you focus on your duties here? Besides, it will test how much you really want to join ShadowClan, and whether you're making the right decision. Or was this just a bee-brained impulse following an argument?"

A smothering wave of embarrassment flooded over Nightheart. Dovewing must have overheard him arguing with his sister at the last Gathering.

"Can't I just catch a whole bunch more frogs?" he asked.

Dovewing let out a *mrrow* of amusement. "You'll thank me later," she assured him. "I wish I'd had this opportunity when I first switched Clans. Closure is a good thing—for you and for your former Clanmates. Besides," she added, "if it ends up not feeling right to say good-bye this way, perhaps that will tell you that you have made a mistake."

Suppressing a sigh, Nightheart had to accept that Dovewing's mind was made up. He didn't try to argue any further; for all he knew, the ShadowClan cats could just be testing how well he would follow orders.

"Okay," he mewed resignedly. "I'm ready when you are."

Dovewing allowed him to take a piece of prey before they headed out of camp side by side. At first Nightheart felt awkward; he had never talked alone with the Clan leader's mate before. Even though they came from the same Clan, Dovewing had left before he was even born.

"What was it like when you left ThunderClan?" he ventured to ask after a while.

"I fell in love with Tigerstar when I was a ThunderClan cat and he was in ShadowClan," Dovewing replied as they padded over the soft layer of pine needles that covered most of the ground in ShadowClan territory. "We weren't allowed to be together, so we kept our relationship a secret for as long as we could. But finally we couldn't hide it anymore, because I was expecting kits. And I began having dreams that the kits would face danger if I birthed them in the Clans."

Nightheart drew in a sharp breath. "What did you do?"

"I followed my instincts and I ran away," Dovewing replied.

"But where did you plan to go?" Nightheart couldn't imagine what would happen to a she-cat and her kits, away from the care and protection of her Clan. "What about Tigerstar?"

"I kept seeing a place in my dreams, a big Twolegplace," Dovewing explained. "I set off to find it. I asked Tigerstar to come, but at first, he was sure he couldn't leave his Clan. ShadowClan was going through a terrible time. After a while, though, Tigerstar came after me, and we raised our kits there for a few moons. The cats we lived with were kind. We might even have stayed, but . . ." Her voice trailed off, her gaze thoughtful.

"Why did you come back?" Nightheart asked.

"Tigerstar was having dreams about ShadowClan and Rowanstar needing him," Dovewing explained. "It turned out that while he was gone, Rowanstar had given up his leadership and ShadowClan had fallen apart. And deep down," she added, "we both knew we wanted our kits to grow up as Clan cats. Clan life has its problems, but it's where we belong."

Nightheart looked at the gray she-cat with added respect. It must have been tough to abandon her Clan and everything she had ever known, especially when she was carrying kits. And maybe even tougher to come back and make a life in a different Clan.

*I thought I made a tough decision,* he thought. *But it must have been even harder for Dovewing when she was carrying kits and didn't have a Clan to accept her.*

"Do you ever regret joining Tigerstar's Clan instead of having him join yours?" he asked.

Dovewing shook her head. "I miss ThunderClan sometimes, especially my kin, but Tigerstar was destined to become ShadowClan's leader. I love him deeply, and I wanted to raise our kits together. And now I truly feel like a ShadowClan cat. I've found Clanmates who are brave and wise and passionate, and I feel loyal to my new Clan. Now, when I go back to ThunderClan, I feel like I'm visiting—ShadowClan is my true home. and I am a ShadowClan warrior. I hope you'll feel the same someday, Nightheart."

Her words made Nightheart think about Sunbeam. Even now she was in RiverClan, carrying out important duties for ShadowClan. She was obviously a respected member of her Clan.

*I wonder if I'll ever achieve that kind of respect in ShadowClan,* he asked himself. *StarClan knows, I was never able to achieve it in ThunderClan.*

When they crossed the border into SkyClan territory, they were careful to stay close to the lake. "I'd rather not meet any SkyClan cats," Dovewing mewed, alertly scanning the edge of the forest. "Leafstar was so hostile to us at the Gathering over Tigerstar becoming RiverClan's temporary leader. Who knows what orders she's given to her patrols?"

Nightheart too pricked his ears and scanned the shadows under every bush and clump of fern. His chest tightened as if he were gripped by a massive paw. But when he tasted the air, the only SkyClan scents were stale, and the grip gradually eased when there was no sign of any SkyClan cats as he and Dovewing swiftly crossed the territory.

Soon the scent of ThunderClan stung Nightheart's nostrils, and he realized with a shock that it smelled alien to him. He had become so used to ShadowClan scent, and he knew that he carried it himself.

*What are they going to think of me, coming into the ThunderClan camp smelling of ShadowClan?*

Dovewing halted at the ThunderClan border and sat down. "We'll wait for a patrol," she mewed, and began calmly to groom herself. Nightheart did the same, thinking that at least he wouldn't turn up in his old Clan looking scruffy and uncared-for. His pelt prickled with apprehension as he wondered which cats would be the ones to find them.

*Please, StarClan, don't let them say anything embarrassing in front of my new leader's mate!*

Eventually a stronger ThunderClan scent wafted over them, the ferns across the border rustled, and a ThunderClan patrol appeared. Lionblaze was in the lead, followed by Cherryfall and Bumblestripe.

"Hey, Dovewing!" Lionblaze greeted his former Clanmate with a welcoming wave of his tail, while Cherryfall trotted up to touch noses with her and let out a pleased purr.

Meanwhile, Bumblestripe had halted, his fur beginning to bristle as he glared at Nightheart. "What's *he* doing here?" he demanded.

Lionblaze gave a start of surprise; clearly he hadn't noticed Nightheart in his joy at seeing Dovewing. "Yes, what are you doing here?" he asked Nightheart; to Nightheart's relief, he sounded more confused than hostile.

It was Dovewing who replied. "I've come to visit Ivypool," she explained. "And Nightheart has business with Lilyheart and some of his kin."

Bumblestripe was clearly not impressed, letting out a low growl. Lionblaze hesitated for a few heartbeats, then gave a brusque nod. "You're always welcome, Dovewing," he meowed. "And I guess Nightheart can come, seeing as he's with you—this time."

Dovewing nudged Nightheart across the border; he dipped his head respectfully to Lionblaze as he padded past.

As soon as they entered the ThunderClan camp, Nightheart was almost overwhelmed by a wave of strangeness. His old home looked the same as always, with cats going about their duties or stretched out to share tongues in the weak leaf-fall sunlight, and yet it looked utterly unfamiliar.

*It hasn't changed,* he realized; *I have. I'm not the same cat.*

He realized too that the gaze of every cat was suddenly fixed on him. It took all his self-control to remain standing at Dovewing's side, his head raised, and try not to show how fast his heart was thumping.

"Lilyheart!" Dovewing had spotted Nightheart's former mentor beside the fresh-kill pile, and beckoned her over with a wave of her tail.

Lilyheart hesitated for a moment and then bounded over to touch noses with Dovewing. "Hi," she mewed. "It's good to see you again."

As she turned to Nightheart, her expression was wary, but not hostile. She didn't speak, but there was a question in her eyes.

"I've come to apologize for how I left," Nightheart responded, the words tumbling over each other in his eagerness to make her understand. "It was rude and inconsiderate of me. But I want you to know that leaving had nothing to do with you. I was unhappy here, but you were a wonderful mentor, and you deserved better than to have your apprentice run off without even saying good-bye or thank you. But . . ." Now it was harder to get the words out. "My heart is in ShadowClan. I hope you can understand."

Lilyheart's gaze had grown thoughtful, and she didn't speak for a few moments. Nightheart waited, his heart thundering so hard he thought it would burst out of his chest.

At last Lilyheart inclined her head. "It took courage to come back and admit that," she declared. "I accept your apology. But there are other Clan members who deserve apologies for the way you left, too."

*That's what I was afraid of.*

"I know," he murmured humbly. "Do you know where I can find them?"

"They're in the warriors' den right now," Lilyheart replied. "But you might find that they're not as ready to talk to you as I was."

*Oh, great! As if this weren't already hard enough!*

Lilyheart led the way across the camp to the warriors' den and stuck her head through the outer branches, calling out to the cats Nightheart needed to see. Then she gave Nightheart a nod and padded away.

Bayshine was the first cat to emerge, his eyes glowing with delight at seeing his old friend. "Nightheart!" he exclaimed. "You're back!"

Nightheart barely had time to feel relieved that at least some cat was pleased to see him before Sparkpelt and Finchlight appeared. They shared the same cool, reserved expression.

"Nightheart." Sparkpelt tilted her head to one side. "But you're not back to stay, are you? Have you quarreled with the ShadowClan cats now?"

"Of course I haven't!" Nightheart protested.

"Then why are you here?" Bayshine asked; his delight faded, replaced by curiosity.

"I would like to know that as well." The voice came from behind Nightheart; he whipped around to see that Squirrelflight had padded up quietly. "Hi, Dovewing," the Clan deputy went on. "Lilyheart told me you were here. I'm sure Ivypool is anxious to see you."

Dovewing dipped her head, her eyes gleaming with anticipation. "I'll go and find her."

"Hey, are you going to leave me here?" Nightheart whispered, alarmed at the thought of being left alone with this group of cats who were all—except for Bayshine—bound to be hostile to him.

"You'll be fine," Dovewing assured him. "I'll be back soon." She headed off without a backward glance.

"So you just came back to . . . what?" Sparkpelt exclaimed, her orange tabby fur fluffing up. "Stroll in here like you can come and go as you please? You *left*, Nightheart! You rejected your name, you rejected your Clan, you . . ." She trailed off, seeming almost too angry to finish.

Nightheart let out a heavy sigh. "What did you expect me

to do?" he demanded. "You never saw me for what I was, just what you thought I should be—some pale imitation of Firestar! If I were in ThunderClan, I'd probably still be picking ticks off the elders. In ShadowClan, I have the chance to be the kind of warrior I've always wanted to be."

"That's if you pass the three tasks," Sparkpelt pointed out. "I certainly hope you have better luck than you did on your assessments."

Nightheart was outraged that his mother would bring up his struggles to become a warrior. And yet it perfectly captured everything he was trying to escape in ThunderClan. "See?" he snarled, letting a gush of anger surge over him. "I passed my assessment, but you can only remember the times I failed. I'm only surprised you didn't remind me that our family is held to a higher standard, and Firestar would be embarrassed. Why should I have stayed?"

To his surprise, Squirrelflight stepped forward, laying her tail on his shoulder in a calming gesture. "Nightheart, take a breath. I'm sorry you were so unhappy here. It's not so much that you should have stayed," she told him, "but that you should have been more open about the way you wanted to leave. If you'd given your Clanmates a real chance to discuss your problems, maybe we could have done something about them, and you would have found that in fact you do belong in ThunderClan."

Nightheart couldn't find the words to respond to that. He could only stare at his paws and respond quietly, "I . . . don't know."

"While you're thinking about that," Squirrelflight continued, her tone surprisingly sympathetic, "there's another cat you should go and see. Bramblestar."

Nightheart nodded. "I will. Thanks, Squirrelflight." Turning to the other cats, he added, "For what it's worth, I am truly sorry about the way I left. But I hope you can trust that I'm doing what's best for me."

"It's all about you," Sparkpelt muttered. "Never mind the cats who care about you."

Nightheart was sure his mother had meant him to hear that, but he chose to ignore it. If Sparkpelt cared about him—if she'd cared while he lived in ThunderClan—then she sure had a funny way of showing it. But this visit was supposed to make peace, not start new quarrels.

With a dip of his head to Sparkpelt, Nightheart turned and followed Squirrelflight up the tumbled rocks that led up the side of the stone hollow to the Clan leader's den. Bramblestar was sitting outside on the Highledge, his head tilted back, his blank gaze fixed on the sky. His pelt was ungroomed, and it seemed to hang on the leader's frame as if it were meant for a much bigger cat.

"Bramblestar, Nightheart's here to see you," Squirrelflight announced.

The Clan leader gave Nightheart a glance; Nightheart saw a flicker of recognition in his eyes, but Bramblestar gave him no greeting, not even a hostile one. "That's . . . nice," he murmured, and went back to staring at the sky.

"Hey, Squirrelflight!" Mousewhisker's voice came up from

the camp below; he was standing in the middle of the clearing with Poppyfrost and Stormcloud beside him. "Where did you want us to hunt?"

"I'll have to see to that," Squirrelflight mewed. "Coming!" she called down to Mousewhisker, and whisked around to run lightly down the tumbled rocks.

Nightheart was left alone beside Bramblestar. For a moment he was unsure what to say, when the Clan leader was showing so little interest in him. "I'm sorry about leaving the Clan the way I did," he declared at last, dipping his head in the deepest respect.

Bramblestar seemed not to have heard him. "Look at those blackbirds." His voice was low, dreamy. "There are so many this season."

"You see, there's this ShadowClan cat—Sunbeam." Nightheart was feeling more and more awkward, finding it hard to understand his former leader's behavior. "She's so brave and beautiful. I love her, and I want to be with her. If it weren't for her, I might have stayed in ThunderClan. I wanted to be a good warrior and make you proud."

Bramblestar still didn't look at him. "Every cat must do what makes them happy," he meowed.

Nightheart felt as if his former leader had clawed him across the face. Bramblestar was his kin; Nightheart had believed that they had a connection, that he mattered to Bramblestar even if he didn't matter to any other cat in the Clan. But Bramblestar didn't seem interested in talking to him at all.

Nightheart didn't know what else he could say. He felt a

massive wave of relief as he saw Dovewing climbing the tumbled rocks and halting at the end of the Highledge.

"Are you ready to go?" she asked.

There was deep meaning behind that question, but Nightheart had no doubt about the answer. "Yes, I'm ready."

He dipped his head once more to Bramblestar and mewed, "Good-bye." Bramblestar didn't even twitch an ear.

Nightheart turned to follow Dovewing. *Now I can go back to where my home is—with ShadowClan and Sunbeam.*

# CHAPTER 10

❧

*The sun had just risen, though* mist still lay in hollows and under the trees, and every blade of grass was furred with frost. Her pelt fluffed out against the chill, Frostpaw followed Harelight to an open stretch of ground not far from the lake, within sight of the Twoleg halfbridge.

"Okay," Harelight began. "Battle training. Today I'm going to explain to you what you should do if your opponent takes you to the ground."

Frostpaw brightened, standing up straighter. *This should be easy!* "I should fight back, right?"

There was a glint of amusement in her mentor's eyes. "Show me what you mean by that."

Stepping forward without warning, he hooked Frostpaw's legs from under her in one smooth movement. She landed on her side; Harelight pressed one forepaw on her shoulder, the other on her ear, pinning her to the ground. Frostpaw bit back a yelp of pain. She tried to free herself, pushing upward with all her strength, but the white tom was too big and heavy for her to shift.

Gritting her teeth, Frostpaw pushed again, straining to

force every last scrap of her strength into her shoulders. Hare-light still didn't move.

*It's* not *easy!* Frostpaw realized, ready to screech with frustration.

"You're wasting energy," Harelight pointed out. "All the effort you're putting into pushing against me is going to tire you out, and if somehow you *do* manage to get out from under me, you'll probably be weak and tired. Your opponent would be able to take you down again quite easily, don't you think?"

Frostpaw could see the logic in what her mentor told her. She gave up pushing, and Harelight stepped back from her.

"Then what should I do?" Frostpaw asked, scrambling to her paws.

"Use your attacker's weight and momentum against them," Harelight explained. "If your attacker is charging forward, don't try to stop them in their tracks. Instead, let them go through you, so you can roll over and get back to your paws."

Frostpaw frowned, feeling thoroughly confused. "I'm not sure what you mean."

"Attack me," Harelight responded. "Then I can show you."

Her pelt prickling with nervousness, Frostpaw charged at Harelight, who didn't try to resist at all as she bore him to the ground. She could feel his body limp and loose beneath her paws, almost like he was dead. As he hit the ground, the force of Frostpaw's attack carried her forward, beyond him, and as she staggered past, the white tom slipped out from underneath her.

Frostpaw felt a paw touch her hindquarters and looked

WARRIORS: A STARLESS CLAN: SHADOW

over her shoulder to see that Harelight was already upright, and in a very good position. From there he could jump right onto her back if he wanted to.

"Now I get it!" Frostpaw exclaimed, nodding eagerly. "Can I try it?"

Harelight patiently guided her through the movements. It took Frostpaw several attempts, with a few painful bumps when she mistimed her move. But eventually she learned how to roll through Harelight's attack the way he had shown her, staying limp until she hit the ground, then stretching out her hind legs to free most of her body so that she could clamber to her paws.

She let out a purr of delight when she finally succeeded. "Fighting is actually pretty simple, really, isn't it?" she meowed.

"It's simple if you're well trained and you know what you're doing," her mentor chided her good-naturedly. "But that requires moons and moons of practice. Are you up for that?"

Frostpaw gave a vigorous nod. "I *definitely* am!"

"I'm glad to hear it," Harelight responded. "Let's get started, then. . . ."

Sunhigh was approaching by the time Harelight decided that they had trained enough. Frostpaw was exhausted, and muscles she'd never known she had were aching, but she was still disappointed at having to stop.

She had mastered how to roll through the initial attack, and she was getting better at pouncing on Harelight's back at the end of the move. She hadn't actually followed up by strik-ing her mentor, but she could see clearly how easy it would be to strike an opponent. When she was on their back, they would be more or less helpless, unable to defend themselves.

When she'd been a medicine-cat apprentice, her legs had carried her over the territory searching for herbs; her paws had gathered them and made poultices. Now it felt strange to think of the wounds she could inflict. For a heartbeat she felt guilty—*that's not what I've been called to do!* Then she reflected that she would only use her claws in the defense of her Clan.

*I feel skilled and powerful,* she thought proudly. *Like a real warrior.*

As she and her mentor headed back to camp, a warm glow was swelling in Frostpaw's chest and belly. It had been hard to decide on becoming a warrior apprentice after training so long with Mothwing. The easier path would have been to follow in Mothwing's paw steps and continue to serve her Clan as a healer, even without communicating with StarClan. But now she knew that the reward was worth the risk; admitting she wasn't a real medicine cat, and starting her warrior training, was the best decision she'd ever made. Good things happened when she was assertive, and she felt more confident than ever before.

"You've worked really hard this morning—you'd better rest for a while," Harelight instructed her when they arrived in the RiverClan camp. "Curl up in your nest and take a nap. Later we'll go out and I'll show you some new hunting moves."

"Great!" Frostpaw responded. "Thanks, Harelight."

Dipping her head to her mentor, she scurried across the camp toward the apprentices' den. But before she reached it, she spotted Splashtail, who was dozing in a patch of sunlight near the Highstump.

*He's been avoiding me,* Frostpaw thought, remembering how he had slipped away from her when she was made a warrior apprentice. *Well, he can't avoid me now!*

She marched across to the brown tabby tom and prodded him awake with a determined forepaw. Splashtail jerked, startled, and Frostpaw saw the flash of his claws briefly extending as he fended off an imaginary attacker.

A heartbeat later his bleary gaze cleared and he recognized her. "Sorry," he meowed, relaxing. "But you shouldn't sneak up on a warrior like that. You could get hurt."

"Not now that I'm being trained by Harelight, I won't," Frostpaw purred.

Splashtail didn't give her an answering purr. He still looked grumpy from being disturbed so abruptly, his shoulders hunched and his tail-tip twitching.

*I can change that, though,* Frostpaw thought.

"The best thing about warrior training is how learning battle moves makes fighting less scary," she told Splashtail. "When I was a medicine cat, the thought of having to fight used to worry me, because all I could think about was getting hurt, and what that would feel like. But now—"

"Warriors still get hurt," Splashtail interrupted her.

"I know that!" Frostpaw rolled her eyes. "But now that I have some idea of how to fight, and the kinds of things I can do so I don't get hurt—or at least not hurt too badly—fighting isn't so scary anymore."

This time Splashtail's only response was a grunt.

"I feel braver than ever," Frostpaw continued. The conviction that there was something she must do was building inside her. Moments before, when she'd returned to camp, she hadn't imagined what she meant to say to Splashtail, but now she had found her confidence and was determined to go through with it. "I'm going to be braver than ever right now."

Splashtail blinked up at her, obviously bewildered. "How are you going to—"

"I like you!" Frostpaw blurted out. "And I think we should be mates. Don't you want that, too?"

For a few endless moments, Splashtail said nothing. Her heart beating fast, Frostpaw vainly tried to read his expression. He didn't look horrified by the idea, but he didn't look all that excited, either.

*Have I made a horrible mistake?*

But even if Splashtail didn't want to be with her, it was better to know now, rather than spend moons vainly padding after him.

*It was still right for me to be brave!*

"What's wrong?" she asked nervously.

Again, Splashtail took a moment before replying. "I like you a lot, too," he admitted at last. "But right now I still think of you as a medicine cat."

Frostpaw huffed out an impatient sigh. "I gave that up. Splashtail, you know that!"

"Yes," Splashtail mewed, nodding. "But it'll be a while before I get used to you being a warrior like me. I'm not much older than you, but you're still an apprentice. It wouldn't be right."

"But once I pass my assessment and get my warrior name—then we can be mates, can't we?" Frostpaw pressed him.

Splashtail's head jerked forward and then stopped, as if he was preventing himself from nodding assent. "Things have been so confused in RiverClan lately," he pointed out, "it's probably best if we don't distract ourselves with such thoughts. Once RiverClan has a new leader, and things have settled down, then we can start to plan for what comes after."

"I suppose you're right," Frostpaw agreed, trying not to feel disappointed. "That sounds sensible."

She said good-bye, her head high even though her whole pelt was hot with embarrassment, and padded over to the apprentices' den to settle herself in her nest. With time to relax, she tried to comfort herself with the idea that Splashtail wanted to think things through and be honest about his feelings.

*You made a great choice, picking such a thoughtful, honest tom for your mate,* she told herself.

But a small, rational voice at the back of her mind reminded her, *He didn't actually say yes to being your mate.*

"He didn't say no, either," Frostpaw meowed crossly, and wrapped her tail over her nose.

# CHAPTER 11

*The sun was starting to go down*, casting long shadows across the forest. Sunbeam, with Nightheart and more of her Clanmates, was standing outside a cave in the hilly territory not far from the Twoleg nest. Every cat was waiting for Fringewhisker to emerge.

Earlier that day, Berryheart and Dovewing had rolled in a patch of wild onions until their pelts reeked of the plants. Then they had ordered Fringewhisker to close her eyes and had led her into the cave.

Sunbeam had a bad feeling about this, the third and last of Fringewhisker's tasks. The brown-and-white she-cat was supposed to find her way out by herself. Normally this would be easy, because she would be able to follow her own scent trail, but Berryheart had been determined to make it difficult for her by flooding the narrow cavern with onion scent. It worried Sunbeam that her mother had obviously enjoyed doing it.

*What will she dream up for Nightheart?*

Nightheart leaned toward Sunbeam, so close that the tip of his ear brushed hers. "What is this feat about?" he murmured, speaking quietly because Tigerstar had explained that he didn't want any cat to make noise that might help guide Fringewhisker out of the cave.

"I heard Berryheart instructing Fringewhisker, just before she led her in there," Sunbeam replied, angling her ears toward the dark gap in the hillside. "She said that a true Shadow-Clan cat ought to know how to move in the dark. It's not just about finding her way back outside. Fringewhisker needs to be one with the darkness. She needs to teach herself to stay calm while walking in shadow."

"Just like Berryheart found her way out easily, after she led Fringewhisker in there?" Nightheart suggested.

Sunbeam nodded agreement. It was hard for her to push away the thought that her mother must have led Fringe-whisker deep within the cave, to an especially difficult spot, to make her task as hard as possible.

"Do you think she'll make me do the same thing?" Night-heart asked.

"I don't know for sure," Sunbeam admitted. "But whatever your next task is, you can be sure it will be just as tough a test of your courage as what Fringewhisker is going through now."

Nightheart's only response was to twitch his whiskers; he didn't look reassured.

Sunbeam felt an unpleasant prickling throughout her pelt as the moments slipped by and Fringewhisker did not appear. A couple of tail-lengths away, Spireclaw was flexing his claws, tearing at the grass, his expression full of anxiety.

At last Berryheart turned toward Tigerstar and Dovewing and broke the silence. "How long do we have to wait before we decide that we've given Fringewhisker more than enough time?" she demanded.

Tigerstar glanced toward the cave entrance, his eyes narrowing. Sunbeam's heart lurched; she was sure that the Clan leader was about to announce that Fringewhisker had failed her vital third task.

But then Sunbeam thought that she could discern another scent beneath the pervasive aroma of wild onion. Her nose twitched. "That's Fringewhisker's scent!" she hissed.

Every cat fell silent, not wanting to speak too loudly in case the former SkyClan warrior heard them. The scent grew stronger and stronger, until at last Fringewhisker staggered out of the cave, blinking in the scarlet light. Her pelt was bristling with alarm and nervousness, her eyes were wide, and her jaws were clamped tightly shut. Sunbeam thought she had never seen a cat look more terrified.

"She's so brave!" she murmured into Nightheart's ear.

Fringewhisker turned to Tigerstar. "Did I pass?" she asked, her voice hoarse.

"You certainly did," Tigerstar replied. "Well done!"

"It took her a while," Berryheart pointed out with a disagreeable sniff.

"It was pretty good for a first attempt." Tigerstar's voice was firm. "I'm sure she'll get used to the shadows and darkness in time. So now . . ." He jumped up onto a nearby fallen log and raised his voice to reach all the cats assembled there. "Fringewhisker has passed her three tasks! Congratulations, Fringewhisker, and welcome to ShadowClan. You are officially one of us now!"

Her Clanmates erupted into cheering. "Fringewhisker! Fringewhisker!" Spireclaw bounded up to his mate and twined his tail with hers, purring too hard to join in the caterwauling.

Sunbeam welcomed her new Clanmate, too, but she couldn't help noticing that Berryheart looked as if she had tasted a piece of crow-food. Her plan had failed: It had made Fringewhisker look even braver, more determined, and more worthy of becoming a ShadowClan cat than she had before, because her tasks had been so hard.

"Berryheart," Tigerstar began as the celebration died down, "have you given any thought to what Nightheart's next feat will be?"

Sunbeam pricked her ears and exchanged a glance with Nightheart, who looked anxious to know what her mother had in store for him. He had good reason to be nervous, Sunbeam thought, after all the obstacles her mother had thrown in Fringewhisker's path.

"Oh, I've been thinking about it," Berryheart responded. "It will involve speed."

"In what way?" Tigerstar asked.

"That's my secret," Berryheart told him, and pressed her jaws together. She wasn't giving anything away, not even to her Clan leader.

Tigerstar led his warriors back to the ShadowClan camp. As they pushed their way through the bramble barrier, the cats who hadn't gone with them to the cave slid out of their dens and gathered in the center of the camp.

"How did it go?" Flaxfoot asked.

"She passed!" Spireclaw announced, his eyes shining with

delight. "She's a real ShadowClan cat now!"

Most of the cats gathered around to congratulate Fringe-whisker, though Sunbeam found it hard to ignore the bristling and hostile glances of some of their other Clanmates, particularly Yarrowleaf and Whorlpelt. They looked as irritated as Berryheart about the way things had turned out.

By the time the clamor died down, the last of the sunlight was gone, and twilight enfolded the camp. Above her head, Sunbeam could see that a single warrior of StarClan had appeared in the sky.

Nightheart's jaws gaped in a massive yawn. "I'm ready for my nest," he meowed.

"Me too," Sunbeam agreed, "but I want to talk to you first."

She led the way into the warriors' den and sat down in her nest. Nightheart settled beside her with his paws tucked under him. So far none of the other warriors had joined them.

"What's on your mind?" Nightheart asked.

"Your next task," Sunbeam replied. As she spoke, Pounce-step and Grassheart slipped into the den, followed by more of her Clanmates returning to their nests to sleep. Disappointed that she and Nightheart couldn't have any more time alone together, she lowered her voice. "You need to relax as much as you can. We don't know exactly what Berryheart has in store for you, but if it involves speed, your muscles need to be loose, not tense or wound up."

"I get it," Nightheart replied. "I'm feeling pretty confident about that, actually. I'm quite a quick cat."

Sunbeam felt a flash of irritation that Nightheart seemed

so calm. "Why aren't you as anxious as I am?" she asked him. "Don't you care? Are you having second thoughts or something?"

Nightheart blinked at her, looking thoroughly confused. "What kind of question is that? I've already completed one task, haven't I? I've been trying to prove how much I want to join ShadowClan and be with you."

Sunbeam began to nod, but Nightheart continued before she could respond. "You seem unsure still," he mewed. "Whatever's bothering you, tell me what it is."

Sunbeam hesitated. Now that she was about to say what was worrying her, it sounded silly, as if she were a kit barely out of the nursery. Yet thinking about what Lightleap had told her about her and Blazefire, how they committed themselves to each other every day, she wondered if she really was being stupid. If Nightheart would make the same commitment to her, perhaps she wouldn't feel so uneasy.

Eventually she managed to force out the words. "You have to understand, this is a big deal for me, too. I never imagined being mates with a cat who wasn't from ShadowClan."

"I know." Nightheart paused, staring at his paws as if there was more he wanted to say. "Your mother spoke to me earlier," he continued. "Before you got back from RiverClan. She really doesn't like me, and she doesn't want us to be mates. She said . . ." He paused again, swallowing as if he had a tough bit of fresh-kill lodged in his throat.

Sunbeam heaved a long sigh. "Why can't she stop sticking her paws in? Come on, Nightheart, tell me."

Nightheart seemed to brace himself. "She said that you had loved Blazefire since you were a kit, and you had never really gotten over him. Is it true, Sunbeam?"

"Of course it isn't true!" Sunbeam snapped out the words without thinking, then hesitated. "Well, it's partly true," she added. "I did love Blazefire when I was a kit. I had a crush on him, and maybe there was some hero worship. He wasn't much more than a kit himself. I assumed we would be mates, and I never realized that we had both grown up into very different cats. I still love him, but as a Clanmate, not as a mate. He and Lightleap are much better suited to each other."

She could tell that Nightheart had begun to relax as he gazed into her eyes. "Then you truly think that I'm the right cat for you?" he asked.

"I do." But Sunbeam's uneasiness was rising again. "I only want to be sure that you think that *I'm* the right cat."

Nightheart stared at her as if he didn't understand a word she had said. "But I've already left ThunderClan, haven't I? I even went back with Dovewing to make a point of saying good-bye to them. I'm risking pain and humiliation trying to complete the tasks your Clan is setting for me. Isn't that enough for you?"

Sunbeam felt heat flow throughout her pelt at how awkward the situation had suddenly become. She realized that Nightheart had a point. He *had* left ThunderClan; if he tried to go back, he would look completely mouse-brained. So if he had made the decision because he wanted to get away from his Clan, and not really about caring for her, he might go on pretending because he had no other choice. And if he failed to earn a place in ShadowClan, he might even end up as a rogue.

"I'm sorry," she mewed, feeling guilty that she had asked him for reassurance. "It's just that even if you succeed and Tigerstar accepts you into the Clan, you know as well as I do that not every ShadowClan cat will be happy about it. Nightheart, you have to convince me that you really want to join."

"Has Berryheart been talking to you, too?" Nightheart asked. "Don't let her turn you against me. Against *us*. She told me that ShadowClan would never really accept me. But that's a risk I'm prepared to take, provided that *you* want me here, Sunbeam. I don't give a couple of mouse droppings for what other cats think of me."

He was so earnest, so determined. Sunbeam loved him all over again. "Of course I want you here, Nightheart. And you're right; we don't have to care what the rest of the Clan thinks. I'm sorry I doubted you."

She realized how different, and how much more challenging, her relationship with Nightheart would be than Lightleap's with Blazefire. Nightheart would always have made this huge sacrifice for her. And they wouldn't always see things the same way; that was easier for every cat when they grew up in the same Clan.

Nightheart waved his tail dismissively, but even though he had accepted her apology, Sunbeam still felt awkward. As they settled down side by side in their nests, curling up to sleep, she had to stifle the urge to apologize all over again.

She was finally drifting into sleep when Nightheart roused

her by prodding her shoulder. "What—" she began, only to be silenced by Nightheart's tail across her mouth.

He leaned over to whisper into her ear. "Where is your mother going?"

Sunbeam opened her eyes and turned her head. In the darkness of the warriors' den she could barely make out the shape of a cat picking their way among the other nests to slip out between the branches of the den. Scent rather than sight told her it was Berryheart.

Every hair on Sunbeam's pelt rose with suspicion. She slid to the edge of the den and peered out. In the moonlight she could see Berryheart clearly, standing near the fresh-kill pile. She seemed to be waiting for something, twitching her tail impatiently.

Nightheart prodded her again and angled his ears farther into the den, where more dark shapes were moving. As they emerged into the open, Sunbeam recognized Snowbird, Whorlpelt, and Yarrowleaf, and even more cats following them. Berryheart led the way out of the camp.

"What are they doing?" Nightheart murmured. "Why are they sneaking out?"

Sunbeam shook her head, confused. She knew that Berryheart and other cats had met secretly before, but never before had they left camp in the middle of the night.

"I don't know what's going on," she admitted.

Nightheart's eyes were gleaming in the near darkness. "We should follow them," he suggested.

For a moment Sunbeam was doubtful. She didn't want to

get caught, or create a problem out of nothing. She would have liked to believe that her mother's actions were perfectly innocent—but she couldn't.

*This doesn't look like a night hunting patrol,* she thought. *If it were, why all the secrecy?*

Her pads were prickling with curiosity, and she knew she couldn't ignore this—couldn't curl up and go to sleep as if nothing was happening.

"Okay," she mewed softly to Nightheart. "But we'll need to be *very* quiet."

# CHAPTER 12

*Every hair on Nightheart's pelt was* prickling with nervousness as he and Sunbeam slipped out of camp and began to follow Berryheart and her group of cats. They were walking along a narrow Twoleg path, heading in the direction of RiverClan.

"We can't take the same path," Sunbeam muttered into Nightheart's ear.

Nightheart understood what she meant. "Yeah, or Berryheart and the others might pick up our scent on the way back."

"This way," Sunbeam mewed, slipping into the undergrowth beside the path and heading in roughly the same direction as the group of ShadowClan cats.

Nightheart followed in her paw steps, hoping that they wouldn't lose their quarry, and hoping even more that no cat in Berryheart's group would realize they were being pursued.

Here, near the edge of ShadowClan territory, the pines were mixed with other kinds of trees, and the ground cover was denser, more like the ThunderClan territory Nightheart was used to. Even so, it was hard to slip through the bracken and brambles without making a noise, and keep his senses alert for the sounds and scents of Berryheart and her Clanmates.

Sunbeam let out an annoyed hiss. "I stepped on a StarClan-cursed thorn," she whispered. "Going this way at night is so hard!"

"Better than being discovered and having to explain ourselves," Nightheart reminded her in response. *If Berryheart found out we were spying on her, she would make my next task impossible!* Then he realized that she might not even wait to assign him his next task. She would probably complain to Tigerstar and get him thrown out of the Clan.

Gradually the trees and undergrowth began to thin out. Nightheart ventured into the open and realized he was at the edge of a clearing; Berryheart and the others had halted at the far side. If they turned in his direction, they would see him, but they all had their heads together, as if they were conferring about something important.

"Get back!" he warned Sunbeam, who had padded up behind him. "Behind that tree!"

In the shelter of a gnarled oak, Nightheart peered out to see that Berryheart and her group hadn't moved; they were still deep in conversation. "What in StarClan is going on?" he murmured. "Is Berryheart leading a night attack on River-Clan?"

"I doubt it," Sunbeam mewed decisively. "She's been so hostile to the idea of us taking over RiverClan, she would never do anything to get us *more* involved. Not unless Tigerstar ordered it. Besides, she hasn't brought enough warriors to attack a whole Clan. But as for what she *is* doing . . ." She shook her head in confusion. "I have no idea."

Finally, Berryheart and the others moved off again, while Nightheart and Sunbeam continued to track them, skirting the clearing and plunging into deep undergrowth again on the far side. Nightheart found that it took all his concentration to stay alert and track the group by their scent and the tiny sounds they made.

Eventually they came to a wide stretch of open ground covered with hard black Thunderpath stuff. At one side was a small Twoleg den; yellow light flowed out from a square gap in one wall.

Nightheart felt his fur fluff up; he had never seen this place before, and he didn't like it. The whole area reeked of Twolegs, and there were other weird smells as well. He picked out several different dog scents, but others he couldn't identify at all.

"Where are we?" he asked Sunbeam.

"This is the greenleaf Twolegplace," Sunbeam told him, speaking low into his ear. "They come and mess about on the lake—don't ask me why. Twolegs are weird."

Berryheart and the others had settled down at the edge of the Thunderpath stuff. Keeping a close watch on them, Nightheart and Sunbeam crouched in the shelter of a clump of bracken. At least the unsettling Twoleg light made it easier to see their quarry.

Nightheart worked his claws into the ground, his heart racing with fear and impatience. "What are they *doing*?" he asked.

"This is the border with RiverClan," Sunbeam replied. "Can't you pick up their scent?"

WARRIORS: A STARLESS CLAN: SHADOW     143

Nightheart tasted the air. Now that Sunbeam pointed it out, he could distinguish the RiverClan border markers, almost drowned by the mixture of Twoleg scents. He picked up the ShadowClan markers, too, and realized with a sudden shock that he had become so familiar with ShadowClan scent that he hadn't even noticed them.

*I smell like that, too,* he thought, remembering his visit to ThunderClan and his surprise that their scent smelled alien to him; a sudden pang went through his heart, as if with the fading of his ThunderClan scent he had lost something precious.

Nightheart twitched his whiskers impatiently as he pushed away his regret. "How long do you think—" he began.

"Shhh!" Sunbeam interrupted. "Some cat is coming."

Concentrating, Nightheart realized that a fresh wave of RiverClan scent was pouring over them from the RiverClan side of the border. He spotted movement in the undergrowth at the far side of the black stretch of Thunderpath stuff, and a moment later a RiverClan cat poked his head out of a clump of long grasses.

"Splashtail!" Nightheart felt Sunbeam tense as she whispered into his ear.

Nightheart crouched watching as Splashtail, spotting Berryheart and her group, emerged into the open and padded toward them. He was followed by Duskfur and Mallownose. All three cats advanced warily, glancing from side to side, their ears pricked and their pelts bristling.

"Those three in particular really hate us being in

RiverClan," Sunbeam murmured. "When Lightleap and I were on duty in their camp, all they did was complain. Oh, StarClan, are they going to *fight*?"

"They're mouse-brained if they do," Nightheart responded. "They're well outnumbered." *And if a fight does break out, do we join in on ShadowClan's side?* he added to himself. *We shouldn't be here at all.* His pelt began to bristle at the thought of how much trouble they would be in if they were discovered.

But when Splashtail and the others reached the Shadow-Clan cats, there was no hostile growling, no claws extended. Instead Splashtail halted in front of Berryheart and bowed his head to her respectfully.

"Greetings, all of you," he meowed; he spoke in a clear voice, as if he had no fear of being overheard, and his words carried easily to Nightheart and Sunbeam in their hiding place. He was standing tall, with his head and tail erect; Nightheart was surprised at how commanding he looked. "Thank you for coming to this meeting," the RiverClan tom continued. "It's good to know that there are cats in Tigerstar's Clan who see the error of his ways."

Berryheart in her turn sounded equally commanding. "We are not moving against Tigerstar," she declared. "He is my Clan leader, and I respect him with every hair on my pelt. This is about making sure that he isn't overburdened by trying to keep a second Clan running smoothly. It will be best for all of us if RiverClan finds their new leader soon."

"I agree," Splashtail responded. "And I'm pretty sure that our new leader will be found any day now."

Berryheart let out a half purr, half growl, as if she was amused and irritated at the same time. "RiverClan needs to find its medicine cat first," she stated. "Have you had any signs about which cat *that* might be?"

Nightheart wondered if Splashtail would be offended by Berryheart's challenge, or by her contemptuous tone, but his voice was even as he replied. "I'm not going to get caught up in looking for signs all over the place. StarClan will choose a new medicine cat for RiverClan very soon. And if that doesn't happen, well . . ." He paused and licked one forepaw reflectively. "I'm sure that we can help them along," he finished.

Nightheart exchanged a startled look with Sunbeam. "What does *that* mean?" he mewed. Every cat in ShadowClan knew by now that Frostpaw was no longer a medicine-cat apprentice, and they had all assumed that RiverClan could do nothing but wait to learn the will of StarClan.

Sunbeam merely shrugged uneasily and did not answer.

Berryheart had already begun to respond. "*Who* the medicine cat will be is important, too," she pointed out. "Splashtail, you must realize that some cat . . . some *suggestible* cat . . . will be helpful to both our Clans."

Splashtail seemed to understand exactly what Berryheart meant. "If the Clanmate I have in mind agrees," he told the ShadowClan cats, "then, yes, she is very suggestible. And I have ways of making her more so."

At his words, Mallownose turned sharply to look at Splashtail. "You're not going to force any cat to do anything, are you?" he asked, sounding thoroughly uncomfortable.

Splashtail tilted his head to one side, narrowing his eyes to give Mallownose a withering stare. "I will do whatever it takes to save RiverClan," he replied coldly. "Nothing comes before that. And if you're not ready, Mallownose, to do whatever needs to be done to push ShadowClan out, perhaps you shouldn't be coming to these meetings."

Mallownose lashed his tail and opened his jaws to retort, then clamped them shut again with the words unsaid.

"We shouldn't overthink this," Berryheart meowed, in a smooth tone that seemed intended to calm the RiverClan cats' hostility. "We all want the same thing: to get Tigerstar out of RiverClan as soon as possible. It's what's best for all our Clans. And once we are separate again, each Clan can sort itself out."

Even though Tigerstar hadn't been his leader for long, Nightheart felt thoroughly unnerved at hearing Berryheart and the other ShadowClan cats actively plotting with River-Clan. *I don't care what she says about respecting Tigerstar. He wouldn't approve of this, and we all know it.*

He shifted uneasily, and accidentally put his paw down on a crackly dried leaf.

Instantly Berryheart whipped around. "What was that?" she snapped.

Nightheart froze, aware of Sunbeam crouching rigid beside him. The silence seemed to stretch out for seasons, until Mallownose meowed, "Probably just a squirrel, or some other prey."

Another unending moment crawled past until Berryheart

finally shrugged and turned back to the others.

Nightheart let out a long breath he had been holding. "We have to get back," he whispered to Sunbeam, angling his ears in the direction of the ShadowClan camp.

Sunbeam hesitated, leaning forward and pricking her ears. Nightheart followed her gaze and stretched forward too, straining to hear. But Berryheart and the others had drawn into a huddle, their meows too soft to be overheard anymore. Glancing at Sunbeam, he saw a look of resignation on her face before she gave a swift nod. Nightheart padded beside her as she headed back the way they had come.

"What do you think Splashtail is going to do?" Nightheart whispered.

"I'm not sure, but what I *am* sure of is that I don't like it," Sunbeam murmured in response, swiveling her ears backward in case any cat was following them. "Is he really planning to fake the discovery of a medicine cat?"

"But that must be against the warrior code," Nightheart objected.

Sunbeam nodded. "Of course it is. It's . . . shocking! But what can we do?"

Nightheart thought about that for a few moments. He couldn't go to Tigerstar and tell him that Berryheart was plotting with RiverClan cats. Because Berryheart was in charge of choosing the tasks that would decide whether he could become a ShadowClan cat, she might accuse him of lying to get rid of her, hoping the tasks would be assigned to some friendlier cat.

As he was thinking, he noticed that Sunbeam had an

uncertain look on her face. "What's the matter?" he asked her.

Sunbeam shrugged, her eyes full of apprehension. "Of course it's wrong to fake a medicine cat who doesn't have a connection to StarClan, but part of me kind of agrees with Berryheart. It *would* be best for both Clans if ShadowClan got out of RiverClan."

"And maybe once they do, then RiverClan could figure out its own medicine-cat problem," Nightheart suggested. "They wouldn't be under the pressure of having a rival Clan ordering them around."

"True," Sunbeam agreed with a sigh. "I just wish my mother weren't having secret meetings behind Tigerstar's back."

"So what do you want to do about it?" Nightheart asked. He knew that he couldn't say a word against Berryheart, but perhaps Sunbeam could. Her Clan might suspect she was biased because of him, but surely they would never think she would accuse her own mother of something so serious, unless it was true.

*Or maybe she's stuck, just like me!*

Sunbeam hesitated before replying. "Berryheart *is* my mother, so I would like to talk to her before we do anything that might cause problems. But right now we need to hurry back to camp. If Berryheart and the others get there before us, they'll wonder where we've been."

With no need for secrecy any longer, they picked up the pace, speeding back along their own scent trail. Neither of them said any more; Nightheart was too unsettled for talking, and he guessed that Sunbeam felt the same.

Memories were crowding into Nightheart's mind—memories of the time in ThunderClan when the false Bramblestar had sown discord and set cat against cat. His accusations of codebreaking had almost torn the Clan apart.

*Almost?* he asked himself. *Maybe we* haven't *truly repaired the damage,* he thought as he remembered how hesitant and listless Bramblestar had been lately. He'd seen ThunderClan cats openly questioning their leader, but he had believed that ShadowClan was more united. Now he wasn't sure that was true. *Have I left one unstable Clan for another?*

# CHAPTER 13

*As Harelight barreled toward her, bearing* her to the ground, Frost-paw slumped beneath him and let every muscle in her body grow limp. The force of her mentor's attack carried him past her; Frostpaw wriggled out from underneath him and rolled upright, then launched herself up onto his back. With her claws sheathed, she raked one forepaw across his ears before jumping to the ground again.

"Did I do okay?" she asked as Harelight turned to face her.

A purr came from deep within the white tom's chest. "I'm impressed, Frostpaw," he told her. "Really impressed. You've learned that move brilliantly."

"Yeah, it was great! You got the timing just right."

Frostpaw spun around at the sound of her brother Gray-paw's voice, and saw him standing under a nearby tree, with Mistpaw and their mentors, Breezeheart and Icewing. She hadn't realized that they had finished their training session and were watching her.

*I'm glad I didn't know. I would probably have messed up.*

"You're really good at this," Mistpaw agreed. "It's weird that Curlfeather was wrong about you being a medicine cat.

But at least now that you're a warrior apprentice, we get to spend more time together."

"Maybe we could all be made warriors at the same time," Graypaw mewed with an excited little bounce.

Frostpaw shook her head, feeling thoroughly embarrassed. "Oh, no, I'll never be ready at the same time as you. I have too much to learn."

"Well, it's not impossible," Icewing meowed. "Harelight tells me that you're making very good progress."

"You are," Harelight agreed. "But if you want your warrior ceremony at the same time as Mistpaw and Graypaw, you'll have to work twice as hard."

"Oh, I will!" Frostpaw assured him fervently, hardly able to believe what her mentor was telling her. "I'll work harder than any cat in the whole forest!"

"This I must see," Harelight purred.

A warm glow filled Frostpaw's body from ears to tail-tip as she and her littermates headed back toward the RiverClan camp with their mentors. The sun was shining and there was a frosty tang in the air. This was going to be a really good day. Winning praise from Harelight and the others was one of the best things she had ever felt; their words filled her with pride at how well she was learning to be a warrior. She had struggled with doubts before she could imagine this life for herself, but she was enjoying every moment of her training. It was hard to believe that she had ever thought she was meant to be a medicine cat.

*Why was my mother so sure I was meant for that?* Frostpaw asked herself. She remembered waking up from dreams in the nursery and telling her mother about them. Curlfeather had immediately been certain that they were visions. *But all kits dream. Mistpaw once dreamed about riding up to the stars in a Twoleg monster! So why was my mother so sure that* my *dreams meant something?*

Frostpaw gave her pelt a shake. She wasn't going to think about that. At last she felt she had set her paws on the right path. She was going to forget about her troubles. As a warrior, she was sure she wasn't going to let RiverClan down.

She could see her new life spreading out before her, a life where she was a loyal RiverClan warrior, and Splashtail was her mate. She had never allowed herself to imagine that before, but now she was sure that was what she wanted.

*I just need Splashtail to agree. . . .*

When they reached the stream that flowed alongside the camp, Frostpaw spotted Splashtail and Lizardtail crouching on the bank, staring intently into the water. As she watched, Lizardtail darted a paw into the water and drew out a wriggling silver fish. He killed it with a neat bite to the back of its head and laid it on the bank.

Frostpaw and the rest of the group padded up to join their Clanmates.

"How are the fish running?" Harelight meowed.

"Not well." Lizardtail prodded the catch he had just made. "That's not big enough to feed more than a couple of cats."

"I see you've been battle training," Splashtail remarked, his gaze flickering across the group of cats and coming to rest on Frostpaw.

"How do you know?" Graypaw asked.

Splashtail let out a small *mrrow* of laughter. "The twigs and bits of leaf in your fur kind of give it away. How is Frostpaw doing?" he added.

"Very well," Harelight replied. "She's learning her battle moves really quickly."

"We'll all be made warriors together!" Mistpaw announced.

Splashtail's ears flicked up in surprise. "Really? Are you sure Frostpaw will be ready for that?"

"We can't make any promises," Icewing responded. "But if she trains hard . . ."

Frostpaw was warmed all over again by the praise of the senior warriors, but she was slightly disappointed that Splashtail wasn't showing more enthusiasm. *The sooner I'm a warrior, the sooner we can be mates.*

"Well, I've fished enough for today," Lizardtail announced, rising to his paws. "I'll take this back to camp." He picked up the fish he had caught.

"I'll come with you." Splashtail rose, too, and took one paw step toward the camp, only to flinch back and let out a screech of pain. "My paw!"

"What's the matter with your paw?" Breezeheart asked.

"I stepped on something!" Splashtail's features were screwed up in a look of agony, and he was holding his paw off the ground. "Great StarClan, it hurts!"

Looking more closely, Frostpaw spotted a sharp stone beside the stream, almost completely hidden by long grass. Treading on it would have been painful, though to her relief she couldn't see any blood.

"You'd better go and see Mothwing," Icewing advised.

Splashtail nodded and hesitantly tried setting his paw down, then flinched and let out another screech. "I can't walk as far as the camp," he meowed, tottering on three paws. "Frostpaw, will you take a look?"

Frostpaw paused for a moment. She didn't like being thrust back into the duties of a medicine cat, but she hated seeing the cat she loved in pain. "Okay," she agreed after a couple of heartbeats. "Lie down so I can get a good look at it."

Obediently, Splashtail lay on his side and stretched out the injured forepaw toward Frostpaw. She peered closely at his pads, licking off a scrap or two of grass. "You're not bleeding," she told him, "so I'm not sure why—wait! There's a nasty bit of grit lodged between your pads. It looks sharp. Keep still while I get it out."

Splashtail kept his paw motionless while Frostpaw dug down with her teeth and tongue until she managed to capture the piece of grit and drop it on the ground. "There!" she exclaimed. "All done!"

While Splashtail gave his paw a good lick, Frostpaw spotted a clump of dock leaves growing at the edge of the bank, and nipped one off its stem. "There, rub your paw with that," she instructed Splashtail. "It's the best cure for sore paws."

"Thanks, Frostpaw." Splashtail gave his paw a thorough rub with the dock leaf, then rose and tested his weight on his injured paw. "It still feels a bit raw, but it's much better. You know, Frostpaw, you have real healing talent. It's a pity that RiverClan will lose your skills—even if you are doing well in your warrior training."

"But I can't get in touch with StarClan," Frostpaw pointed out, disappointed that Splashtail was questioning her decision again, especially in front of her littermates, her mentor, and Icewing, who was the nearest thing RiverClan had to a leader.

"I know you've been saying that," Splashtail responded, "but are you *sure* your visions aren't real? What if you gave it more time?"

Mistpaw stared at Splashtail, then at Frostpaw. "We love it that you're going to be a warrior," she meowed, "but I sort of wish you were still a medicine cat, too."

"Well, I can't be both!" Frostpaw snapped, upset that her littermate was joining in on Splashtail's side.

"It's just that we don't want to believe Curlfeather was so wrong," Graypaw explained.

Frostpaw's frustration spilled over. "I *am* a warrior, not a medicine cat!" she snapped, lashing her tail and scraping her claws through the grass. "I'm the one who gets to decide! No cat knows what goes on inside my mind except me."

"She's right," Harelight meowed, stepping up to Frostpaw's side, while Icewing murmured agreement. "Suppose we all leave her alone and start minding our own business and getting on with our own duties."

Splashtail dipped his head. "I'm sorry, Frostpaw," he mewed. "You're just too good at too many things."

"We're sorry, too," Graypaw murmured.

Frostpaw let herself relax, feeling her anger drain out of her like water sinking into dry ground. "It's okay," she mewed.

"Good. So if that's over, are we going back to camp or not?"

Lizardtail grumbled around the fish he was still holding.

"You can," Splashtail replied. "I think I'll stay and rest my paw for a while. I could do some more fishing. Does any cat want to join me?"

"Every hair on my pelt is aching from the beating this apprentice gave me," Harelight replied, with a humorous gleam in his eyes as he gazed at Frostpaw. "And I'll be surprised if she has the energy."

"We're all ready for a break," Icewing agreed, "The apprentices trained really hard this morning."

"I'd like to stay," Frostpaw ventured, optimism bubbling up inside her again. "And I still have *plenty* of energy." *Fishing with Splashtail! What could be better?* "I need to work on my fishing skills, if I'm going to catch up with Mistpaw and Graypaw."

Harelight gave her an amused look, as if he guessed that she wanted to stay with Splashtail. "Sure, stay and get some practice," he told her. "Fishing is an important skill for a RiverClan cat."

"Great!" Splashtail meowed.

For a heartbeat Frostpaw wondered why he sounded so pleased, when he had been arguing that she shouldn't give up being a medicine cat. *Maybe he does like me,* she told herself.

"Come and sit here by me, Frostpaw," Splashtail added, waving his tail invitingly.

Frostpaw plopped herself down at once, saying good-bye to the other apprentices and their mentors, who headed back to the camp with Lizardtail.

The last time she and Splashtail had talked together was when she had told him she wanted them to be mates. Splashtail hadn't agreed—though he hadn't refused, either. Now Frost-paw wondered whether he had made his mind up, seeing that she might be a warrior soon.

*At least he's happy to go fishing with me!*

Crouching on the bank of the stream, with the water swirling by just below their paws, Frostpaw kept glancing at Splashtail, trying to see if he felt as excited as she did to be fishing together. But Splashtail had his gaze fixed on the slowly flowing water.

As the moments slipped by, Frostpaw felt her pads begin to prickle with impatience. "Isn't this great?" she asked eventually. When she'd been a medicine cat, she had never gotten to fish with him, or hunt with him, or do anything except treat him when he got sick or injured. Now she loved feeling as if they were equals; there was so much more they could do together now that they were both warriors—or soon would be. "Doesn't it feel right, us being warriors together?" she prompted him.

Splashtail's ears gave an irritated twitch. "Shhh!" he hissed. "The fish will hear you."

Frostpaw blinked, stung by the blunt rebuke, and doubt-ful that the fish would hear anything over the sound of the water. But then, she reminded herself, she had no idea what it was like to be a fish; perhaps they could hear everything from beneath the surface. She was still new to fishing, and Splash-tail must know what he was doing. *I'm here to learn from him,* she reminded herself. She clamped her jaws shut, determined not to make another sound.

A heartbeat later, Splashtail's ears pricked forward;

Frostpaw realized that he had seen something. Stretching out her neck, she spotted a silvery gleam in the water: a big fish lazily swimming past.

Splashtail leaned forward and swiped out a forepaw, trying to hook out the fish. But with a flick of its tail, the fish slid away. Almost without thinking, Frostpaw flashed out a paw in turn, and felt her claws sink into the fish's scaly skin. Leaping back, she pulled it out onto the bank, where it lay flapping and wriggling until Splashtail killed it with a swift bite.

"It's huge!" Frostpaw exclaimed, triumph bubbling up inside her. *Much bigger than the one Lizardtail caught.* "They'll be so pleased with us when we take it back to camp."

Splashtail didn't look at her. "Congratulations," he grunted.

Frostpaw guessed that he was embarrassed about missing when he'd tried to catch the fish, especially when an apprentice then caught it instead. *I didn't want to annoy him, but that wasn't my fault.*

The fish was so big that Frostpaw wasn't sure she could carry it back to camp, and she didn't want to ask a grumpy Splashtail for help. Finally she sank her teeth into the back of its head and let its body trail underneath her belly as they headed home.

"I'm sorry I snapped at you just now," Splashtail meowed after a few moments; he was limping on the injured forepaw, and Frostpaw guessed it might still be hurting. "About the fish hearing you."

"It's okay," Frostpaw mumbled around her mouthful of fish; her jaw was aching from the weight of her catch. She set it down for a moment. "I wasn't upset." *Even though I was, a bit,* she added silently to herself.

"I had a lot on my mind," Splashtail admitted. "I can't stop thinking about what you said to me before. It's hard to wrap my mind around you not being a medicine cat anymore, but . . . I do like you, Frostpaw. Maybe we could be mates, if you really do become a warrior. I just need time to accept it."

As Frostpaw picked up her catch again, she felt a purr gathering in her chest; she was so happy that at last Splashtail was seeing things the way she did. *This is exactly what I wanted to hear! My plans are actually working out!* For a moment she wished that her mother were here to see how happy she was, even if Curlfeather could never have imagined she would have a life as a warrior. *But this feels right. . . .*

Even so, a tiny part of Frostpaw wished that Splashtail sounded more excited about it.

"But, despite everything, Frostpaw," Splashtail continued, "I'm still not completely convinced that you're not a medicine cat."

Frostpaw's purr died in her throat. She opened her jaws and let the fish fall to the ground. "Are you serious? Are you *still* meowing on about that?" she asked, feeling anger well up inside her. "Do you think you know better than I do whether I'm a medicine cat? How does that work? Do you live in my head? I *know* my visions weren't real!"

"Mothwing heals our Clanmates without having visions," Splashtail reminded her gently.

"But that's different," Frostpaw insisted. "And it's why

RiverClan's next medicine cat *must* have visions, or our Clan won't have any connection to StarClan. Can't you see how important that is? Besides," she added, when Splashtail didn't respond, "the only reason I ever thought about being a medicine cat was because my mother convinced me that I *did* have that connection. If Curlfeather hadn't brought it up, who's to say that I would ever have thought of it myself?"

Splashtail shook his head, clearly unconvinced. Frostpaw felt her fur begin to prickle with anger that he refused to see something that was completely clear to her.

"Visions or not, you were a very good healer," he pointed out. "Look how you fixed my paw."

*Any cat could have done that,* Frostpaw thought.

She glanced down at the fish she had caught—the fish Splashtail had missed. "I'm going be a very good warrior, too," she declared. "You heard what Harelight said about how my training is going."

"Of course you'll be a good warrior," Splashtail responded. "You're clever and quick and strong, and you'd be good at anything you tried. It's just taking me a while to get used to, that's all."

In spite of his praise, Frostpaw felt as if she had swallowed a huge lump of crow-food and it was lodged in her belly. "Do you *want* me to be a medicine cat or something?" she asked. "Because, to be honest, I'm kind of relieved not to be anymore. And if I *were* a medicine cat, we couldn't be mates."

Splashtail hesitated a moment, his gaze darting in all directions. "I told you, it's just taking me some time to get used to.

But hey"—he flicked her ear with the tip of his tail—"we have time to work all this stuff out, right?"

"I suppose," Frostpaw muttered.

"In any case," Splashtail went on, "we would have to wait until you were given your warrior name before we got together. We have time to make sure that the warrior's path is the right one for you. That's the most important thing to me."

"But I *know*—"

"I care about you," Splashtail interrupted, as if Frostpaw hadn't spoken. "I care too much to be okay with you maybe making the wrong choice. You have to make the right one, even if it means we might not get to be mates. Frostpaw, it's all about what's best for RiverClan."

"I've already made my choice, and I know it's the right one," Frostpaw asserted, annoyed that Splashtail wasn't listening to her. She faced him and tried to put all her certainty into the tone of her voice. "I told you, I'm going to be a warrior." Then, without waiting for Splashtail to respond, she picked up her catch again and stalked off, back toward the camp.

A moment later Splashtail appeared at her side; he must have hurried to catch up with her. "So you're not having any weird dreams? You're not seeing signs anymore?"

Even though sunlight still sparkled on the stream, Frostpaw felt as though gray clouds surrounded her, darkening her day. She dropped the fish again to ask, "Why are you so obsessed with me having visions? Don't you want me to be a warrior?"

"It's not about what I want," Splashtail responded, an

irritated edge to his tone. "Or what *we* want. It's about what's best for the Clan. And—"

"I'm so tired of hearing that!" Frostpaw interrupted. "I matter too, not just the Clan! And I know I'm a warrior. It was really only Curlfeather who was convinced I was a medicine cat," she continued. "She read a lot into my dreams, but I think it was just a coincidence that I dreamed of Jayclaw before he died, or that I dreamed of a thunderstorm a couple of days before there was one. Maybe Curlfeather just really *wanted* me to be a medicine cat for the sake of the Clan, and I was too young to question what she told me."

*And maybe that's why Splashtail is insisting on it,* she added to herself. *He's putting the good of RiverClan above what he wants for himself. Maybe he thinks I'm being selfish, because I'd rather be a warrior and his mate than be a medicine cat. But I'm really not!*

She waited, struggling with frustration, for Splashtail's reaction, but he only stared at her and didn't speak.

"I know it's hard to accept," she went on, trying not to feel intimidated, "but I know my visions weren't real. I was just imagining I was communing with the spirits of our warrior ancestors. The only explanation I can think of is that my mother was too excited at the idea that I would be our Clan's medicine cat."

When she finished speaking, Splashtail still went on staring at her, for so long that Frostpaw began to wonder if he was angry about what she had told him.

Finally, he shook his head a little. "I guess we just have to wait and see," he meowed with a sigh. "Maybe there's still time for StarClan to give you a real sign."

Frostpaw opened her jaws to protest, hardly able to believe what she had heard. *Does he still not get it?* She hadn't stopped liking Splashtail, and she was trying to understand his feelings. *But could he be any more annoying?* She didn't know what else to say; she had told him over and over that she was training as a warrior now, and she was looking forward to a future where they were warriors of RiverClan together, and mates.

But Splashtail didn't wait for her to speak. "Don't let your doubts change your feelings toward your mother," he advised her. "Curlfeather loved you so much—maybe she saw something in you that you haven't seen in yourself . . . *yet.*"

Without giving Frostpaw the chance to respond, he picked up the fish and headed off toward the camp.

Frostpaw followed, musing on his advice about Curlfeather. She was sure she had never had the gift of a medicine cat, but it was good to think that her mother's certainty had been based on love. *I'll never know what Curlfeather was thinking, but I'm going to believe the best of her.*

Still, Splashtail's words hadn't changed her mind. What she knew about herself was the truth.

*I guess it will just take time for him to start seeing me as a warrior. But that's okay,* she thought, padding along in his paw steps. *We have time. . . .*

# CHAPTER 14

*Crouching at the edge of the* warriors' den, her paws tucked under her, Sunbeam stared across the camp. Nightheart was sunning himself a few tail-lengths away, and farther off, beside the fresh-kill pile, her mother was sharing prey with Yarrowleaf and a couple of other cats from the group who had met with the RiverClan warriors. Sunbeam almost felt that the force of her gaze should burn Berryheart's pelt, but her mother seemed quite unaware that she was being watched.

Sunbeam hadn't spoken to her mother all day, because she had no idea what words would come out of her mouth. But after what she and Nightheart had overheard the night before, she knew she would have to talk to her soon. Even so, the thought of having such a conversation with her mother made her feel chilled from her ears to the tips of her claws. Nightheart's presence in the camp, and her previous quarrel with Berryheart over her hostility to outsiders, had already strained their relationship to the breaking point.

Taking a deep breath, Sunbeam decided that she would ask Berryheart to walk with her, so that they could talk well away from any listening ears. But then, she asked herself, wouldn't every cat in the camp know that something was going on?

*Maybe I should think of an excuse to tell them before I head off.* For a few heartbeats Sunbeam wondered what excuse would work best, before giving her pelt a shake and an irritated twitch to the tip of her tail. *Mouse-brain!* she scolded herself. *You're perfectly entitled to talk to your mother, and tell any cat who asks to mind their own business.*

Full of new resolve, Sunbeam rose to her paws and took a few paces toward Berryheart. But as soon as she moved, Nightheart sprang to his paws and bounded up to intercept her.

Sunbeam noticed that the black tom looked more nervous and uncertain than he had the night before. "Are you okay?" she asked.

"I'm just wondering . . ." Nightheart stared at his paws, then raised his head to meet Sunbeam's gaze. "Is what we saw worth causing trouble in ShadowClan?" he asked. "We might be being too hasty. Or maybe we . . . misunderstood."

"I'm not going to cause trouble," Sunbeam assured him. "I'm going to talk to Berryheart about what we heard at the secret meeting last night, that's all. I need my mother to put my mind at ease."

"At ease?" Nightheart kept his voice low, but Sunbeam guessed that he would have liked to yowl the words across the whole camp. "Those cats were plotting a way to fake a new medicine cat for RiverClan, just to get Tigerstar out of their fur. Whatever any cat thinks about what Tigerstar is doing over there, that doesn't change the fact that he's the leader of

ShadowClan. To go against his orders is against the warrior code."

"Hey—a heartbeat ago you were wondering if we misunderstood," Sunbeam mewed. "Make your mind up!"

"That's the problem," Nightheart confessed. "I don't know *what* to think!"

"I know, I know." Sunbeam soothed him with a touch of her tail on his shoulder. "I have doubts about what Tigerstar is doing as well, but I would never discuss them with another Clan."

Nightheart gave a swift, furtive glance around the camp. "Berryheart might say that of course I would accuse her of being up to something," he muttered, "because she's in charge of the tasks."

"You could be right," Sunbeam admitted. Berryheart was so hostile to the idea of taking in cats from other Clans; she might try anything to prevent it. "But I promise I'll keep you out of it."

Nightheart sighed, and when he spoke, his voice was heavy with resignation. "I know I can't stop you," he mewed. "In fact, I agree with you. I think you should talk to your mother. But I want you to be sure of what you're doing before you do it."

At his words, Sunbeam clenched her jaws on a growl that wanted to escape her muzzle. She *had* been sure before Nightheart came over. Now she felt herself wavering, which wasn't what she had intended at all.

"Go and hunt or something," she told Nightheart. "Behave as if this has nothing to do with you." Then she headed over to where Berryheart was just finishing up her prey beside the fresh-kill pile.

"Can we take a walk?" she asked.

Her mother twitched her whiskers in surprise before meowing, "Sure."

Sunbeam led the way out of camp and along the same path that Berryheart and the others had followed the night before, toward the Twoleg halfbridge. Their stale scent still hung around it; Sunbeam tried her best not to show she noticed it, so as not to make Berryheart suspicious.

Finally, when the bridge was in sight, she sat in the shelter of a clump of bracken and wrapped her tail around her paws. Berryheart sat beside her, a curious glint in her eyes.

"This feels very serious," she mewed.

"It *is* serious," Sunbeam responded. She paused long enough to take a deep breath, trying to ease the tightness in her chest, then continued, "I followed you and the others last night. I heard what you said to Splashtail and the other RiverClan cats."

Berryheart's ears flicked up and she narrowed her eyes as she gazed at Sunbeam. "Did you indeed?" she murmured.

"I did." Now that Sunbeam had confessed, she felt her courage returning. "How could you plot against Tigerstar?" she demanded. "Does Splashtail intend to force some cat to *pretend* to be the next medicine cat for RiverClan? Berryheart, what are you *doing*?"

"I don't have to explain myself to you," Berryheart snapped, her anger clear in her slowly rising shoulder fur. "What do *you* think you were doing, spying on me? Do you mistrust me so much?"

Sunbeam had to choke back a *mrrow* of amusement. "It seems I was right to!" she retorted.

Berryheart glared at her for a moment longer, then cautiously surveyed the forest all around them, her ears pricked for the sound of movement and her jaws parted to taste the air. "I'm not plotting to depose Tigerstar," she meowed when she had made sure that no other cat was in earshot. "Nothing like that. What you overheard was just a meeting of like-minded cats who think it's best for every Clan if RiverClan is left alone to deal with its own problems. If we keep our noses in their Clan's business much longer, it will only cause conflict. All I'm trying to do is keep ShadowClan safe."

"But Splashtail implied that he could *create* a new medicine cat for RiverClan," Sunbeam protested. "What does that mean? Is he going to make some cat fake visions from StarClan?"

Berryheart interrupted with a dismissive wave of her tail. "RiverClan's medicine cat is RiverClan's business," she declared. "Which they can sort out for themselves once they're out from under Tigerstar's control. That's where we agree with Splashtail, and that's all I'm fighting for."

Sunbeam sagged with relief to hear that that was all her mother intended. What Berryheart had said sounded almost exactly like her own thoughts. But the comfort lasted for only a few heartbeats before her worries crept up on her again like ants crawling through her pelt.

"Tigerstar says he isn't looking for a conflict," she pointed out. "So why do you think you need to conspire with River-Clan to avoid one?"

Berryheart tilted her head, gazing at Sunbeam with a mixture of love and pity in her eyes. "Sometimes I forget that you're still a young cat," she meowed. "Tigerstar might not be looking for conflict, but that doesn't mean that conflict won't come, whether he wants it or not. Think about the way the RiverClan cats have been talking and acting."

Reluctantly, Sunbeam had to nod agreement. She had seen enough of RiverClan's hostility when she and Lightleap had been on duty in their camp.

"And then there's Leafstar, don't forget," Berryheart continued. "She was making a point of displaying her claws in front of the other Clan leaders."

*That's true,* Sunbeam admitted to herself. At the emergency Gathering, the SkyClan leader hadn't tried to hide her anger at what Tigerstar was doing.

"But she couldn't get another leader to support her," Sunbeam meowed. "And SkyClan won't attack alone. So what do you mean?"

Berryheart was silent for a moment, while her expression hardened, the love and pity in her eyes giving way to irritation. "Don't be so naive," she scolded Sunbeam. "Remember what Leafstar said? That they would reassess the situation at the next Gathering. Without a little prod from me and my group, do you think Tigerstar will have withdrawn from RiverClan by then?"

Sunbeam couldn't find words to answer. She knew that Tigerstar wasn't even close to stepping back from RiverClan, that he was as committed as ever to keeping a ShadowClan presence within their territory. And he wasn't wrong; when she had been on duty in RiverClan with Lightleap, she had found it impossible to ignore how disorganized the Clan was.

"Besides," Berryheart went on, "leaders change their minds all the time. How do we know what's being discussed in WindClan or ThunderClan? All it would take is for Harestar or Bramblestar to have a change of heart and decide they agree with Leafstar."

"Surely they wouldn't . . . ," Sunbeam protested, though she sounded feeble even to herself.

"No cat knows what might happen," Berryheart declared. "Remember what it was like before the Clans realized that Bramblestar was being controlled by Ashfur. The Clans fought each other in a terrible battle; so many innocent cats died. And this could be much worse, because the conflict isn't about one cat. Do you understand how important it is to avoid more bloodshed?" Her voice grew softer, more persuasive. "It's even more important now that you love a ThunderClan cat. Do you want to see Nightheart's loyalty tested?"

Sunbeam stared down at her paws, not wanting to answer. She found it hard to admit, even to herself, that Berryheart might be right.

Berryheart waited for a few heartbeats, then continued when Sunbeam didn't speak. "Don't you think Squirrelflight sounded willing for ThunderClan to join SkyClan at the Gathering? She's Bramblestar's mate as well as his deputy; if any cat can change his mind and get him to agree, it would be her. And if two Clans agree, what then? Would that convince

WindClan to go along?" She let out a snort, half-amused, half-contemptuous. "It probably would, because WindClan is true to its name, and always waits to see which way the wind is blowing. And then what would ShadowClan be facing?" She didn't wait for Sunbeam to find an answer. "We'd be facing the combined strength of three Clans . . . fighting for our lives, and for what? All for the sake of *RiverClan*—cats who aren't even our Clanmates. Do you really think that's a sensible thing for ShadowClan to do?"

"No—no, of course not, but . . ." Sunbeam stammered. "What about the other medicine cats? Surely StarClan must have something to say about all this trouble in RiverClan?"

Berryheart shook her head. "I heard Puddleshine reporting to Tigerstar after the last half-moon meeting," she mewed. "None of the medicine cats were able to get any information. They all reached their own Clanmates in StarClan territory, but none of the warrior spirits would tell them anything about RiverClan." Her mouth twisted wryly, and she let out a snort of amusement. "Except they were all upset that Tigerstar has taken over RiverClan's territory. So think about that, Sunbeam—my group and I are doing the will of StarClan!"

Sunbeam wasn't at all sure that she agreed. *Yes, ShadowClan should leave RiverClan*, she reflected. *But openly—honorably—not because of plotting with other cats by night.* "What did Tigerstar say about that?" she asked. "He must care that StarClan doesn't support his plan."

Berryheart sighed. "Tigerstar is hardheaded, as you know. When Puddleshine told him this news, he quickly dismissed it. He says he's only caring for RiverClan until they can take care of themselves—it isn't a takeover."

Sunbeam shook her head. *But it is,* she thought, *or it certainly feels like one to RiverClan.* Still, if StarClan couldn't get through to Tigerstar, she didn't like her own odds.

"Of course," Berryheart continued, "all this makes Mothwing even more certain that StarClan is useless. According to Puddleshine, she's thinking that maybe she won't attend any more of the half-moon meetings."

Sunbeam thought that over. Whatever Mothwing might think, it would make sense that the spirits of their ancestors wouldn't discuss the affairs of a different Clan with the medicine cats. But then how would RiverClan ever find out what they should do? Mothwing didn't speak to StarClan at all, and apparently didn't want to, while her apprentice, Frostpaw, had changed her mind and was a warrior apprentice now. It seemed as if there was no way out for the beleaguered Clan.

"Maybe StarClan is angry with RiverClan," Berryheart suggested.

Sunbeam shook her head. *If they ever got angry, it would more likely be with us.* "I remember how Ashfur tried to convince the Clans that StarClan wasn't communicating with us because they were angry," she mused, half to herself. "But Ashfur was lying. When the Lights in the Mist traveled to StarClan, they were told that StarClan had never been angry, and would never cut off the living world out of spite."

"So StarClan must want RiverClan to contact them directly," Berryheart responded. "That's why it's so important for RiverClan to find their own way to reach StarClan. Each Clan should be in control of their own destiny. After all, their Clanmates still bear the scars—in their bodies and their hearts—from when they were under the control of Darktail."

Sunbeam had been born outside Clan territory, when her mother and father had fled from Darktail. Her mother rarely spoke of his fearful rule, but Sparrowtail had told her that he had played a huge part in her parents' lives, and had even killed her sister, Needletail, who had drowned long before Sunbeam was born.

"Many cats died," Berryheart went on, a shudder of horror passing through her, "including my own daughter, Needletail. I mourn her every day, and regret that I didn't do more to save her. So many cats were killed, in fact, that our whole Clan's way of life almost collapsed and disappeared into nothing. You almost missed being raised as a Clan cat," she told Sunbeam, turning an intense gaze on her. "If Tigerheart hadn't found us near the abandoned Twoleg den where we were sheltering, we would still be living there as rogues. And we were there because I followed Darktail away from ShadowClan. It was the worst decision I ever made, and I'll never stop regretting it. That evil cat did his best to destroy our Clan, and he took the thing most precious to me. I can't let that happen again. I'll protect ShadowClan with my last breath!"

"I understand why you and the others feel the way you do," Sunbeam admitted. "I can't imagine what it must have been like to lose so much. But there's no Darktail to threaten us now. And I still don't think going behind Tigerstar's back is the right thing to do."

"So you want to tell him?" Berryheart's voice was harsh. "Sunbeam, ever since you were a kit, you've been obsessed with following the rules, but you're old enough now to understand that life isn't always neat and orderly. Sometimes you have to accept that things are messy."

"But there's no need to *make* them messy," Sunbeam muttered, digging her claws into the ground.

"Is that what you think I'm doing?" Berryheart stretched her neck forward so that she was nose to nose with Sunbeam. "No! Sometimes an honorable warrior has to step up and do what's right, step up and protect their Clan. That's all that I and the others are trying to do. Are you really going to stand in our way?"

"I never meant—" Sunbeam began to protest, but Berryheart ignored her.

"How will you feel, Sunbeam, if a moon from now, Shadow-Clan is tangled in a fight with *three other Clans?*"

Sunbeam didn't know how to answer. She knew that she didn't want to go running to Tigerstar to tell him what she had discovered. *That went so badly last time.*

"Fine, I won't tell," she meowed at last. "As long as you and your group are just talking to each other, and not raising claws against your Clanmates."

"Of course we're just talking," Berryheart snapped. "We would never do anything more—and you should know that."

Sunbeam bowed her head in acceptance, but at the same time she sensed prickles of dread and frustration in her chest. She felt as if she wasn't being strong enough. An ominous apprehension hung over her head like a storm cloud about to unleash its fury. She tried to comfort herself by remembering Berryheart's promise that she was trying to prevent a battle, so that no cat would get hurt.

But Sunbeam couldn't convince herself. She wondered whether her mother was wrong, and whether what her group was doing would cause some terrible disaster, instead of preventing it.

*Have I just given up my chance to do something to stop it?*

Then Sunbeam told herself she was being mouse-brained. She didn't need to say something right away, because Berryheart and her supporters couldn't force change overnight. Tigerstar would always be Clan leader, and she could always tell him if anything changed and she thought Berryheart had gone too far.

When she and Berryheart returned to camp, Sunbeam noticed Lightleap looking at her curiously, a question in her gaze. Quickly Sunbeam looked away; she was certain she could never talk to her friend about what she and Nightheart had overheard. Lightleap was Tigerstar's daughter, and she would want to tell her father at once.

Then Sunbeam spotted Nightheart crossing the camp with prey in his jaws. When he had dropped it on the fresh-kill pile, he returned to the patch of sunlight where he had been dozing earlier.

*Of course—I can always talk to Nightheart!*

The burden of her stress and her confused feelings seemed to grow lighter as she padded across to the black tom. Whatever might happen next, it was a relief to have a cat she could relate to in her own Clan.

# CHAPTER 15

*Nightheart wasn't convinced by Berryheart's assertion* that all she and her group intended to do was talk. It felt *wrong* not to tell Tigerstar about Berryheart and her allies conspiring with RiverClan cats behind his back. He was uncomfortably aware that most of the ShadowClan cats weren't sure of his loyalty yet. *After all, I abandoned ThunderClan, so why should they trust me here in ShadowClan?* Keeping secrets from their leader seemed likely to prove that he couldn't be relied on.

At the same time, he knew he was the last cat who should be making accusations against Berryheart. The whole Clan had seen her hostility toward him. Even if Tigerstar believed him, he might see him as a troublemaker who had no place in ShadowClan.

If any cat was to report to Tigerstar, it ought to be Sunbeam, but Nightheart understood why she was reluctant. After all, so far Berryheart and the others had only talked to some RiverClan cats. They hadn't acted against any of Tigerstar's orders. And whatever RiverClan did about their medicine cat, it was RiverClan's business.

"I know it's harder for you, with Berryheart being your

mother," he told Sunbeam. "Of course you don't want to get her into trouble."

"Does that mean *you* want to—" Sunbeam began nervously.

"No, I promise I'll stand by your decision," Nightheart assured her. "I won't say a word about what we overheard, if that's what you think is best. But we should still keep an eye on Berryheart and her group."

"Yes, sure," Sunbeam agreed at once. "Maybe everything will be fine, as long as they're just talking and not starting fights."

"Maybe." Nightheart wasn't convinced. *I wish I were sure that we're doing the right thing.*

"There's something else Berryheart said," Sunbeam continued. "She thinks there's a good chance that the other Clans will attack ShadowClan if nothing changes before the next Gathering."

"And that's only days away." Nightheart felt a small worm of apprehension stir in his belly. "It's unlikely that Tigerstar will change his mind before then—unless RiverClan gets a new medicine cat or a leader. Like *that's* going to happen," he finished gloomily.

"True," Sunbeam agreed. "But I can't imagine that the other Clans would attack us over this. Most cats are too sensible—at least, I believe they are. I just hope that Berryheart and her group don't feel like they have to do something rash if nothing changes before the Gathering."

"What could they do?" Nightheart wondered. "They can't force Tigerstar's paws."

"I don't know. . . ." Sunbeam blinked unhappily. "But Berry-heart has been pretty creative with the tasks she's thought up for you and Fringewhisker. And I'm not sure I trust that Splashtail at all."

"I certainly don't," Nightheart declared. "And you're right about your mother, but I don't think she has time to do any-thing really dreadful. Except for my next task." His mouth twisted wryly. "I'm sure she's thought up something really grim for tomorrow."

"You'll be fine," Sunbeam assured him. "I wish I could say the same about RiverClan. The thing is," she confessed, "Tigerstar *should* pull out of there. I agree with Berryheart on that, at least, if not with the way she's going about it. . . ."

She fixed her gaze on Nightheart, her eyes liquid with unhappiness. A shiver went through him as he realized all over again what a beautiful cat she was. *But this isn't the time to think about that.* He leaned toward her and gave her ear a lick.

"It'll be okay," he reassured her.

Sunbeam heaved a long sigh. "It bothers me because I've never doubted Tigerstar's decisions on something serious before," she mewed sadly. "I've always trusted him to do the right thing for our Clan."

"Well, this time I think he's wrong, too," Nightheart meowed. "ShadowClan shouldn't be taking over RiverClan, it's no wonder that the RiverClan cats resent it. Though I do believe that Tigerstar means well, and he doesn't want to take RiverClan over for good, just guide them while they find a new leader."

Sunbeam nodded agreement. "He isn't grabbing for power, but I wish he weren't so hardheaded," she murmured. "He never listens to any arguments against his own point of view."

Nightheart remembered the last few times he had spoken with Bramblestar. "Better to be stubborn than to act like you don't even care about your Clan," he muttered. "At least Tigerstar is ready to fight for what he believes is right."

Wisps of morning mist still drifted through the forest, and the grass stems were heavy with dew, when Berryheart led the way out of camp on the following day. Nightheart padded along at her shoulder, his heart racing as he wondered what new task she had devised for him. Most of the ShadowClan cats were following them, including Tigerstar himself.

Once again Berryheart chose the path that led toward the halfbridge and the greenleaf Twolegplace, halting at the edge of the clearing where, according to Sunbeam, the Twolegs set up their pelt-dens. Nightheart knew that usually the Twolegs only came there in greenleaf, when the weather was warm, but now one small pelt-den still remained, in the center of the clearing.

Nightheart wrinkled his nose at the strong scent of Twoleg, and felt a tingle of apprehension at an underlying smell of dog. Scanning the clearing, he spotted the Twoleg at the far side, its back turned to them as it fussed with a small fire, adding the acrid tang of smoke to the other unfamiliar scents. He couldn't see any sign of the dog.

Turning to face Berryheart, Nightheart saw a look of

satisfaction in her gaze, as if she was pleased with herself.

"Okay," he meowed. "What do I have to do?"

"Your next task," Berryheart replied, raising her voice so that the cats crowding up behind them could hear, "is to steal something out of the pelt-den without being caught by the Twoleg."

Nightheart felt a pulse of alarm, though he did his best to hide it. He hadn't expected a challenge that would involve Twolegs, much less dogs, and he wasn't at all confident that he would be able to pull it off.

He was aware of some uneasy muttering from the Shadow-Clan cats. Dovewing pushed her way to the front of the crowd. "That's unnecessarily risky," she pointed out, her gaze challenging Berryheart. "And it isn't something that a ShadowClan cat would do. The whole point of these tasks is for Nightheart to prove that he can be a ShadowClan cat."

"I agree," Tigerstar meowed, coming to stand beside his mate. "Twolegs are dangerous, and no Clan cat would mess with one unless there was a good reason. Choose something else, Berryheart."

Nightheart felt his pelt begin to prickle with hope that Berryheart would obey her Clan leader and he wouldn't have to do the task after all.

But Berryheart wasn't going to back down as easily as that. "This *is* a good reason," she insisted. "I'll admit we don't usually go near Twolegs. But this test will need stealth, and stealth is one of the most important skills of a ShadowClan cat. And another important skill is speed, which Nightheart will need to escape if the Twoleg spots him."

"But what about that dog?" Blazefire objected, sniffing the air. "A cat would have to have bees in their brain to go anywhere near a dog if they didn't have to."

"The dog is not part of the challenge," Berryheart retorted. "Can any cat *see* a dog? No? Okay, then, it won't interfere."

Nightheart was disappointed to see Blazefire turn aside with an angry shrug. He let out a sigh of resignation; obviously Berryheart wasn't going to change her mind.

"Yeah, Berryheart is right," Yarrowleaf meowed. "The tasks are *supposed* to be difficult and dangerous."

Berryheart shot a sidelong glance at Fringewhisker. "Otherwise," she mewed, "we might find ourselves accepting cats who aren't fully committed to ShadowClan."

At Berryheart's comment, Fringewhisker's mate, Spireclaw, lashed his tail furiously and opened his jaws to protest, but Fringewhisker laid her tail across his mouth and gave a tiny shake of her head. Spireclaw subsided, though he still fixed Berryheart with a sullen glare.

Nightheart saw that Tigerstar was still looking doubtful, but he obviously wasn't going to insist that Berryheart change the task. *I have to do it, so I might as well make the best of it,* he thought.

Summoning all his resolve, Nightheart stepped up to face the Clan leader. "I can do it, Tigerstar," he declared. "It'll be fine."

Tigerstar hesitated a heartbeat longer, then shrugged. "Okay, go for it," he agreed. "I put Berryheart in charge of these tasks, and if you don't object, Nightheart, then there's no reason to question her choice."

Berryheart took a pace back, a smug look on her face, and

waved her tail toward the pelt-den. "Off you go, then," she mewed.

Nightheart took a deep breath and braced himself for the challenge. Slinking out of the undergrowth, pressing his belly to the ground as if he were stalking prey, he kept a wary eye on the Twoleg, which still had its back to him. A breeze had risen, scattering the last scraps of mist, and it blew toward Nightheart; he guessed the Twoleg wouldn't be able to scent him.

*But what about the dog?*

Nightheart could still smell it, but he couldn't see it anywhere; maybe Berryheart was right, and it wasn't here right now.

Paw step by paw step, Nightheart crept across the clearing, his belly fur brushing the ground, hardly daring to breathe until he reached the pelt-den. Part of the pelt was folded back to make an opening; Nightheart poked his head through the gap and peered around, looking for something he could steal.

More pelts covered the den floor, and at the far side were piles of strange-looking Twoleg stuff: a few hard, shiny things like upturned leaves, and a roll of something weird and fluffy at the very back.

None of that looked like something he could carry back to the ShadowClan cats, but in the middle of the den floor was a small Twoleg pelt lying by itself; it was just the right size for him to carry easily.

"Thanks, Twoleg," he breathed.

Darting into the den, Nightheart gagged at the stronger

scents of Twoleg and dog. He snatched up the small pelt, wincing at the weird taste. As he spun around to make his escape, he couldn't believe how easy the task had been so far.

But before Nightheart could leave the pelt-den, a loud yapping broke out behind him. His fur bristling, he looked back to see that what he had thought was a roll of weird fluffy Twoleg pelts had reared up and shown itself to be a tiny but very angry dog.

*No wonder the dog scent was so strong in here!* he thought, briefly frozen in shock.

The dog charged at him, still yapping and baring sharp-looking teeth. Before Nightheart could pull himself together and flee, it grabbed the other end of the pelt and tugged at it. Determined not to lose his loot, Nightheart dug all four sets of claws into the ground and yanked back. For a few terrifying heartbeats they pulled the pelt back and forth, until suddenly it tore in two and Nightheart staggered back with half of it dangling from his jaws.

At the same moment, light flowed into the den as the Twoleg yanked the flap open, yowling something. Nightheart streaked between the Twoleg's legs, still clutching his half of the small pelt in his teeth, and dashed back across the clearing to where the ShadowClan cats were waiting.

*Is this fast enough for you, Berryheart?*

He risked a glance over his shoulder and saw that the tiny dog was still chasing him, yapping fit to burst, until the Twoleg ran after it, scooped it up, and carried it back into the pelt-den.

Nightheart's heart was pounding as he rejoined the other cats. They scattered around him as he plunged into the undergrowth.

"Back to camp!" Tigerstar yowled.

When he reached the ShadowClan camp, Nightheart was panting, his legs trembling from shock and exertion. Most of his Clanmates had already arrived; Tigerstar was standing in the center with Berryheart by his side, and Sunbeam hovering nearby.

Nightheart took a moment to calm himself, worried that the chaos at the end of his task meant that he hadn't been stealthy enough. Then he padded across the camp with his head and tail held high, to lay his piece of pelt at Tigerstar's paws. By now thin tendrils were trailing off it, and it was damp with his spit. Tigerstar bent his head to sniff it and reared back with a disgusted expression on his face.

"I completed the task," Nightheart announced, dipping his head respectfully.

"You did nothing of the sort!" Berryheart objected, glancing indignantly from Nightheart to Tigerstar and back again. "You were supposed to demonstrate stealth, but you filled the forest with that racket."

"*And* you were caught by a dog and a Twoleg," Whorlpelt pointed out. Some of Berryheart's other allies, crowding around the black-and-white she-cat, muttered agreement.

"They didn't *catch* me," Nightheart argued, glaring at Whorlpelt with narrowed eyes.

"And *you* promised that the dog wasn't part of the task."

Sunbeam glared indignantly at her mother. "But it was right there, *in the pelt-den!*"

*And maybe she set that up deliberately,* Nightheart thought, clenching his jaws to stop himself making the accusation aloud.

Berryheart's only response was to whisk her tail angrily.

Turning back to Tigerstar, Nightheart took a calming breath and continued, "My task was to steal something from the pelt-den, and I did that." He angled his ears toward the soggy half pelt.

"Yes, you did complete the task," Tigerstar declared, to Nightheart's relief. "The first part of your test, before you entered the pelt-den, was very stealthy. And on your way back, I've rarely seen a cat move so fast. You also showed admirable bravery, which is a very important quality for a ShadowClan cat. And now," he added, "get that disgusting object out of my camp."

As Nightheart picked up the half pelt, he saw Berryheart flicking her tail in annoyance. She padded up to him as he exchanged a glance with Sunbeam, seeing anxiety in the young she-cat's eyes.

"You may have talked your way out of that one," Berryheart mewed. Her tone was pleasant, for the sake of her Clanmates nearby, though her eyes were ominous. "But I still have one more chance to keep you out of ShadowClan."

# CHAPTER 16

❧

*The sun was still shining,* but a chilly breeze riffled the surface of the pool near the spot where Frostpaw had gone fishing with Splashtail a few days before. Now she was crouching beside Harelight, and so far she hadn't managed to catch a thing.

The gleam of a small fish just below the surface caught Frostpaw's eye. Leaning down, she swiped her paw at it, but the fish swam away with a flick of its tail as if it were laughing at her.

"I don't understand!" she complained, turning to her mentor. "I caught that big fish so easily when I was with Splashtail. What am I doing wrong now?"

"Don't be so impatient," Harelight meowed. "Stay as still as you can, slow your breathing, and make sure your shadow doesn't fall on the water. Then, when the fish is calm beneath you, that's the time to strike."

"I'll try," Frostpaw responded.

She leaned over the water, making sure that her shadow was stretching away from her across the bank, and concentrated on spotting another fish.

At first all she could see was her own reflection: her pale

gray pelt and her wide, watchful eyes. Then the surface of the pool seemed to shimmer, and when the glittering light cleared away, the water had vanished. Frostpaw froze, biting back a cry of alarm.

*What's happening? Where are the fish?*

Instead of the pool, a stretch of undergrowth lay in front of her, and her heart thumped as she recognized where she was. She was seeing the territory through another cat's eyes, creeping forward toward the ravine where she and her Clanmates had found Reedwhisker's body.

Part of Frostpaw wanted to yowl in terror at what was happening to her, but the cat whose body she inhabited was cold and controlled, focusing on . . .

*Reedwhisker!*

Another pulse of terror shook Frostpaw when she saw the Clan deputy just ahead, still alive and uninjured. He was concentrating on some prey Frostpaw couldn't see, slipping among the stems of fern with silent skill.

As they reached the top of the ravine, Frostpaw's cat exploded into motion, leaping onto Reedwhisker's back and scoring their claws through his pelt so deeply that blood gushed out.

Reedwhisker let out a screech of alarm. Rearing up and twisting, he threw his attacker off his back and spun around to face them. Alarm throbbed through Frostpaw when his eyes widened with shocked recognition. He struck out at Frostpaw's cat, but he was clearly confused; he wasn't putting much strength behind his blows.

*This is a cat he doesn't want to hurt,* Frostpaw realized.

The attacking cat lowered their head and barreled toward Reedwhisker, forcing him toward the edge of the ravine. Frostpaw saw the ground begin to crumble away under his paws. As he fell, Reedwhisker made a frantic effort to save himself, digging his claws into the grass and trying to haul himself up.

His attacker sprang forward, thrusting at him with head and shoulders. Reedwhisker's grip gave way, and he let out a despairing yowl as he plummeted down into the ravine. Then there was silence.

Frostpaw's cat padded up to the edge and looked down. Reedwhisker's broken body lay stretched out on the rocks, his head at an awkward angle, just as it had been on the day Frostpaw and the others had found him.

*He didn't fall!* she realized with a pulse of pure terror. *He was pushed! He was murdered!*

Frostpaw stood frozen with shock and fear, unable to tear her gaze away from the terrible sight. Gradually she realized that the other cat had left her; she was herself again, though still trapped in the same fearful moment.

*I don't know how to get back!*

Gasping for breath, Frostpaw tried to calm herself, though deep shudders were coursing through her whole body. All she wanted was to collapse onto the ground and hide her head beneath her paws. Then she sensed that another cat was standing beside her; she whipped around, half expecting to be hurled into the ravine along with Reedwhisker.

But it was the former deputy himself who stood next to

her. His black pelt was misted over with stars, and stars glittered at the tips of his ears and his claws. His gaze was full of sorrow as he looked at her.

"There is a darkness in RiverClan," he told her. "Closer than you think."

"What do you mean?" Frostpaw couldn't stop her voice from shaking. "Who was that cat?"

But before Reedwhisker could reply, she blinked and found herself back on the bank of the stream, with Harelight giving her an exasperated look.

"Are you okay, Frostpaw?" he asked. "I've been trying to get your attention, but you were just staring into the water. There was a fish there, just asking to be caught, if you had tried."

Frostpaw gazed at him, unable to find words to respond. Vomit was rising into her throat. *Surely that must have been a real vision.* And it was the worst vision Frostpaw could imagine. Things were even worse for RiverClan than they had thought. Their deputy hadn't accidentally fallen to his death. Some cat had killed him.

Everything Frostpaw believed had suddenly changed. *Why now?* she demanded silently. *Why me? I don't want to have real visions!*

Then she realized that this wasn't about her or what she wanted. It was bigger than that: It was about the good of her Clan.

Who would have tried to murder Reedwhisker? He had been a good deputy, brave and loyal and hardworking. He would have made a brilliant Clan leader. What reason could any cat have had for killing him?

Deep shudders coursed through Frostpaw's body, from her ears to the tips of her claws. She remembered how she had watched her mother being torn apart by dogs when she was on her way to the Moonpool to receive her nine lives and become RiverClan's new leader.

*But what if that attack wasn't random? What if Curlfeather was murdered too?*

Frostpaw remembered Curlfeather's last words as the dogs were pulling her down: *Trust no cat!* She remembered too that prey bones had been found on the moor close to where she and Curlfeather had first encountered the dogs. Did that mean that the same cat who killed Reedwhisker could have lured the dogs there?

Frostpaw's chest felt so tight that she could hardly breathe. Had she been so worried about a new leader for RiverClan that she had failed to notice a murderer among her Clanmates?

*What am I supposed to do?*

All these thoughts raced through Frostpaw's mind in a few heartbeats. Harelight was still looking at her with concern in his eyes.

"Are you okay?" he repeated.

"I—I'm not feeling well," Frostpaw stammered. "I think I'd better go and see Mothwing."

"Do you want me to come with you?" Harelight asked.

Frostpaw shook her head. What she wanted most of all was some time alone to think about what had happened. "I'll be fine, thanks," she mewed.

Her head whirling, Frostpaw stumbled back to camp. She'd been so sure that she wasn't meant to be a medicine cat. She was *happy* being a warrior apprentice.

*I have to tell Mothwing—but what in StarClan's name can I tell her?*

Frostpaw knew that she should tell her former mentor and her Clan about her vision, but she wasn't sure that any cat would believe her, after the way she had insisted that all the visions she had previously reported weren't real. She knew she had to work out what had happened in her own mind, before she told her story to any cat.

*Or was this even a real vision?*

Knowing she had tricked herself into believing in her earlier visions, Frostpaw could hardly trust her reactions now, even though this vision had *felt* completely different, much more real, more like the visions Puddleshine had described to her. Yet even he had never mentioned walking in the paws of another cat.

*Maybe Mothwing will know what to do.*

As Frostpaw reached the camp, she passed by her littermates, Mistpaw and Graypaw, heading out with their mentors. They called a greeting, and Icewing gave her a friendly wave of her tail. Frostpaw's throat felt dry as she responded. She remembered Reedwhisker in her vision, telling her "The darkness is closer than you think," and thought again how Curlfeather had warned her, just before she was killed, to trust no cat.

Reedwhisker had known the cat who'd murdered him; he'd been surprised, and he had fought back clumsily. Did that mean his killer was a Clanmate? Frostpaw shivered from ears to tail-tip at the thought.

*Maybe I'd better not tell any cat what I've seen. Not even Mothwing. Not just yet.*

Crossing the camp, Frostpaw leaped down from the bank to the entrance of Mothwing's den beside the stream. Mothwing was just inside, trickling juices of horsetail onto one of Mallownose's forepaws.

"Thanks, Mothwing," Mallownose meowed. "That feels better already."

"Good," Mothwing responded. "Stay off it for today, and come to see me again if your paw starts to swell. And don't pick up any more thorns," she added as Mallownose thanked her again and tottered off on three paws.

"Hi, Frostpaw." Mallownose dipped his head in greeting as he passed her.

"Hi," Frostpaw murmured, unable to stop herself from thinking, *Was it you?*

"Well? What do you want?" Mothwing's tone was sharp, and the look in her amber eyes was unfriendly.

Frostpaw realized that her former mentor still hadn't forgiven her for telling the truth and choosing to become a warrior apprentice. "I've got a bellyache," she replied.

Mothwing sighed. "Lie down," she instructed. "Have you been eating crow-food?"

"No," Frostpaw replied, stretching out on the pebbles so that Mothwing could feel her belly. She was still churning inside from the shock of her experience, but she couldn't tell Mothwing that. "I don't know what caused it."

Mothwing let out a grunt and vanished into her den, to reappear a moment later with a sprig of watermint. "Eat that," she ordered.

Frostpaw licked up the leaves obediently and sat up.

"Mothwing . . . ," she began hesitantly, "I've been thinking about Reedwhisker and the wounds he had when we found him. You examined his body. Do you think those were typical injuries that a cat might get from a fall onto rocks?"

Mothwing's tail flicked with annoyance. "What's this about? You don't need to worry over learning about injuries, now that you've turned your back on becoming a medicine cat."

That was true enough, and Frostpaw fumbled for words, not knowing how to respond.

Mothwing's gaze softened slightly. "There's no use in going over the past," she told Frostpaw. "We all miss Reedwhisker, but he's dead. He's never going to be our leader. And we won't know who will be until we have a sign from StarClan."

"The other medicine cats haven't heard anything?" Frostpaw asked.

Mothwing shook her head. "At the last half-moon meeting all the medicine cats focused on getting a sign—any sign—to tell us what ought to be done about RiverClan. They all reached StarClan and spoke with the spirits of their warrior ancestors. But the spirits refused to answer any questions about RiverClan. Only about ShadowClan, and how they shouldn't be here—but we all know that anyway. Not even Jayfeather could get anything more out of them—and whatever we might think about Jayfeather, he is the cat with the strongest connection to StarClan." She gave an irritated whisk of her tail. "What's the *point* of StarClan, if they won't help us?" she growled.

Frostpaw felt slightly encouraged that Mothwing had unbent enough to tell her what had happened. "So there's no good news?" she mewed.

"Not about a new leader," Mothwing replied, then added, sounding more cheerful, "But Havenpelt is expecting Sneeze-cloud's kits. Kits are always something to look forward to."

*But we don't want kits born into chaos,* Frostpaw thought. *We need a leader and a deputy, and we need them soon.* She felt ready to despair; she had believed that all these worries were behind her, but now the burden was weighing on her shoulders once again.

"Now off you go to the apprentices' den," Mothwing meowed briskly. "Rest until you feel better—and no more food until sunset."

"Yes, Mothwing. Thank you."

As she headed for her den, Frostpaw felt more uneasy than ever, and more alone. She couldn't tell Harelight what had happened, and she was frustrated that her visit to Mothwing hadn't helped her at all. She looked around at all her Clan-mates, so familiar as they went about their daily tasks, cats she had known all her life.

*Who can I trust?* she wondered anxiously. *What am I supposed to do, when there's no cat I can share this with?*

And there was another question that she could not answer, more troubling and even more terrifying: *Who is the darkness in RiverClan?*

# CHAPTER 17

*The moon was riding high in* a sky streaked with cloud as the last of the cats pushed their way through the bushes into the clearing around the Great Oak. Sunbeam sat beside Nightheart in the midst of the heaving, murmuring mass of cats and gazed up at the Clan leaders in the branches above her head.

Usually Sunbeam looked forward to Gatherings and the chance to meet friends from other Clans and hear news from all around the lake. But not tonight. It worried her that the full moon had arrived without anything changing for River-Clan or ShadowClan. Tigerstar still had no intention of leaving RiverClan, not while RiverClan had found a medicine cat who could help them discover the will of StarClan.

*What will happen? Is Berryheart right that another leader will turn against us and we'll end up fighting a battle?*

A shiver ran through Sunbeam at the thought. It seemed wrong to fight another Clan because Tigerstar insisted on interfering in RiverClan's affairs. Memories crowded in on her of the battle between the Clans, and the later battle against the impostor Ashfur—could the peace they had achieved be broken so soon after that terrible time?

She worried about Nightheart, too. If ThunderClan went into battle against ShadowClan, he would have to fight against his former Clanmates—his family and friends. Berryheart had been right that his loyalties would be tested, perhaps to the breaking point.

*Oh, please, StarClan, don't let that happen!*

The ThunderClan leader was sitting in a fork between a branch and the trunk of the Great Oak. An inert bundle of rumpled tabby fur, he had his gaze fixed on his paws.

*Bramblestar won't want to fight.* Sunbeam tried to comfort herself with the thought, but it was followed immediately by another, not comforting at all. *Squirrelflight might persuade him.*

Harestar, last of the Clan leaders, leaped up into the tree. There was no RiverClan leader except for Icewing, sitting not in the Great Oak, but beside Cloverfoot in the deputies' place on the roots. More RiverClan cats were clustered together at the edge of the crowd, watching the proceedings with a defiant air, as if they expected some cat to challenge their right to be there.

Splashtail was one of them, reminding Sunbeam of how he had told Berryheart that he could fake a medicine cat. *Has he done anything yet?* she asked herself. Mothwing was the only RiverClan cat to join the other medicine cats, so it looked as if she didn't have a new apprentice yet.

Tigerstar stepped forward to the end of his branch. The other leaders had already given their reports, and Sunbeam sensed a quickening of tension in the cats around her as the ShadowClan leader prepared to speak.

"Prey is running well in ShadowClan—" he began.

Instantly several voices interrupted him; Hawkwing, the SkyClan deputy, made himself heard above the rest. Sunbeam winced at his stern tone. *Oh, no . . . it's starting.*

"Tigerstar, just what is going on between you and River-Clan?" Hawkwing asked. "When you say prey is running well, do you mean just in ShadowClan, or in RiverClan as well?"

"ShadowClan is still in RiverClan, and prey is running well for both of us," Tigerstar replied. His voice was calm, but Sunbeam knew him well enough to realize that the quivering of his whiskers revealed how hard he was finding it to hold in his irritation. She dug her claws into the ground, trying to hide her misgivings; the way that Hawkwing wouldn't even let Tigerstar finish his opening speech was a sure sign of how upset the other Clans were. "We have no plans to leave until a new RiverClan leader is found," the ShadowClan leader continued. "We are *helping* RiverClan."

*Do I believe that?* Sunbeam asked herself, exchanging an uncomfortable glance with her mother, who was sitting a couple of tail-lengths away.

Harestar leaned forward, his brown-and-white pelt scarcely visible among the brown leaves that still clung to the oak. "We've learned that StarClan doesn't share your view," he meowed. "Do you believe you know better than them?"

Tigerstar didn't flinch. He stood tall, pushing out his chest in defiance. "I believe my intentions were misrepresented to StarClan," he replied. "As I have explained endless times, *this is not a takeover.* I am *helping* RiverClan."

Hawkwing flicked his tail in annoyance. "Does *RiverClan* see it that way?" he asked, his voice full of concern.

Tigerstar nodded toward the RiverClan she-cat on the roots below. "Icewing? Perhaps you could answer Harestar."

Icewing rose to her paws, and Sunbeam leaned forward eagerly. Sunbeam hadn't known Icewing well during the brief time she was part of ShadowClan, but while Sunbeam was in the RiverClan camp, she had seen how level-headed and capable Icewing was. She worked well with Cloverfoot. Sunbeam was sure that the white she-cat would say something worth hearing.

"While RiverClan is eager to find our new leader," Icewing responded, raising her voice to address all the cats, "we are still at peace with ShadowClan. Tigerstar is involved in our affairs only to help, as he said. I'm sure he will leave as soon as our leadership is settled."

Sunbeam could see that the old she-cat believed what she had said, but it was obvious that some of her Clanmates didn't agree.

Duskfur sprang to her paws. "*I* don't believe a word of what Tigerstar says!" she snarled.

"Neither do I!" That was Splashtail, his shoulder fur bristling. "ShadowClan doesn't belong in our camp!"

"They shouldn't have any say over our affairs," Mallownose hissed. "They should leave!"

Tigerstar waited for the protests to die down, but before he could speak, Leafstar rose, looking down at him from a branch just above his head. "How is RiverClan planning to select a new leader?" she asked. "Have they been in touch with StarClan?"

While the SkyClan leader was speaking, Sunbeam looked over at Mothwing, sitting among the other medicine cats; her amber eyes were sparking with anger, and the tip of her tail was twitching. But she said nothing, and it was Tigerstar who responded.

"Frostpaw has become a warrior apprentice," he meowed. "She no longer believes she has a connection to StarClan. Right now, RiverClan doesn't have any contact with StarClan at all."

At her Clan leader's words, Sunbeam felt a prickle of the same disbelief and horror that she had experienced when she'd first learned about Frostpaw giving up her calling. *How can a Clan go on existing without any connection to StarClan?*

All around her the cats from the other three Clans, who hadn't known about Frostpaw until now, erupted into startled exclamations and yowled out questions.

"What were her visions, then?" some cat demanded.

"Did she lie to every cat?"

"Of course she didn't lie," Tigerstar retorted, raising his voice above the clamor. His amber eyes gleamed balefully from his place in the Great Oak. "She's young. It can take time for a cat to discover their true place in their Clan."

The yowls died down, giving way to murmurs of surprise as Crowfeather rose from where he sat with the other deputies on the oak roots. "What you say is true, Tigerstar," he began coolly. "But it's also true that a Clan is much weaker if they have no medicine cat. You wouldn't have encouraged Frost-paw to become a warrior, would you, to make it easier for you to take over her Clan?"

"How dare you!" Tigerstar growled.

Before Crowfeather could respond, another voice cut across the ShadowClan leader's words. "Take that back, Crowfeather!"

To Sunbeam's astonishment, Frostpaw had bounced to her paws and rushed forward to glare at the WindClan deputy, her fur bushing out in fury. Until then, Sunbeam had believed she hadn't come to the Gathering; she must have been hidden among her Clanmates. Sunbeam felt a spurt of admiration that such a small, young cat who would dare to stand up to the formidable WindClan deputy.

"No cat made the decision for me!" she snapped. "It was all mine. I didn't lie to any cat, but I made a mistake. Tigerstar had nothing to do with it."

Crowfeather dipped his head toward her. "I'm glad to hear it," he meowed, sitting down again.

"We should all leave Frostpaw alone," Leafstar put in, with a warm glance at the young apprentice. "None of this is her fault. But it leaves RiverClan in an even bigger mess," she added to Tigerstar. "And gives even more reason for you to get out of RiverClan now, since there's no end in sight."

Even though she didn't like it, Sunbeam had to admit that Leafstar was right, that Frostpaw's decision had left River-Clan in an even worse state. She knew Tigerstar wouldn't be leaving any time soon.

*And how long can ShadowClan go on like this? Most of us want to stay on our own territory, not go trekking off to keep watch over RiverClan. And we want our deputy back!*

With another glance at Berryheart, Sunbeam wondered if her mother had been right all along.

Gazing at the group of RiverClan warriors, Sunbeam remembered what Splashtail had promised in his meeting with Berryheart and her followers. He had seemed certain that a new medicine cat would soon emerge. *Will it be now?* Sunbeam asked herself, feeling her pelt prickle with anticipation. But no RiverClan cat spoke.

As the muttering died down at last, the ThunderClan warrior Twigbranch rose to her paws, looking up at the leaders with a troubled expression. "Is this like Shadowsight's visions from Ashfur?" she asked. "Was Frostpaw being led astray?"

Tigerstar shook his head. "No, it was all just a misunderstanding," he reassured her. "Not false visions sent by some other cat."

"Then in that case," Leafstar pointed out, an edge to her tone, "RiverClan has no way to select a new leader. And it seems as if there's no foreseeable end to ShadowClan's occupation of RiverClan."

With a glance at Nightheart, Sunbeam twitched her tail nervously, remembering how Leafstar had argued for forcing ShadowClan out at the previous Gathering. She seemed heartbeats away from suggesting the same thing now.

Tigerstar simply shrugged. "So what do you suggest, Leafstar?" he asked. "I can't create a connection between

RiverClan and StarClan. We'll just have to wait."

*Is he for real?* Sunbeam asked herself, a thrill of annoyance passing through her pelt. Tigerstar was more or less daring Leafstar to mount an attack. *Our lives are at stake. Why won't he try to pacify her?*

Once again there was an outcry from the RiverClan cats and some cats from other Clans, too. Splashtail had risen, arching his back and hissing at Tigerstar as if he was going to jump into the Great Oak and attack him. "Are you saying you'll keep ordering us around for however long it takes?" he snarled.

Among the ShadowClan cats, Sunbeam spotted Berryheart lashing her tail in fury; when she followed her mother's gaze across the clearing, it was fixed on Splashtail.

"There must be another way!" Duskfur yowled. "A senior RiverClan warrior could lead until StarClan shows us their will. Icewing is already doing most of the leader's tasks."

Tigerstar shook his head impatiently. "That's exactly what got RiverClan into this mess," he snapped. "Not having a real, StarClan-approved leader. I don't understand why you're so upset," he added. "I've been very paws-off so far."

"That's a lie!" Mallownose screeched. "Cloverfoot and other ShadowClan warriors are still staying in our camp, ordering us around."

Leafstar let out a gasp of outrage. "Is that true?" she demanded, sliding out her claws as if she would have liked to take a swipe at the ShadowClan leader. "You have your deputy actually running RiverClan? I think you've overstepped, Tigerstar."

"Cloverfoot is only there to advise," Tigerstar explained.

Sunbeam could tell that her leader was barely holding in his temper. She had always known he was arrogant, but she hadn't believed he would be so uncaring about the prospect of cats losing their lives in battle.

"Icewing is working with her to make sure RiverClan is still responsible for its own decisions," Tigerstar continued. He angled his ears down toward the oak roots, as if to prove that Icewing had status with the Clan deputies.

"If Icewing can do that—and every cat knows she can—why do we need Cloverfoot and the others at all?" Duskfur demanded.

"Yeah," Podlight added. "You're treating us like kits still in the nursery!"

Leafstar turned to Bramblestar and Harestar, raising her voice to be heard over the complaints from the cats below.

"In answer to my earlier question, Tigerstar's actions clearly *aren't* acceptable to RiverClan," she pointed out. "And he has no plans to leave. When he first took over, you both said you would wait and see what happened. Well, we *have* waited. And *nothing* has happened. So now are you ready to *make* Tigerstar leave RiverClan?"

"I'd like to see you try!" Tigerstar retorted, his bristling fur showing he was at the end of his patience.

Sunbeam felt her muscles cramp with tension. *Are we going to have to fight the other Clans?* she wondered. *Here at a Gathering— breaking the truce? And in defense of something that I agree is wrong?*

She almost hoped that both leaders would turn against Tigerstar. That would surely make him see how stupid he was being, because ShadowClan couldn't fight off all four of the other Clans. But even if only one more leader turned against him, that could end in war. And if that leader was Bramblestar, Nightheart would be in a terrible position.

Sunbeam turned toward him, seeing her anxiety reflected in his eyes. Then he gave her a firm nod, as if he was reassuring her that he would stay with her, with ShadowClan.

She wasn't sure she should feel relieved as Harestar dipped his head politely to Leafstar. "No," he replied. "The situation is peaceful. I see no reason to shed blood over it. Besides," he added, "everything Tigerstar has said shows that he truly is planning for this to be temporary."

"That's true," Tigerstar agreed, with a nod of gratitude to the WindClan leader. "I have no intention of staying in RiverClan. For StarClan's sake, it's difficult enough running one Clan!"

Leafstar gave her whiskers an irritable twitch as she turned to Bramblestar. "What do you think?" she asked the Thunder-Clan leader.

Sunbeam felt her belly cramp with tension. Bramblestar turning against ShadowClan would be the worst possible outcome. She tried to comfort herself with the thought that ThunderClan was still recovering from the damage Ashfur had caused. They must be weakened, easier for ShadowClan to defeat.

*What am I thinking?* she asked herself. *I don't want to fight at all!*

Bramblestar blinked thoughtfully; Sunbeam wondered if he had actually been paying attention to the argument. "I agree with Harestar," he meowed at last. "There's no reason for the Clans to fight. This will work itself out."

Sunbeam had hardly a moment to feel relieved before Squirrelflight spoke, making her belly lurch with renewed alarm.

"Maybe you should think that over one more time!" the ThunderClan deputy yowled from her place on the oak roots. "I think—and many of our Clanmates think—that Leafstar is right. We need to get ShadowClan out of RiverClan. By force, if necessary. Bramblestar, surely you can see that this is a problem!"

Shock pulsed through Sunbeam at the ThunderClan deputy's words. "Squirrelflight must feel strongly about this," she whispered, turning to Nightheart. "Or she would never contradict her leader in the middle of a Gathering. Do they often disagree like that?"

Nightheart's gaze was clouded. "Lately, they do," he replied. "It's been a relief in ShadowClan to see how Tigerstar and Cloverfoot work together."

*That's going to be a problem,* Sunbeam reflected. *I just hope Bramblestar sticks to his decision and isn't influenced by Squirrelflight.*

"I don't want to see any more bloodshed," Bramblestar responded, his amber eyes sad as he gazed down at his deputy—who was also his mate. "Haven't we all seen enough of fighting?"

*Why doesn't he shut her down?* Sunbeam wondered. *They shouldn't be having this argument in front of every cat.*

Squirrelflight lashed her tail irritably. "Sometimes Clans

have to fight," she asserted. "There's no surer way for a Clan to be destroyed than for its leader to be afraid of battle."

Bramblestar heaved a deep sigh. "In that case," he mewed, "maybe you're better suited to be leader than I am."

A disbelieving silence fell on the clearing, as if every cat were enfolded in ice. Bramblestar hadn't sounded angry; he had sounded as if he meant it.

Sunbeam turned to Nightheart. He was shaking his head, his eyes wide. She didn't think she had ever seen him this upset. She leaned into his shoulder comfortingly, and heard him whisper, "No."

"You said it was normal for them to disagree," Sunbeam murmured.

"Yes, but not like this," Nightheart responded. "I can't believe that Bramblestar is so lost that he doesn't want to be leader. And he said it in front of the whole Gathering!"

Sunbeam gave his ear a lick, trying once more to comfort him. At the same time, she hoped that Bramblestar didn't mean what he had just said. She needed him to hold out against Leafstar and refuse to join an attack on ShadowClan.

After what seemed like seasons of frozen shock, Crow-feather's cool voice broke the silence. "It seems like maybe there are two Clans without a leader."

Squirrelflight whirled around to face him where he sat next to her on the oak roots, her lips drawn back in a furious snarl. Crowfeather's fur bushed up in response.

"Stop!" Hawkwing intervened, pushing Crowfeather aside to get between him and Squirrelflight. "We can't break the full-moon truce without angering StarClan."

Looking up, Sunbeam spotted a wisp of cloud dangerously close to the moon, but as the furious deputies subsided with no more than glares between them, it drifted away again.

"ThunderClan will not join your attack, Leafstar. I want peace more than anything," Bramblestar continued. "We have seen too much horror in recent moons." His shoulders drooped; suddenly he looked old and tired. "If we don't stop fighting, the fighting will never stop."

Silence, more thoughtful this time, spread throughout the Gathering. Glancing around, Sunbeam saw her own anxiety reflected on the faces of cat after cat. *There's something wrong with Bramblestar.* It was one thing for a leader to want to avoid battle, but quite another to sound so fearful and exhausted as he admitted to the other Clans that he was tired of fighting. Even though Sunbeam was glad that Bramblestar had refused to fight, she could tell that he wasn't himself. *What does that mean for ThunderClan?*

Glancing at Nightheart, she saw him staring up at Bramblestar, his gaze fixed on the ThunderClan leader as if there were no other cat in the clearing, his expression deeply worried.

Sunbeam's pads prickled uneasily to see how preoccupied Nightheart was with his former leader. Did it mean that he was regretting his decision? "That was tense," she commented softly into his ear. "But at least Bramblestar sided with Tiger-star."

In spite of her reassurance, Nightheart's anxiety did not seem to fade, and he made no response.

"I appreciate your support, Bramblestar." Tigerstar briefly looked a little surprised, then dipped his head to the Thunder-Clan leader as though nothing unusual had happened. *He must realize how weird that was,* Sunbeam thought. *But at least it was weird in his favor.* "I promise that my only purpose is to protect RiverClan and help them through this difficult time," Tigerstar continued. "I have no intention of becoming their leader myself. I don't even like fish," he added. No cat reacted to the feeble joke.

"The Gathering is at an end!" Harestar called out.

Sunbeam could almost hear a collective sigh of relief as cats immediately began to leave through the bushes, heading for the shore of the island. But she noticed too that many cats glanced back, casting puzzled or apprehensive glances at the ThunderClan leader.

She spotted Berryheart with her followers, all of them looking frustrated, and wondered what her mother would do now. It was clear that the other Clans weren't going to inter-vene, so would Berryheart decide that talking wasn't enough?

Berryheart and Whorlpelt had their heads close together; Sunbeam eased herself nearer and caught a few words coming from her mother's mouth. "It's time to step up our plan-ning...."

Sunbeam felt every one of her muscles growing tense. *We have to watch her—even more closely!* she thought. "Nightheart—"

But when she turned toward the black tom, he wasn't by her side anymore. Instead she saw him heading toward the departing ThunderClan cats. She hurried across the clearing, dodging around the other cats making for the encircling bushes, until she caught up to him.

"Nightheart, what are you doing?" she asked. "Our Clanmates are leaving for home. And I need to talk to you."

But after a single glance, Nightheart turned away from her. "Sorry," he muttered. "I have to talk to my sister."

Sunbeam watched him pad away, hardly able to believe that he had dismissed her like that. She felt tension building inside her until she felt as if she might explode.

"Oh, StarClan!" she sighed aloud. "Why won't you help us? Why won't you send a new leader for RiverClan?"

# CHAPTER 18

Nighteart raced after the departing crowd of cats, his gaze flickering to and fro as he searched for his sister. He had always known that Bramblestar and Squirrelflight argued, but not like that, and not in front of every cat at the Gathering. And Bramble-star had seemed so defeated, not like a Clan leader at all.

*I have to know whether everything is all right.*

At first Nighteart couldn't see Finchlight among the crowd of her Clanmates. Desperate to find her, he thrust his way through the mass of cats, ignoring the hisses of protest, until he spotted her waiting for her turn to leave through the bushes. He bounded up to the edge of the group and signaled to her with a wave of his tail.

Finchlight's expression darkened as she saw him, but she slid out of the cluster of her Clanmates to stand at his side. "What is it, Nighteart?" she asked, an edge of irritation in her voice.

"I need to know what's going on," Nighteart explained. "Bramblestar doesn't seem like himself at all. He doesn't sound like ThunderClan matters to him anymore. And why are he and Squirrelflight arguing in front of the other Clans?"

He was prepared for Finchlight to ask him what business it was of his, now that he had left to become a ShadowClan cat, but as he spoke, he saw her expression soften and anxiety gather in her eyes.

"Things aren't great in ThunderClan," she confessed, with a swift glance around to make sure no cat could overhear. "Squirrelflight and Bramblestar are arguing a lot. More than usual." She shook her head fretfully. "You're right that Bramblestar doesn't really seem to care about the Clan anymore. Maybe it *would* be better if Squirrelflight took over as leader."

Nightheart blinked at her, taken aback to hear her put the idea into plain words. His anxiety about his old Clan and his new one felt like tendrils bound tightly around his chest. "Back when we were young," he meowed, "I remember Bramblestar as a confident leader. It's true that he has changed since everything happened with the Dark Forest. But if Squirrelflight becomes leader, she'll want to help Leafstar push ShadowClan out of RiverClan. Do you—do your Clanmates—really want to fight against ShadowClan?"

There was uncertainty in Finchlight's eyes, but she replied readily. "Tigerstar can't be allowed to take over RiverClan."

Nightheart hesitated before he replied. He really believed that Tigerstar had no intention of taking over. But he suddenly realized that if Squirrelflight became Clan leader, and tried to drive ShadowClan out of RiverClan, then he would have to fight against ThunderClan. Against his own former Clanmates and his family.

He swallowed hard, the knowledge like crow-food lodged in his throat. *I can't imagine doing that!* "I think ThunderClan ought to respect Bramblestar after all he's been through," he told Finchlight. "Not turn against him like this."

Finchlight lashed her tail. "If you think I appreciate you sticking your nose in," she snapped, "you're wrong. A cat who really wanted to help would come back, instead of abandoning his Clan."

Before Nightheart could reply, she turned away from him. The crowd was clearing by now, and she was able to join her Clanmates who were thrusting through the bushes on their way to the shore of the island.

Getting ready to follow her, Nightheart realized that the ShadowClan cats were approaching. Sunbeam was padding along in the rear, a hurt look on her face. Yarrowleaf had reached the bushes ahead of the rest, and was standing nearby, watching him with suspicion in her eyes.

"Is everything okay?" she asked.

"Sure," Nightheart replied, trying to sound unconcerned. "I was just talking to my sister."

Yarrowleaf's eyes narrowed. "That's fine," she mewed, "as long as you remember which Clan you're trying to join."

At the same moment, Tigerstar called out to his cats, waving his tail to gather them together for the journey home. As Nightheart joined the others, ready to follow their leader out of the clearing, he glanced back, surprised to see Bramblestar still standing beside Squirrelflight at the foot of the Great Oak. Squirrelflight was meowing something to him, but

Bramblestar didn't seem to be listening.

Bramblestar and Tigerstar looked very much alike, and Nightheart remembered that they were kin. But while Tigerstar was striding forward, bright-eyed and confident, Bramblestar stood with stooped shoulders, looking tired and defeated.

Nightheart hadn't changed his mind; he still intended to be a loyal ShadowClan cat. But as he crossed the tree-bridge and followed his new Clanmates home, he couldn't shake off his grief for the Clan he had abandoned.

Nightheart crouched in the undergrowth just outside the ShadowClan camp. Sunbeam was beside him, so close that their pelts were touching. He couldn't see the rest of the ShadowClan warriors, but he knew they were there, watching and waiting. . . .

The moon had set, and the warriors of StarClan had winked out, one by one. Yet dawn did not break. A dull, pallid light lay on the forest; it reminded Nightheart of all the stories he had heard about the Dark Forest. He shuddered.

Then a powerful smell wafted over him, coming from the direction of the lake: ThunderClan and SkyClan scents mingled together. Sunbeam whispered, "They're here."

Heartbeats later Nightheart spotted the slim shapes of cats slinking furtively through the trees, bearing down on the ShadowClan camp. At the same moment, Tigerstar rose up out of a clump of fern.

"ShadowClan, to me!" he yowled. "Attack!"

Nightheart sprang forward, Sunbeam next to him and the warriors of ShadowClan keeping pace with them on either side. The invaders abandoned their stealthy approach and leaped forward to meet them, yowling a challenge.

As the two sides clashed and broke up into knots of furiously tussling, screeching cats, Nightheart lost sight of Sunbeam. Instead he found himself face-to-face with his sister, Finchlight. He raised a paw, but he couldn't make himself strike her. Finchlight didn't even pause; she reared on her hind paws and raked his ears with both forepaws. "Traitor!" she snarled.

Nightheart froze, feeling blood trickling from his ears, while Finchlight vanished into the heaving mass of cats. All his instincts were telling him to flee, that he couldn't fight against his Clanmates and his kin, yet he knew that if he did, he would betray ShadowClan.

While he hesitated, he felt another cat barrel into him from behind, carrying him off his paws. Squirming around to look his attacker in the face, he saw with horror that the cat was his mother.

"Coward! Mange-pelt!" Sparkpelt growled. She parted her jaws, aiming her fangs at his throat.

Nightheart summoned all his strength and pushed her off, his claws instinctively sheathed. In desperate panic he plunged away, not back to the shelter of the camp, but further into the thick of the battle. Cats shoved and battered at him from all sides so that he could scarcely breathe.

He was beginning to think that he couldn't stay on his paws any longer, that he would collapse and let himself be trampled, when he found himself in an open stretch of ground, covered in a soft coating of pine needles. The sounds of the battle had faded to an eerie wailing; the little clearing was surrounded by a writhing, pulsating wall of fur, where glittering claws and eyes flashed in furious combat.

A single cat crouched in front of Nightheart. As he approached, he recognized the tabby fur and the amber eyes raised to stare at him.

*Bramblestar!*

Nightheart knew what his duty was. The ThunderClan leader seemed to be wounded or weakened; Nightheart could strike the blow that would end his life and give victory to ShadowClan.

He padded forward with one paw raised, and saw recognition flow into Bramblestar's eyes. "Don't I know you?" the ThunderClan leader murmured. "I thought I knew a promising young warrior once. . . . He looked a lot like you."

*I can't! I can't kill him!* But even as the thought passed through his mind, Nightheart drew back his paw to deal the killing blow, and extended his claws.

Bramblestar waited, only acceptance in his calm gaze.

"I can't! I can't!" Nightheart was shaking as he choked the words out. "I can't!"

Then a mist rose and engulfed him, the forest, and Bramblestar. Nightheart found himself thrashing around in his nest in the ShadowClan warriors' den.

Sunbeam was looking down at him, concern in her gaze. "Nightheart, what's the matter?" she asked. "What in StarClan's name are you meowing about?"

\* \* \*

After the fearful nightmare of the battle, Nightheart had tried to settle down again, but sleep had only come in snatches, along with more disturbing dreams. At last he gave up, crouching in his nest as he listened to the quiet breathing of the ShadowClan warriors around him. He was nervous about his third task, which was to take place at sunhigh. Berryheart was bound to make it as difficult as possible.

But along with his apprehension about the task, Nightheart was kept awake by his worries for Bramblestar. The night before, on their way back to camp, Sunbeam had tackled him for speaking to ThunderClan after the Gathering.

"What am I supposed to think?" she demanded angrily. "What is any cat supposed to think, when you're always going off to talk to ThunderClan cats?"

"Not *always*," Nightheart defended himself. "And not just any ThunderClan cats. That was my sister. Am I supposed to ignore her? Besides, I wanted to find out what's going on in ThunderClan—or what's going on between Bramblestar and Squirrelflight."

Some of Sunbeam's anger seemed to fade. "No," she sighed. "I understand why you would want to talk to Finchlight. But it's like we said the other night—ShadowClan cats won't trust you if they think you're still loyal to ThunderClan. You have to be more careful."

Nightheart could see her point, remembering how Berryheart had told him that he would never be accepted as a real ShadowClan cat. "I promise you, I'm loyal to ShadowClan— and to you," he had assured her. "But I'm worried about Bramblestar. You saw what he was like."

Sunbeam nodded. "I'm worried too," she admitted. "Especially if Squirrelflight persuades Bramblestar to go to war with us over RiverClan."

"Then Bramblestar needs to stay leader," Nightheart had declared.

He knew most cats would tell him that he had no business being concerned about ThunderClan when before nightfall he would be a ShadowClan warrior. But he couldn't help remembering his discussion with Sunbeam. If somehow he could convince Bramblestar to stay on as leader, he could maybe prevent war between ThunderClan and ShadowClan.

*That must be important to ShadowClan.*

Nightheart sat up and began to groom scraps of bedding out of his pelt. An idea was growing inside his head, like a bud swelling before it expands into a flower. He wanted to go to ThunderClan and speak to Bramblestar. If he could help the Clan leader regain some of his confidence, then they could avoid a battle. And that would protect ShadowClan too.

Part of Nightheart felt that he was being totally mouse-brained for thinking that Bramblestar would listen to him: a young cat without much experience who had abandoned the Clan of his birth. The last time he had visited the Thunder-Clan camp, with Dovewing, had been a disaster. But then, he told himself, pushing away the prickle of doubt, this time he really wanted to say a true farewell to his old Clan. Besides, Bramblestar had listened to him in the past. Nightheart had always felt a connection between him and the ThunderClan leader.

He glanced aside to where Sunbeam was still sleeping in

her nest with her whiskers rippling as she snored gently. He didn't wake her; he was afraid that maybe she would talk him out of going. Even though she would want him to try convincing Bramblestar to stay on as leader, she also wouldn't want him to risk missing his task.

*I can't take the chance of talking to her. Anyway, I'm sure to be back by sunhigh, ready for whatever Berryheart can throw at me.*

The morning mist was clearing away, and the lake had a milky sheen in the strengthening light as Nightheart bounded along the edge. Remembering the tension at the previous night's Gathering, he kept a wary eye out for SkyClan cats as he crossed their territory, but all was quiet. The border markers were strong and fresh, suggesting that the dawn patrol had already passed.

Finally Nightheart reached the ThunderClan border and sat there to wait in the shelter of an elder bush. He was hardly settled when a wave of ThunderClan scent washed over him and Lionblaze emerged from the undergrowth at the head of the dawn patrol; Sorrelstripe and Molewhisker were with him. Nightheart's anxiety eased at the sight of Sorrelstripe; she'd practically raised him, and had been one of just a few former Clanmates to encourage him when he'd felt no cat could see him for who he was.

"Nightheart?" The golden tabby warrior, however, didn't sound pleased to see him. "What do you want?"

Nightheart rose to his paws and dipped his head politely. "I'd like to speak to Bramblestar, please."

"You've got some nerve!" Molewhisker burst out. "Deserting

your Clan and then sneaking back and demanding to talk to our leader!"

"I'm not *sneaking.*" Nightheart felt anger rising inside him; it was a struggle to keep his voice even. "I just want to see Bramblestar. It's important."

Lionblaze's amber eyes were unfriendly as he looked at Nightheart, whose respect for the golden tabby warrior made it hard for him to meet that stern gaze.

"I can't imagine what you would have to say to our leader that could possibly be important," Lionblaze declared in a chilly tone. "No, we're not taking you to our camp. And don't even *think* about crossing the border on your own." He was already turning away to continue the patrol.

"No, wait—" Nightheart began desperately.

"Lionblaze, I think we should let him come," Sorrelstripe meowed, slipping ahead to intercept her Clanmate before he could stalk off. "I know Nightheart well, and he is an honorable cat who I trust. Whatever he's come for, it must *really* be important. He may have information that we need to know."

"You mean he might be betraying ShadowClan now?" Molewhisker sneered.

*I'd really like to claw that cat's ears off,* Nightheart thought, surprised that Molewhisker was being so hostile. *It's because he's a loyal ThunderClan cat,* he added to himself, keeping his claws sheathed and all four paws on the ground.

"I don't believe Nightheart is betraying anybody," Sorrelstripe replied calmly, looking Nightheart up and down. "In fact, he looks like he's come into his own in ShadowClan. He looks much more confident than I've ever seen him. I think we should listen to what he has to say."

Nightheart met Sorrelstripe's gaze, trying to communicate with his eyes how much her approval meant to him. *Finally, someone from ThunderClan sees how far I've come!* Meanwhile Lionblaze was looking thoughtful; after a couple of heartbeats he gave Sorrelstripe a nod. "Okay," he agreed, his voice still cold. Turning to Nightheart, he added, "Put one paw wrong, and I'll make you wish you'd never been kitted."

Leaving Sorrelstripe to finish marking the border, Lionblaze led the way back to the ThunderClan camp. Nightheart followed with his head bowed and his tail trailing, trying to look as humble and unthreatening as he could. He was acutely aware of Molewhisker treading hard on his paws, and hoped the brown-and-cream tom wouldn't find something sarcastic to say when they reached the camp.

When they arrived in the stone hollow, Nightheart expected that Lionblaze would escort him over to the tumbled rocks that led up to Bramblestar's den on the Highledge. Instead the golden tabby tom crossed the camp straight to where Squirrelflight was grooming herself just outside the warriors' den.

"Look what I found on our border," Lionblaze announced.

Nightheart felt himself shrivel inside as Squirrelflight looked him up and down with unfriendly green eyes. Memories flashed into his mind of how she had failed him on his second assessment, and how angry she had been when he left. He had massive respect for the ThunderClan deputy, but somehow they always managed to get off on the wrong paw. She hadn't been too unfriendly when he'd visited with Dovewing, but he still found Bramblestar much easier to talk to.

"I thought you already came to say one last good-bye," Squirrelflight declared. "What are you doing here *again*?"

"I'd like to speak to Bramblestar, please," Nightheart responded, keeping his voice as low and even as he could in an effort to sound respectful. "It's important."

"Is it indeed?" Squirrelflight's mouth twisted. "Then why don't you tell me what's on your mind, instead of bothering the Clan leader?"

Nightheart didn't know what to reply. What he had to say to Bramblestar wouldn't impress Squirrelflight at all. It might be the last thing she wanted to hear.

"It's not—" he began desperately.

"Nightheart!" Bramblestar's voice interrupted him. Looking up, Nightheart saw the tabby tom outside his den, leaning over the edge of the Highledge. His whiskers quivered with relief, especially when he realized that Bramblestar was looking more alert than he had at the Gathering. "I thought I heard your voice," Bramblestar continued. "Come up so we can have a talk."

Squirrelflight looked up at her mate, her eyes chips of green ice. "Have you forgotten that Nightheart has chosen to join *another Clan*?" she demanded.

"He is still our kin," Bramblestar responded, "no matter which Clan he calls home." He beckoned with his tail. "Come on up, Nightheart. You're welcome here."

Nightheart cast an awkward glance at Squirrelflight, then ran lightly up the tumbled rocks to join Bramblestar on the Highledge.

"So," Bramblestar began, leading the way into his den and settling himself in his nest of moss and bracken. "What brings you here, Nightheart?"

"I wanted to talk to you." At first Nightheart was afraid that he might sound arrogant, thinking that he could advise a cat of Bramblestar's stature. But then he realized that was the point: that a cat who had achieved as much as Bramblestar had no need to feel discouraged. "I looked up to you so much when I was a kit," he continued, gathering confidence. "The elders told us so many stories about all the brave things you did. Weren't you one of the cats who traveled to the sun-drown-place and then found this new home for us by the lake?"

Bramblestar let out a small sigh. "That was many seasons ago."

"Yes, you were as young as me then," Nightheart went on eagerly. "And you were already doing amazing things! Then when you became Clan leader, you saved the Clan from the Great Storm, and you led the Clan against Darktail when he invaded the forest. Bramblestar, you're such an inspiring cat! The whole of ThunderClan depends on you."

As he spoke, Nightheart had hoped to see the light of a new resolve kindle in Bramblestar's amber eyes. Instead, his former leader was beginning to look even more tired and defeated, as if the memories were draining his strength. Nightheart hadn't seen the capable, determined Bramblestar since his return from the Dark Forest. He wondered whether having Ashfur take over his body for so long had hollowed him out somehow, so that the cat who had returned to life was not the bold leader he had been.

"What are you thinking, Bramblestar?" he asked, after he had fallen silent and yet the ThunderClan leader had not responded.

Bramblestar heaved another sigh. "I can't imagine doing those things for my Clan now," he confessed. "That seems like another lifetime. Yes, I've done so much, given so much to my Clan, but now I wake up every morning, and I just feel . . . exhausted. Somehow I feel as though my paws are leading me back to the darkness in the Place of No Stars. I'm never sure how I will make it through the day."

"But you never have to go back there," Nightheart objected. "You're done with all that."

"Not in my mind," Bramblestar sighed. "It's so difficult to forget what I saw there, and sometimes it floods my thoughts out of nowhere, as though I've never really left."

Nightheart could hardly bear to see the sadness in the Clan leader's eyes. His dream came vividly back to him: how in it, Bramblestar had been so ready to accept his death.

"Have you talked about this to Squirrelflight?" he asked. "Maybe she—"

Bramblestar shook his head. "No. I try not to mention it, because it upsets her. Besides, she wasn't there for as long, and she was never driven out of her body. Maybe that's why she doesn't seem as haunted by it as I am. I can't let it drain her strength as it's drained mine."

As the Clan leader spoke, Nightheart began to realize that Bramblestar was going through something more serious than just being weary and despondent, something that couldn't be banished with a few encouraging words. He had heard stories about the Dark Forest, but he had never been there, and he knew that it must be much more terrifying in reality. He would have liked to hear about it from one of the Lights in the Mist, the cats who had recently experienced it, but they were all so much more senior, so hard for him to talk to. He couldn't even imagine it, and that meant he couldn't really imagine what Bramblestar was suffering.

*This is all beyond me,* he thought. *Why did I ever think I could help?*

"Have you spoken to a medicine cat about this?" he asked. "Maybe Alderheart or Jayfeather could help."

"I've tried, but it's difficult," Bramblestar sighed. "Alderheart is my son, and Jayfeather . . . well, Jayfeather and I have a complicated relationship. I wouldn't feel comfortable talking frankly to either of them about this. Besides," he added, as Nightheart opened his jaws to protest, "what could they do to help? No herb will blot out everything I've seen. No poppy seed will make me forget the Dark Forest."

Nightheart could find nothing more to say. He felt mouse-brained now for thinking that he could talk Bramblestar out of this darkness with a few stirring words. Every cat knew that the Dark Forest changed you. That was one of the challenges the Lights in the Mist had faced, fighting in the Dark Forest for so long, and his brave leader had been trapped there for moons, far longer than the rest of them. How would any cat react to that? Of course the experience had drained him of the energy he needed to lead his Clan.

Every muscle in Nightheart's body began to tense with worry for Bramblestar . . . and for ThunderClan. How would Bramblestar be able to face a threat to the Clan if he could barely face a normal day as leader?

"About two moons ago," Bramblestar continued, "I asked Jayfeather to take me to the Moonpool. I wanted to know if StarClan had any guidance for me. We went at night, without telling any cat."

"And did StarClan send you a message?" Nightheart asked.

Bramblestar nodded. "Leafpool spoke to Jayfeather. She told him that I must prepare myself to make a sacrifice. I assumed that she meant I must soon die. I have no idea how many lives Ashfur drained from me, so it could mean giving up my last life."

"Is *that* why you don't want to go into battle with Shadow-Clan?" Nightheart asked, thinking that he had begun to understand Bramblestar's state of mind.

The ThunderClan leader turned an intense amber gaze on him, and Nightheart realized that he hadn't understood at all. He felt ashamed of himself for assuming that his Clan leader would be such a coward. "I—I'm sorry—" he stammered.

Bramblestar waved the apology away with a tiny gesture of one forepaw. "I'm not afraid of dying," he mewed. "How could I be, when so many friends are waiting for me in StarClan?

What I am afraid of is starting a war I may not be able to finish, and leaving ThunderClan in such a fragile state, with Squirrelflight thrown into leadership without warning. And yet whatever I decide, my death is waiting for me, like a badger crouching across my path. How can I lead my Clan with that weighing on me?"

Suddenly Bramblestar's refusal to fight Tigerstar seemed understandable. Dangerous, but understandable. *But what if the problem wasn't just Tigerstar being stubborn?* Nightheart asked himself. *What if it was something more dangerous: another Ashfur, or Darktail, or the first Tigerstar?*

Nightheart had come to ThunderClan to convince Bramblestar to stay on as leader. That would help Thunder-Clan, and keep ShadowClan from being attacked. *I thought I could help every cat I care about at once.* But now he realized that he cared too much about Bramblestar to push him into remaining leader if that condemned him to so much suffering every day.

*I'm not choosing ThunderClan over ShadowClan,* he assured himself. *I'm just doing what any decent cat would do in my position.*

"I came here to try to encourage you," Nightheart meowed after the silence had dragged out for several heartbeats. "I wanted to convince you to be a strong leader again. But if you're truly struggling that much . . . have you considered stepping down? Maybe that's the sacrifice Leafpool spoke of—not dying, but giving up your leadership."

Slowly Bramblestar shook his head. "I know what I said at the Gathering," he murmured ruefully. "And maybe I meant it then, with so many cats demanding action against Tigerstar. But in all seriousness, I can't be the leader who gave up and abandoned his Clan. I know how ThunderClan feels about Pinestar, who gave up his leadership to be a kittypet, and brought shame on himself and his Clan."

"But you—" Nightheart tried to interrupt.

Bramblestar ignored the attempt. "Now that you're in ShadowClan," he continued, "you must know about Rowan-star, who gave up *his* leadership. After that, ShadowClan fell to pieces and became part of SkyClan, until Tigerstar came back."

"But you're not abandoning your Clan if you're doing it for their own good," Nightheart pointed out. "You're not like Rowanstar; you've got a strong deputy to take over. No cat could possibly be angry with you, or think you were acting shamefully, after all you've been through."

Bramblestar blinked thoughtfully, then let out another sigh. "True, Squirrelflight would make an excellent leader," he admitted. "We don't always see things the same way, but there's no cat I trust more to do what is right for the Clan. Maybe that *is* what Leafpool meant. . . ."

The leader's deep amber gaze rested on Nightheart for a few heartbeats; Nightheart felt his love and respect for this profoundly suffering cat fill him to overflowing, like rain spilling into an upturned leaf.

"Did Tigerstar send you?" Bramblestar asked abruptly.

"No," Nightheart replied, shocked that the Clan leader might think that. "I'm here as a ThunderClan cat. A *former*

ThunderClan cat," he corrected himself hastily. "And as your kin, Bramblestar."

"I'm grateful for what you've said," Bramblestar meowed. "And I promise you I'll think about it. Maybe you're right." He rose from his nest, and Nightheart realized that he was being dismissed. "I hope things work out for you in Shadow-Clan," Bramblestar continued. "And with Sunbeam. I've always seen something special in you, Nightheart, and I think you deserve happiness."

Nightheart picked his way down the tumbled rocks, inwardly shaking from the stress of his talk with Bramblestar. *I had some nerve, talking like that to the leader of another Clan!*

At the foot of the rocks, Finchlight, Bayshine, and Myrtle-bloom were waiting for him, crowding eagerly around him as he jumped down the last couple of tail-lengths.

"What did you need to talk to Bramblestar about?" Bayshine asked.

"Yeah," Myrtlebloom added. "What did he say to you?"

Nightheart knew there was no way he could tell them about what had passed between him and Bramblestar in the Clan leader's den. "I'm sorry," he mewed, trying to sound friendly. "It's not really my right to talk about it."

To his relief, his former Clanmates seemed to accept that.

"It's great that Bramblestar was willing to talk to you." Finchlight looked reluctantly impressed. "You must mean a lot to him."

Nightheart ducked his head, feeling embarrassed at his sister's praise. "I hope so. He means a lot to me. It's been good seeing you again," he continued. "But I have to go now."

"What?" Myrtlebloom's eyes stretched wide in surprise. "You came all this way, just to turn around and run back to ShadowClan?"

"We hoped you wanted to stay." Bayshine's tone was hurt.

"If you're a ShadowClan cat now, why do you care about ThunderClan's business so much?" Finchlight asked, a challenge in her gaze. "Maybe you're not really meant to be a ShadowClan cat. Have you ever thought of that?"

Nightheart could only dip his head. "I have to go," he repeated.

An image of Sunbeam came into his mind: her beautiful eyes, the sheen on her fur. A hollow place opened up inside him at the thought that she would be upset if she knew what he had said to Bramblestar.

As he crossed the camp, Nightheart looked around at ThunderClan—at his kin, at his friends, at his former mentor, Lilyheart, who was watching him sadly on his way out. He thought of Sorrelstripe and her kind words when they'd met on the border. When he had left his Clan, he had seen these cats only as enemies, or as obstacles keeping him from what he wanted to be. But now he saw them as the real cats they were. He realized how deeply he cared about them, even though he hadn't always agreed with them. It hurt more to leave now than when he had first stormed out to go to ShadowClan.

*I wish there were a way to please them, and to please Sunbeam. But right now I can't think of one.*

When Nightheart pushed his way out of the thorn tunnel,

he suddenly saw how short the shadows were on the forest floor. Looking up, he saw that sunhigh was not far off.

*Oh, great StarClan, no! I'm going to be late for my task!*

His heart pounding, Nightheart took off, racing through the trees and along the shore of the lake. He knew that Berryheart would insist that he had failed if he didn't get back to the ShadowClan camp on time, and Sunbeam would never forgive him.

But as he ran, Nightheart still thought back to his conversation with Bramblestar. If he had convinced Bramblestar, then Squirrelflight would become the new leader of ThunderClan. And that meant that ThunderClan would probably join Leafstar in fighting ShadowClan.

*I told myself that Sunbeam comes first—but is that true, if I've just pushed my new Clan into war?*

# CHAPTER 19

Crouching in the long grass, the sound of the nearby stream in her ears, Frostpaw was lost in her vision of Reedwhisker. *What am I going to do?* In the couple of days since she had witnessed the deputy's murder and heard his warning, she hadn't been able to stop looking at her Clanmates, pondering which one of them might be Reedwhisker's killer. She didn't even want to be in camp anymore; she felt such a sense of danger when she set paw there.

*Duskfur?* she wondered. The old she-cat had clearly wanted to be leader, yet she had been pleased when her daughter, Curlfeather, was chosen instead. *Mothwing?* But it seemed unlikely that the medicine cat who'd trained her could ever be a murderer. *Owlnose?* Frostpaw forced back a snort of laughter at the very thought. If she knew anything about Owlnose, it was that he *didn't* want to be Clan leader.

But eliminating those three cats still left Frostpaw with a whole Clan of suspects. *I've known them all my life. But how much do I really know about any of them?*

"Frostpaw!" Harelight's sharp voice broke into her thoughts. "What's the matter with you? That mouse practically ran over your paws."

His rebuke jerked Frostpaw back to the hunting patrol; ashamed, she admitted to herself that she hadn't even seen the mouse, nor scented it. "Sorry," she apologized to her mentor and to Podlight and Havenpelt, the other cats hunting with them. "I was thinking about something else."

Harelight rolled his eyes. "Then maybe start to think about feeding the Clan," he meowed. "Come on, let's try closer to the lake."

Frostpaw followed obediently, forcing herself to pay attention to the sounds and scents of nearby prey, but she was still worried. Her vision wasn't something she could just ignore. She knew that sooner or later she would have to do something about it, but she shrank from making the decision on her own. She needed to tell some cat, but she had no idea how to work out who she could trust.

Harelight halted at the top of a bank that sloped gently down toward the lake. "This is a good place for voles," he meowed. "Let's spread out and see what we can find."

Frostpaw found a spot with particularly lush vegetation overhanging a sandy hollow where two or three holes led back into the bank. Crouching low among the leafy steams, she forced herself to concentrate and push her worries to the back of her mind.

Soon a whiskery nose poked out into the open, sniffing the air. The rich scent of vole swept over Frostpaw, carried by a breeze from the lake. *And that means the vole can't scent me,* she told herself, tensing her muscles, ready for a pounce.

For a moment she thought the vole had gone back into its

burrow. Finally its head emerged, then its whole body, as it headed for the lake.

It didn't get far. Frostpaw launched herself from the top of the slope, all four sets of claws extended, and thumped down on the vole, gripping its shoulders and killing it with a bite to the throat.

"Thank you, StarClan, for this prey," she mewed.

"Hey, Frostpaw, that was great!" Harelight was looking down at her, approval in his eyes. "You see what you can do, once you wake up a little."

Harelight had also caught a vole, while Podlight and Havenpelt had several mice between them. The patrol headed back to camp, carrying their prey. Frostpaw was glowing inside from her mentor's praise, aware once more of how much she was enjoying her warrior tasks.

*But maybe I'll have to give them up soon,* she thought, dejection washing over her again.

As the patrol approached the camp, the peaceful sounds of the gurgling stream and the wind in the trees were shattered by a sudden earsplitting screech.

"Great StarClan, what's that?" Harelight exclaimed.

He began to run; Frostpaw and the other two cats raced after him. Frostpaw felt her fur beginning to bristle; she was afraid that fighting had broken out between her Clanmates and the ShadowClan interlopers.

*Please, StarClan, not again!* she begged. *Not more injured cats!.*

The screeching continued, and Frostpaw realized that she wasn't hearing a fight: this was the sound of a single cat in pain. As the patrol burst into the camp, she spotted Scorch-fur, one of the ShadowClan warriors, writhing on the ground near the fresh-kill pile. His jaws were gaping open, and he was clawing frantically at the inside of his mouth.

Frostpaw bounded across the camp and dropped her prey on the fresh-kill pile before turning toward the wounded warrior. "What happened?" she asked Shimmerpelt, the cat nearest to her.

"He was eating a mouse, and somehow there was a thorn in it," Shimmerpelt explained.

"Serves him right!" Duskfur yowled.

"Yeah," Brackenpelt agreed. "He shouldn't be in our camp in the first place."

The two she-cats were blocking Mothwing from reaching the injured cat; Mothwing looked irritated as she tried to dodge around them, but she didn't seem ready to thrust her Clanmates aside.

Frostpaw slipped past Shimmerpelt and crouched down beside the writhing Scorchfur. "Stop making that awful noise," she snapped. "Any cat would think a fox had gotten you. Keep still and let me see what the problem is."

To her relief—and a little surprise—Scorchfur obeyed her. Peering into his open jaws, Frostpaw spotted a huge thorn firmly driven into the inside of his cheek.

"Okay, keep your mouth stretched as wide as you can," Frostpaw ordered.

She slid her paw between Scorchfur's teeth and delicately inserted one claw at the side of the thorn. A groan came from deep within Scorchfur's chest, but he didn't move. Frostpaw gave a gentle tug; she felt the thorn shift, and with a second tug she managed to hook it out. Blood flowed out after it, and Scorchfur collapsed, trembling.

"You did a good job." Mothwing had come to stand beside Frostpaw, who thought she could see annoyance in the medicine cat's amber eyes.

Guilt flooded over Frostpaw. *In an emergency, I acted like I was the medicine cat,* she thought. *No wonder Mothwing isn't pleased with me.*

"Okay, Scorchfur," Mothwing meowed brusquely. "Come with me to my den, and I'll give you some horsetail to stop the bleeding. And for StarClan's sake, watch what you're putting into your mouth next time."

Frostpaw watched them go, then began to scratch a hole in the earth of the camp floor, meaning to bury the thorn so it couldn't do any more damage. While she was digging down, she heard a cat pad up behind her and meow, "Icewing, I want a word with you." Frostpaw recognized Cloverfoot's voice; the ShadowClan deputy didn't sound pleased.

"Okay, I'm listening." That was Icewing, as calm and polite as usual.

"I believe some cat put that thorn in the piece of prey, and then made sure my warrior would get it," Cloverfoot meowed.

"Don't you think that's a bit unlikely?" Icewing asked, her voice still mild.

"No, I don't!" Cloverfoot snapped. "I know very well there's a group of RiverClan cats here who are plotting against

ShadowClan. Don't you dare deny it!"

By now Frostpaw's ears were twitching. She concentrated on digging far deeper than she really needed to, and hoped that neither of the senior she-cats was paying her any attention.

"I wouldn't dream of denying it," Icewing responded. "I know perfectly well that something is going on, but there isn't much I can do about it. They're organizing behind my back. Believe me, Cloverfoot, I'm keeping my eyes and ears open. Meanwhile, the best thing you can do is warn your warriors to be on the alert."

Cloverfoot let out a snort and stalked off. Frostpaw dropped the thorn into the hole and patted the soil down neatly on top of it. Her mind was racing. *Some RiverClan cats are plotting against ShadowClan . . . and they're not above hurting ShadowClan cats.* This was a new problem. Could she justify keeping her vision secret? Or would revealing it cause even more chaos? Would it push the tension in the camp toward violence?

*What am I going to do?*

As she cleaned the soil from her forepaws, Frostpaw spotted Splashtail sitting alone just outside the warriors' den. *Should I talk to him?* she wondered. *Can I really trust him?*

Then Frostpaw told herself that she was being mouse-brained to hesitate. Splashtail was a young cat, not much older than she was, so he couldn't seriously have any plans to be made Clan leader. He had always been on her side, too. Still, Frostpaw reflected, if she told him about her vision, he would be convinced that he had been right all along: that she was truly meant to be a medicine cat. And that would mean they couldn't be mates.

*But I need to talk to some cat. I trust Splashtail, and he'll help me work out what to do.*

Her mind made up, Frostpaw felt relieved as she bounded across the camp to Splashtail's side. He had always been her friend; he might be the only cat she could trust. She didn't have to deal with this alone.

When she reached Splashtail, dipping her head in response to his friendly greeting, Frostpaw made sure that no cat could overhear them. She even stuck her head into the warriors' den, to be certain that no cat was drowsing inside. She was especially careful that Cloverfoot and the other ShadowClan warriors staying in the camp were nowhere to be seen.

"Why all the secrecy?" Splashtail asked, his eyes glimmering with amusement.

"There's something I have to tell you," Frostpaw mewed. "Something very important."

Splashtail blinked at her, a pleased expression spreading over his face. "You know you can tell me anything," he responded. "Any decision you make, I'll support you."

Leaning close to him, Frostpaw began to tell Splashtail about her vision. "I was fishing, staring down into the water," she meowed. "And then . . . suddenly I wasn't there anymore."

Splashtail frowned, looking puzzled. "What do you mean?"

"I don't know how to explain it," Frostpaw went on. "I wasn't by the stream; I was on our territory, not far from the ravine where we found Reedwhisker's body. And—you're not going to believe this, Splashtail—I was inside another cat."

"You were *what*?" Splashtail gasped, staring at her. "How is that even possible?"

"I don't know," Frostpaw replied. "I only know that's what happened. I was inside another cat, looking out of their eyes, and they were carrying me along, heading for the ravine. And then I saw Reedwhisker. He was alive still, hunting, and then . . ." Her voice choked and she had to take a breath before she went on. "Then the cat who was carrying me attacked him, and flung him over the edge of the ravine."

She paused for Splashtail to respond, but at first her Clanmate said nothing, only looking at her with eyes stretched wide and jaws gaping. After a few heartbeats he gave his pelt a shake. "You saw . . . ," he began in a hoarse whisper, then let his voice die away again.

"Reedwhisker fought back," Frostpaw went on, "but he wasn't trying hard. I thought that he recognized the cat and was too shocked to defend himself properly. Then the edge of the ravine crumbled away, and he fell."

"And what happened then?" Splashtail asked, finding his voice again. "Was that the end of it?"

Frostpaw shook her head. "No. The other cat—the one I was inside—left me there, and I was myself again. And then Reedwhisker reappeared, and his fur was full of stars! He told me there was a darkness in RiverClan. That was when I found myself back beside the stream, with Harelight scolding me for daydreaming."

"That's . . . amazing," Splashtail commented when she

finished. He seemed to be recovering from the shock of hearing Frostpaw's story, gazing at her with a look of intense interest. "This cat that you say was . . . carrying you. Did you see them?"

Frostpaw shook her head. "No, I told you, I was *inside* them."

"But you might have seen their forepaws. Or part of their chest fur. Enough to know the color of their pelt or the size of their claws."

That was true, Frostpaw thought. She concentrated hard, trying to remember, but in the end she had to shake her head again. "I was so scared, I don't think I noticed."

"And you say Reedwhisker recognized this cat?" Splashtail continued.

"He seemed to," Frostpaw replied. "And he wasn't fighting well, as if he wanted to defend himself, but without hurting his attacker. I thought maybe the cat was a Clanmate." Her voice shook as she finished. "One of us."

"Oh, come on!" Splashtail protested. "It doesn't make sense for a *RiverClan* cat to have attacked him. Maybe it was a cat he knew from another Clan, or a rogue. There are plenty of cats out there who would like to weaken RiverClan! ShadowClan, for a start."

"No," Frostpaw declared. "I could see it in Reedwhisker's eyes. This was a cat he knew well. He never saw the attack coming."

Splashtail nodded slowly, as if he was accepting her reasoning at last. "You could be right. But are you *sure*? I believe what you're telling me, but well . . . you thought you were having visions before, and then you decided they were just your imagination. How do you know it was really Reedwhisker showing you this from StarClan?"

Bright leaf-fall sunshine covered the camp, but for Frostpaw it might as well have been the darkest day of leaf-bare.

"I'm sure," she replied. "I wish I weren't."

"If you're having a real vision now," Splashtail mewed thoughtfully, "then maybe your other visions were real, too. Maybe we should go back to Owlnose. Surely he would agree to be leader if he knew StarClan had *really* chosen him."

Frostpaw bit back a hiss of annoyance. *Hasn't he understood anything I've been telling him?* "Those visions *weren't* real," she insisted. "But this one was. I can't describe it, but they're different. I'm *sure*, Splashtail."

"But if this was a false vision as well," Splashtail went on, without paying attention to her assurance, "and you tell the Clan, who knows what trouble it could cause? Every cat might panic, and that would make things worse in RiverClan. We're already suffering. Or maybe they won't believe you, after you changed your mind and started your warrior training."

"I'm sure it was a real vision this time," Frostpaw repeated. "Now that I've had one, I'm more certain than ever that the others *weren't* real. This was so much clearer; I was actually *there* when Reedwhisker was killed."

Splashtail licked one forepaw and drew it over his ear. "You'll still have trouble convincing the rest of the Clan," he pointed out.

"I know," Frostpaw admitted. "And I'm not sure what good it will do to tell them. It's not like I have any idea who was behind Reedwhisker's murder. And you're right, Splashtail, that things are difficult in RiverClan just now. I don't want every cat suspecting each other."

Splashtail was silent for a few heartbeats, deep in thought. "Is there a medicine cat you can talk to about this?" he asked.

"Not Mothwing," Frostpaw mewed instantly.

"No, you need a cat who knows about visions," Splashtail agreed. "It's so important for RiverClan to find a medicine cat that you'll need to have some cat backing you up. And maybe they could help you learn more about what StarClan wants from you."

"That's a really good idea!" Frostpaw instantly felt more cheerful. *I knew I was right to confide in Splashtail!*

"So is there any cat?" Splashtail prompted her.

Frostpaw thought for a moment, letting the other medicine cats pad through her mind. Puddleshine and Shadowsight had both been kind to her, but ShadowClan was too close to the problem. Alderheart was kind, too, but Frostpaw admitted to herself that she was a bit scared of Jayfeather, and she couldn't tell one without the other. The same went for Frecklewish and Fidgetflake, who had come to RiverClan to help Owlnose get his nine lives, and had seen what a mess everything was. *That just leaves WindClan. . . .*

"I could ask Whistlepaw, the WindClan medicine-cat apprentice," she suggested at last. "She was always friendly to me when we met at Gatherings and the half-moon meetings. And she's been training longer, so she knows more about StarClan."

"But she's an apprentice," Splashtail objected. "Does she

know *enough*? Why not Kestrelflight?"

"I think Whistlepaw has enough experience," Frostpaw responded. "Besides, it might be better to talk to an apprentice rather than a full medicine cat. I don't want to bring the Clan leaders into this—at least not yet—and the full medicine cats would probably insist on telling their leaders. But I think Whistlepaw would be willing to keep it secret, at least for now."

"Okay, that might work," Splashtail agreed, his eyes gleaming with approval. "So how do you want to do it?"

Frostpaw let herself imagine walking into the WindClan camp and asking to speak to their medicine-cat apprentice. But she wasn't a medicine cat herself anymore, so she didn't have the right to do that. Harestar or Crowfeather would be sure to demand an explanation.

"It will have to be done secretly," she meowed.

Splashtail nodded. "That means at night."

For a couple of heartbeats Frostpaw quailed inwardly at the thought of leaving the safety of her camp and trekking across WindClan's moors in the dark. Then she remembered that only a day had passed since the Gathering, and if the sky was clear there would be bright moonlight.

"Okay, I can manage that," she meowed. "I'll sneak along the lakeshore past the horseplace, and then head up the hill to WindClan's camp. With any luck, I'll be able to persuade whichever cat is guarding the camp to fetch Whistlepaw out to speak to me in private."

"And if she thinks you've had a real vision?" Splashtail asked.

"Then tomorrow I'll tell the rest of RiverClan," Frostpaw replied.

"It's a good plan." Splashtail rested his tail on Frostpaw's shoulder and looked deep into her eyes. "You should be careful, though," he added. "There's so much tension between the Clans just now, you wouldn't want to run into any cat unexpectedly."

"I will be," Frostpaw promised, warmed by the young tom's concern for her.

*Tonight,* she decided. *Tonight I'll go to WindClan.*

# CHAPTER 20

*Sitting beside the fresh-kill pile in* the ShadowClan camp, Sunbeam nibbled reluctantly at a frog. She hadn't eaten that day, but she still didn't have much of an appetite. Her belly was roiling with nervousness, because this was the day of Nightheart's third task, the task that would decide whether he was allowed to stay in ShadowClan.

Sunbeam would have been anxious enough if that was all. But when she'd woken that morning, she had found Nightheart missing from the warriors' den, and now, with sunhigh approaching, there was still no sign of him. Before this, Nightheart had never left camp without telling her, and his absence now felt terribly wrong.

Worries kept racing through Sunbeam's head like startled mice. She managed to choke down a couple of bites of her frog, and looked up as Tigerstar strode across the camp to halt by her side. Berryheart padded along at his shoulder.

*What if Berryheart said something to him that scared him off?* Sunbeam wondered, glancing at her mother as if she could read her intentions from her expression or the way she held herself. *Or what if he had second thoughts, and decided he would be happier in ThunderClan after all?*

She remembered how worried Nightheart had looked at the end of the Gathering, and how he had gone to talk to his sister as the cats were leaving. Later they had talked about that, and he had assured Sunbeam that he was committed to her, and to ShadowClan.

*But what if he changed his mind?*

"Nightheart's task is set to begin in a few moments," Berryheart announced, with a glance up at the sun. "So where is he?"

Sunbeam forced down another mouthful. "He . . . he left camp to take a walk," she responded. "He said it would help him to get energized."

"Hmm . . ." Berryheart looked as if she didn't believe a word that her daughter was meowing.

"Well, in that case," Tigerstar suggested, "maybe we should head for the place where the task will happen."

Berryheart paused as if she wanted to object, and declare that Nightheart had failed as soon as the last moments before sunhigh slid away. "All right. It's not far," she agreed at last. "Just outside the camp. Nightheart will be able to follow our scent trail."

She led the way out into the forest and through the pines as far as the other side of the Twoleg path. Tigerstar walked beside her, and Sunbeam joined her Clanmates who were crowding after them. Their glowing eyes and quivering whiskers told her how eager they were to see Nightheart tackle his final challenge.

*Eager to see him succeed . . . or eager to see him fail?* she wondered.

Berryheart came to a stop at the foot of a tall pine tree. The rest of the Clan gathered around in a ragged circle, but there was still no sign of Nightheart.

"You're sure he's coming?" Berryheart meowed, turning to Sunbeam.

"Of course I'm sure!" Sunbeam declared, though with every moment that passed it was less true.

Her belly was churning harder than ever. She wondered once again whether Nightheart was abandoning her. *But why would he? We were getting along so well. . . .* And even if he had changed his mind, surely he would have told her, not just disappeared without even a word of good-bye.

*What if something has happened to him?* Sunbeam felt as if her anxiety were going to pull her apart like a piece of prey fought over by a pack of rogues. She could imagine him trapped under a rock, or dangling from a branch somewhere in the forest, or swept away and drowned in the lake.

*What could keep him away when he knows how important this is?*

Sunbeam kept catching her mother's eye, and could see that Berryheart seemed almost satisfied, as if she had known this would happen, or at least was pleased it had. Unable to go on looking at her, Sunbeam turned her head away.

"Well, Berryheart, while we're waiting," Tigerstar meowed, "why don't you explain to the rest of us what the task is?"

Berryheart gave the Clan leader a sharp look. Sunbeam guessed that she had been about to announce that Nightheart had failed, and she wasn't pleased that there was an extra delay.

"Down that tunnel," Berryheart began, waving her tail at a yawning gap that opened up among the pine roots, "there are a couple of rats nesting. Nightheart must go down there and fight them off. Then he must catch three pieces of prey. And lastly, he must climb this tree and collect one egg from that pigeon's nest up there. If he can do all that, and bring the egg back unbroken, then he can be a ShadowClan cat."

Sunbeam stared at her mother, shocked, while gasps came from the rest of the assembled cats. Even for Berryheart, that was such a difficult task, with so many different parts. She knew her mother wanted Nightheart to fail, and now she had made it almost inevitable that he would.

*If he even shows up.*

"That's really three tasks, isn't it?" Tigerstar asked, with a doubtful look at Berryheart.

Sunbeam felt a sudden hope that her Clan leader might insist on changing the challenge, or dropping one of the sections. But the hope died almost at once as Berryheart responded.

"It's similar to Fringewhisker's second task," she mewed, with a dismissive wave of her tail.

"It feels awfully difficult, though," some cat objected from the crowd.

"Difficult is the *point*," Berryheart insisted. "This is Night-heart's *last task* before joining ShadowClan. How many more times do I have to say that it shouldn't be easy! He has to *earn* his place among us. ShadowClan cats are strong, and swift hunters, and good, agile climbers. If Nightheart is meant to be one of us, he can do it. Provided he bothers to turn up," she added, echoing Sunbeam's thought.

A long, awkward moment of silence followed Berryheart's

words. Glancing up at her Clanmates, Sunbeam spotted Light-leap and Blazefire giving her pitying looks. Her fur grew hot with embarrassment, and she fixed her gaze on the ground.

Frustration was swelling inside her as the moments slid past. *What is Nightheart doing?* Even if he still intended to meet his last challenge, he had to know how humiliating it would be for her, that he would show up so late. It was as if he didn't care.

"Tigerstar, it's obvious that—" Berryheart began.

At the same moment Sunbeam heard the rustling sound of a cat racing through pine needles. Nightheart appeared from the direction of the camp, hurtling along with his belly fur brushing the ground and his tail streaming out behind him. Murmurs of surprise rippled through the assembled cats.

Nightheart skidded to a halt beside Sunbeam. "Sorry!" he panted. "I went out to clear my head, and then I followed your scents here. Is this where my task will be?"

With a disappointed twitch of her whiskers, Berryheart began explaining the challenge to him. "You need to go down this tunnel." She gestured to it with her tail. "A couple of rats live there, and you have to fight them."

"Okay, I can do that." Nightheart sounded confident.

"Then you need to catch three pieces of prey."

Nightheart's eyes widened and his ears twitched up. Sunbeam could see that he was surprised that there was a second part to the task, when the first part was already difficult.

"After that . . . ," Berryheart continued, "you see that pigeon's nest, high up in the pine tree? I want you to bring an egg down, unbroken. If you can do that, you can be a Shadow-Clan warrior."

Nightheart rolled his eyes, but to Sunbeam's relief he didn't make any kind of sarcastic comment. It wouldn't take much to convince Berryheart to add a fourth part to the task.

While her mother was speaking, Sunbeam kept trying to catch Nightheart's eye, hoping to get some sense of where he'd been, but when at last she managed to lock gazes with him, he looked distant, as if there were a barrier behind his eyes.

*It's just nerves,* Sunbeam tried to reassure herself.

She and Nightheart had trained together to make him as skillful as a ShadowClan cat could be, and he was ready. The task would be difficult, but there wasn't a single part of it that he couldn't do. Soon he would pass, and they would be able to begin their life together.

*I can't wait!* Sunbeam thought, surprised at how very important Nightheart had become to her over such a short time.

"Okay, get ready," Berryheart meowed to Nightheart. Turning to the crowd of watching cats, she added, "For this first part, no cat must help him, even if he struggles with the rats. If you do"—she let a hard gaze rest on Sunbeam— "he will fail the task."

Sunbeam returned her mother's glare. The warning meant nothing to her. If Nightheart was in serious danger, she would jump in to help him, no matter the cost.

Nightheart plunged into the gap among the pine roots, letting out a furious screech, as if he was daring the rats to come and fight him. The sound was followed by faint scrabbling and chittering, and after a few heartbeats a shriek of pain, abruptly cut off.

Sunbeam drew in a sharp breath. *Was that a rat, or was it Nightheart?*

A moment later the black tom reappeared, scrabbling backward into the open. He held the limp body of a rat in his jaws and tossed it aside at Berryheart's paws. He was dragging the second rat out with him, its fangs fastened just behind his shoulder.

Nightheart twisted and struggled in an attempt to throw the rat off, but it still clung to him, raking its claws across his chest and shoulder. He let out gasps of pain; blood was trickling from several wounds. Nightheart kept swiping at the rat, but its position made it hard for him to get full force behind his blows.

Finally, when Sunbeam was already bracing herself to intervene, Nightheart let himself go limp and thumped down on top of the rat. Now that it was pinned beneath him, he slashed at its eyes; with a wail of pain the rat let go and struggled out from underneath Nightheart. He staggered to his paws, gasping for breath, and watched the creature as it limped off into the trees.

"Do I need to kill it?" he asked.

Tigerstar replied before Berryheart had a chance to. "No, that looks like defeat to me."

Despair threatened to overwhelm Sunbeam as she gazed at Nightheart's pelt, glistening with blood. She wondered whether Berryheart had put the most dangerous part of the challenge first, so that Nightheart would be weakened for the two remaining tasks.

*I wouldn't put it past her. . . .*

"Okay, then, three pieces of prey." Nightheart gave a nod, breathing heavily, then pointed with his tail at the dead rat. Sunbeam thought he was deliberately trying to sound confident. "Can I count that one?"

Several *mrrows* of laughter came from the crowd of cats, though Sunbeam's belly cramped; Berryheart wouldn't tolerate Nightheart being disrespectful.

"Three *more* pieces of prey." Berryheart's voice was icy. "All different."

*That wasn't what she said at first,* Sunbeam thought. *Oh, Nightheart, don't annoy her any more. Do you* want *her to fail you?*

"Okay, you got it." Nightheart waved his tail and prowled off, deeper into the trees.

Sunbeam felt as if several seasons passed before Nightheart returned, dragging a squirrel. He laid it beside the rat, then disappeared again to return almost immediately with a sparrow.

When Nightheart left for the third time, he bounded off in the direction of the lake. Berryheart was shifting her paws impatiently, and Sunbeam wondered how long her mother would wait before she declared that Nightheart had failed this part of the task.

But not many heartbeats slipped by before Nightheart returned. This time his prey was a frog. "Will that do?" he asked as he dropped it beside the rest of his catch. He passed his tongue several times over his jaws, as if he was trying to get rid of an unpleasant taste; Sunbeam had yet to persuade him to enjoy frogs.

Berryheart looked as if she had accidentally swallowed crow-food. "It will," she meowed.

Nightheart dipped his head and turned to the pine tree, gazing up into the branches at the pigeon's nest. It was lodged many fox-lengths above the ground, precariously balanced on a flimsy branch that would never bear a cat's weight.

*I'd bet a month of dawn patrols that's exactly why Berryheart chose it.*

But Sunbeam knew that Nightheart had experienced this before, when she'd shown him the territory. He would find a stronger branch just above or below, and approach from there, as he had when they'd collected honey from the abandoned bees' nest.

Now Sunbeam's nervousness changed to excitement. Her heart was thumping so hard that she thought the whole Clan must be able to hear it. Nightheart had almost finished his tasks. He was almost a ShadowClan warrior.

For an instant Nightheart's gaze met hers, and Sunbeam could see the love for her glowing there. She felt warm from nose to tail-tip, thinking about the life they would have as soon as he finished. *We're finally going to be mates, and live together in ShadowClan forever!*

Nightheart leaped into the tree and clawed his way up the trunk, his muscles bunching and stretching strongly. But when he reached the flimsy branch that held the nest, he paused. *What is he doing?* Sunbeam waited for him to climb a little higher, to a thicker branch just above. Instead he stepped out onto the weak branch and dropped into a hunter's crouch.

Sunbeam heard the shocked intake of breath from her Clanmates around her. She was as surprised as any of them, sliding out her claws and digging them hard into the ground.

*He knows better than that!*

Berryheart, however, was following Nightheart's progress with a look of satisfaction. Sunbeam could see how pleased she was that her plan was working out.

Nightheart crept outward from the trunk until he was a couple of tail-lengths from the nest. The branch began to sway and creak ominously. Sunbeam knew it would never bear his weight once he ventured closer. She felt sick with fear for him; if Nightheart fell from such a high branch, he could be seriously hurt, or even killed.

"Go back, you stupid furball," she whispered. "Take the thicker branch!"

Instead of retreating, Nightheart made the worst possible decision. He lunged for the nest as if he could catch it before the branch broke. But he only knocked the nest free. There was a sickening crack as the branch gave way and everything—the nest, the branch, and Nightheart himself—began plummeting downward.

"No!" Sunbeam couldn't stifle her yowl.

Nightheart was falling, his body twisting and his legs flailing at the air. In the last few heartbeats before he crashed to the ground, he managed to snag his claws into a sturdier branch; he hung with his hind legs and his tail waving helplessly before he hauled himself to safety. The nest, however, slammed to the ground and all the eggs shattered. A dark hollow of disbelief opened up inside Sunbeam as she watched Nightheart look down at the wreckage and then sadly meet her gaze. Moons seemed to pass before he began climbing down the tree.

"Bad luck," Berryheart mewed as he leaped down the last tail-length and landed in front of her. "I'm afraid you've failed."

For all her sympathetic words, the brightness in Berry-heart's eyes told Sunbeam that she was pleased.

"I'm sorry." Nightheart dipped his head to Tigerstar and then to Sunbeam. "I really tried. But maybe I'm not meant to be a ShadowClan cat."

Tigerstar nodded in agreement, his expression regretful. "You made a valiant effort," he told Nightheart. "I would have been happy to welcome you into my Clan. But rules are rules. You must leave our territory now." He cast an understanding glance at Sunbeam and added, "Take all the time you need to say good-bye."

Nightheart dipped his head respectfully to the Clan leader, then padded over to Sunbeam. The rest of the Clan gathered to head back to camp, some of them aiming sympathetic looks at Sunbeam as they left.

"That was a really good try," Blazefire meowed, with a dip of his head to Nightheart. "No cat could have done better."

Sunbeam led Nightheart away from them, away from the ruins of the nest that showed so painfully the ruin of all her hopes.

Her head was whirling, and she felt as if the ground might give way under her paws. She still couldn't believe this was happening. She had been so sure that Nightheart would pass the tests, once he showed up to take them.

When she halted, Nightheart stood gazing at her, dejection in the droop of his head and his tail.

"What was *wrong* with you?" Sunbeam demanded, anger pushing aside the numbness of shock. "We practiced moving around in trees! You knew not to approach along the weaker branch. You're smarter than that, Nightheart. You fought those two rats!"

Nightheart stepped closer to her. Gazing into his eyes, she could see that he didn't look disappointed or frustrated, only sad and regretful. Sunbeam realized that what he had done was no mistake. So much emotion was shaking her, she wanted to crouch down with her paws over her ears and wail like a lost kit.

"You're really leaving, aren't you?" she challenged him. "You meant to leave me. You *wanted* to!"

Nightheart ran his tail along her back; she shuddered deeply at his touch. "I'm sorry . . . so sorry," he choked out. "I wish I could have told you. I *wanted* to, but there was no time—I only realized this morning. And I knew I had to fail the task. If I'd just left, every cat would have said it was because I didn't want to be with you anymore. And I do, Sunbeam, oh, I do. I care about you so much. This is the hardest thing I've ever had to face." He paused and gulped in air as if he had just surfaced from deep water. "But . . . I need to be in ThunderClan right now. I've had trouble with my kin and my former Clanmates, it's true. But they need me. And I think I've grown enough to finally be the warrior I've always wanted to be. When Dovewing took me to ThunderClan to say good-bye, she said that after a while, going to ThunderClan felt like just visiting any other place, because ShadowClan was home. I've tried hard to get there, but . . . I can't. Each time I go back, I feel it a little more strongly. *ThunderClan* is my home. I just wish . . . I wish I didn't have to leave you to get there."

Sunbeam lashed her tail furiously. "So you were just playing with me," she accused him. "*You* came to *my* Clan and made me care about you, Nightheart. I didn't ask you to do that!"

"I'm so sorry," Nightheart mewed. "I never expected to feel this way. I came to ShadowClan because I thought you were the best cat I'd ever met. I still do. But . . . ThunderClan needs me now, more than they ever have before. And I can't leave my Clan."

"I don't believe this," Sunbeam hissed. "All I've heard from you since we met is how ThunderClan misunderstands and disrespects you!"

"That's true," Nightheart admitted. "But . . . I think now I can make them see the warrior that I *am*, not the warrior that they expected me to be. I plan to stand up for myself more, to speak up when I feel misunderstood. It may not be perfect. But I realize how much I still care for my Clanmates. And I think I have to try."

Sunbeam took a deep breath; she felt as though anger and grief were tearing her apart. "If that's true," she whispered, "then I've nothing more to say to you. You broke my heart."

Nightheart blinked slowly. Sunbeam could tell that he was hurting, too, but she turned her back on him and stalked away before he could say any more.

*If he's not going to tell me he's staying—and how can he, now that he failed the task?—then it doesn't matter. I don't need to hear it.*

Berryheart was waiting for her at the side of the Twoleg path. Sunbeam braced herself for the inevitable gloating that Nightheart was finally leaving their Clan.

But, to her surprise, Berryheart's gaze was sympathetic, and when she spoke, she sounded sincerely concerned. "I'm so sorry, Sunbeam. I know you cared about him."

Sunbeam didn't reply, just let herself sink into her mother's comfort and compassion. It felt good.

"You know, you can't trust cats outside ShadowClan," Berryheart continued. "Better to stick with the cats we know."

Only that morning, talk like this would have infuriated Sunbeam. But now, as she pondered a future without the cat who'd stolen her heart, she couldn't help wondering whether her mother was right.

About everything.

# CHAPTER 21

❧

*Watching from behind a pine tree,* Nightheart saw Sunbeam meet with Berryheart on her way back to the ShadowClan camp. He could only imagine what they were saying, or how Berryheart would be turning Sunbeam against him.

*Like I haven't turned her against me all by myself.*

A wave of misery suddenly shook him from ears to tail-tip. *What have I done?* He couldn't shake off the pull he felt to go back to ThunderClan, but for the first time, he had a clear-eyed view of what he had given up. The bravest and most beautiful cat in all the Clans could have been his, forever, if only he hadn't thrown away his final task.

Nightheart began the long, lonely trek along the lakeshore, back to the ThunderClan border, only to halt as abruptly as if he had walked into a tree. *Will ThunderClan even take me back?* A chill ran through him from whiskers to tail as he realized that he didn't know. *What if I've made a huge mistake? I could end up as a rogue!*

He had expected that it would be hard to leave Sunbeam, but he hadn't been prepared for the empty, hollow feeling inside him as he wondered how he would face the next few days—no, the next few moons—without the only cat he felt had really understood him.

Going back to ThunderClan, Nightheart knew, would be returning to the Clan that had weighed him down with its expectations because of his kin. They had never seemed truly able to look past that to see *him*. It had been wonderfully freeing to be part of ShadowClan, where he was just another warrior. Except that Berryheart and her followers, he reminded himself, had seen him as an interloper.

But Nightheart knew that he had the power to make ThunderClan see him as he was. Bramblestar saw it, and Sorrelstripe saw it. He'd seen a flicker of recognition in Finchlight's and Squirrelflight's eyes, too. He was Nightheart, a ThunderClan warrior, and now he had to make them see that ThunderClan needed him. *But will they take me back?* he wondered. *Bayshine is still my friend, and I think Lilyheart would be on my side.* But his heart cramped with pain as he realized he couldn't be sure of his mother and his sister. *Even Squirrelflight might have objections.*

By the time Nightheart reached the ThunderClan border, the sun was going down. He crouched there to wait, feeling chilled by more than the stiff breeze as the scarlet light faded from the sky and the surface of the lake and twilight enfolded the forest.

At last the sound of rustling in the bushes and a wave of fresh ThunderClan scent alerted him to the arrival of the evening patrol. Cherryfall and Eaglewing emerged into the open and halted, exchanging a glance of surprise, as they spotted him.

"You again?" Eaglewing mewed.

"I suppose you have more important news to share with Bramblestar." Cherryfall's tone was teasing rather than hostile, but she still didn't sound welcoming.

"I do," Nightheart responded. "I want to rejoin Thunder-Clan."

Cherryfall's tail curled up with amusement. "So you failed your tasks in ShadowClan? Suddenly being part of Firestar's Clan isn't so terrible after all?"

Nightheart considered telling her that he had failed his final task on purpose, but he knew that would make it look as if he didn't truly love Sunbeam. He didn't want to say anything that would embarrass her.

He met Cherryfall's gaze evenly. "I see things differently now," he meowed.

Cherryfall let out a derisive snort.

"Bramblestar ought to hear this, at least," Eaglewing pointed out. "You carry on with the patrol, Cherryfall, and I'll take Nightheart back to camp."

Cherryfall paused, then gave a curt nod. "Okay."

Nightheart crossed the border and followed Eaglewing through the undergrowth in the direction of the camp. As soon as they were out of earshot of Cherryfall, Eaglewing turned to him.

"Don't listen to her," she murmured. "It's brave of you to come back. You must have known that cats would react like that."

"She was right about one thing," Nightheart confessed. "I did fail my final task."

Eaglewing blinked in surprise. "Really? I didn't expect that. You know, I've always thought there was more to you than what the Clan saw," she mewed. "Maybe now you'll have the chance to show them."

Her support raised Nightheart's spirits. "I feel like this is the place for me after all," he told her.

But Nightheart's new confidence didn't survive the trek through forest that should have been familiar to him and yet now was suddenly alien. His apprehension about his Clan's reaction, his fear of being driven out to live Clanless, began to bubble up again.

Emerging behind Eaglewing from the thorn tunnel, Nightheart spotted Alderheart and Jayfeather sorting herbs outside their den. Alderheart looked up and gave Jayfeather a prod in the side. Jayfeather started, then opened his jaws to taste the air. "Great StarClan, not him again!" he exclaimed.

The sound of his voice alerted Stormcloud and Twigbranch, who were sharing prey beside the fresh-kill pile. Their heads swiveled in Nightheart's direction; Nightheart saw their surprised looks, but couldn't make out whatever it was that Twigbranch murmured to her companion.

By now more cats had emerged from the warriors' den and were heading toward him. Bumblestripe and Lionblaze were in the lead; Nightheart knew he couldn't expect a friendly welcome from them. He looked in vain for Sparkpelt or Finchlight, and so far there was no sign of Squirrelflight.

Nightheart stood erect, trying to look confident, as his former Clanmates began to gather around. Their hostile glances and bristling fur told him he wasn't welcome.

"What are you doing here?" Lionblaze demanded.

"Yeah, go back to the pine forest!" Bumblestripe hissed. "We don't need ShadowClan rejects in our camp!"

Molewhisker's lips curled back in disgust. "You stink of ShadowClan!"

Eaglewing gave Nightheart a regretful nod and headed out again to rejoin her patrol. Nightheart braced himself and faced the crowd of hostile cats.

"I need to speak to Bramblestar," he announced, "or whoever is in charge."

At first no cat spoke. Nightheart wondered if that meant that Bramblestar had already stepped down as leader. He swallowed apprehension—would Squirrelflight would have the last word on whether to take him back?

"You'll be waiting a while, then," Shellfur responded at last. "He and Squirrelflight have been talking in Bramblestar's den since sunhigh."

Nightheart could guess what that meant, but he tried to look surprised. "Is that so? What about?"

Every cat shrugged or exchanged bewildered glances; clearly none of them knew.

A moment later, Nightheart spotted Sparkpelt thrusting her way through the crowd to stand in front of him. "What are you doing here?" To Nightheart's relief her tone wasn't angry; she sounded as if she really wanted to know. "You're not . . . you must just be here to . . . ?"

"To rejoin," Nightheart replied simply. "Or to ask to rejoin. I came because I realized I belong here."

His mother's eyes softened at his words. "Really?" she mewed, unable to hide how touched she was. "That's all I've wanted to hear, so badly!"

*I was so wrong about her,* Nightheart realized, feeling a pulse of pure joy pass through him. *I thought she was angry because I'd betrayed the Clan . . . but she was hurt because she missed me!*

"I always belonged here." Nightheart found it hard to choke the words out. "I will always care about ThunderClan more than any other Clan. I tried and tried to convince myself that I belonged in ShadowClan, because the cat I love is there. But I don't. My kin are here. Speaking of which . . . ," he added, "what's happening with Bramblestar?"

Sparkpelt's expression darkened. "By now every cat must know what things are like between Bramblestar and Squirrelflight," she replied. "It's probably another fight, but I'm sure they'll show themselves soon."

Nightheart thought that his mother was trying too hard to seem confident. He could share her pain; not only were Bramblestar and Squirrelflight her Clan leader and deputy, but they were also her parents.

To his surprise, Sparkpelt went on gazing at him for a moment, then leaned forward nervously and nuzzled his shoulder. "I'm glad you're here," she murmured. "And . . . I'm sorry I was so hard on you that you felt you had to leave. I feel I never got it quite right, being your mother."

"It wasn't all your fault . . . ," Nightheart responded, beginning to feel thoroughly embarrassed.

"I wasn't there when you were younger," Sparkpelt

continued, stroking her tail along his side. "And I feel guilty for that. I suppose I was hard on you because I was hard on myself. I thought that maybe if I pushed you harder . . . maybe I could make up for all the time I wasn't there. But it didn't work, did it? It only pushed you away."

Nightheart didn't know what to say. "I . . . I only wanted you to see me for who I was. *Nightheart*, not Flameheart."

Sparkpelt met his eye. "I see you, Nightheart," she purred. "I promise to do better this time."

Nightheart felt his throat burning as he forced the words out. "Thank you."

He spotted Bayshine approaching and looked up, thankful to be distracted from the intense encounter with his mother; his friend's fur was bushing out with excitement, and yet his eyes were wary.

"I knew you would figure it out sooner or later," Bayshine mewed. "You're ThunderClan, the greatest Clan there is!"

"I am, Bayshine," Nightheart agreed. "You were right all along."

Finchlight padded up and touched noses with Nightheart, then stood back and gazed at him with her head tilted. "What about Sunbeam?" she asked. "Weren't you leaving to be her mate?"

Another pang of grief at what he was losing shook Nightheart to the tips of his claws, but he forced himself to speak calmly. "That won't be happening now, but I still care a lot for her. Sunbeam is a very special cat."

Unexpectedly, Finchlight pressed her muzzle to his shoulder and let out a sympathetic purr. Nightheart began to hope that now that he had returned they could be friends again.

"Maybe you'll find a special cat in ThunderClan now," Sparkpelt suggested.

"No," Finchlight put in before Nightheart could respond. "Nightheart should take his time. Hearts don't heal so quickly."

Nightheart looked at his sister in surprise; she had spoken as if she had experienced loss herself. *How many things about my sister are there that I don't know?* he asked himself. When he'd lived in ThunderClan before, he had always been focused on his own concerns. *Maybe that can change now.*

Nightheart realized that the cats around him were shifting, turning away, and muttering comments among themselves. He looked up to see that Bramblestar and Squirrelflight had emerged from the leader's den and were standing side by side on the Highledge.

"Let all cats old enough to catch their own prey join here beneath the Highledge for a Clan meeting!" Squirrelflight yowled.

Most of the cats were already out in the clearing. Nightheart spotted Daisy emerging from the nursery, while Jayfeather and Alderheart turned away from the herbs they had been sorting and sat side by side in front of the brambles that screened their den. The elders slipped out from beneath their hazel bush; Nightheart could make out Cloudtail's white pelt glimmering in the twilight.

"We have an announcement to make," Squirrelflight declared when all the cats had assembled. She stepped back, dipping her head to Bramblestar.

Bramblestar padded forward until he stood at the very edge of the Highledge. "I have decided to give up my leadership," he told his Clan.

He paused, but not a single sound greeted his words; every cat was staring at him as if they couldn't believe what they were hearing, and were too stunned to respond.

"Squirrelflight and I will go to the Moonpool tomorrow night to announce our plan to StarClan," Bramblestar continued. "I don't know for certain what will happen, but I expect that Squirrelflight will become Squirrelstar. And I can think of no cat more suited to lead ThunderClan."

At last the cats on the ground below him erupted into a turmoil of gasps, yowls, and hisses.

"What? He's going to renounce his leadership, after all he's been through?"

"That's probably *why* he's renouncing his leadership."

"But Firestar chose him! How can he say he knows more than Firestar?"

The comments and debate raged all around Nightheart, who stood bewildered, hardly recognizing the Clan he had come home to. Glancing at his sister, he saw her give a firm nod, as if she knew that was the right decision. Sparkpelt, however, simply looked stunned.

Eventually Molewhisker raised his voice to be heard above the rest of the Clan. "StarClan gave you nine lives, Bramblestar!" he yowled. "How can you be so bold as to tell them they were wrong?"

"I'm humbled by StarClan's faith in me," Bramblestar

replied, looking down at his warrior with understanding in his amber eyes. "But I don't have that faith in myself any longer. I've seen too much in the past few moons . . . too much fighting, too much bloodshed. I'm not the cat I was before, and I cannot lead like I once did. I want only peace, and that's not the right frame of mind for any leader, because a Clan must be willing to protect our kits and elders, and stand proud among the other Clans."

"But what will you do?" Flipclaw questioned. "Are you going to leave us?"

"No. I'll retire to the elders' den, if StarClan agrees," Bramblestar meowed.

"It is possible for a leader to renounce their leadership," Squirrelflight pointed out. "Rowanstar and Pinestar did it."

"And Rowanstar's abdication destroyed ShadowClan," Twigbranch objected. "At least until Tigerstar returned to become leader."

"But ShadowClan didn't have Squirrelflight," Bramblestar responded, with a glowing look at his mate and deputy. "She is an amazing warrior, brave and resourceful, and she loves her Clan; she will be a remarkable leader. She already led ThunderClan when I was trapped in the Dark Forest. Now she will keep ThunderClan safe and together."

For a moment utter silence spread throughout the clearing. It was Bayshine who broke it, yowling out, "Bramblestar! Nightheart is back!"

As all eyes turned toward him, including Bramblestar's and Squirrelflight's, Nightheart felt his fur grow hot with embarrassment. He wished that he could sink into the earth of the camp floor like a drop of rain.

Bramblestar's gaze was warm with welcome, but Squirrelflight fixed Nightheart with a wary look. "Why?" she asked.

Nightheart braced himself, knowing that he had to speak out boldly. "I admit I failed my last task in ShadowClan," he meowed. "But that's not my only reason for coming back. I've realized that I belong here. I am, and I've always been, a ThunderClan cat at heart."

Lionblaze let out a snort, half mocking, half disdainful. "Of course you realized you were meant to be in Thunder-Clan once that was your only option!"

"But it's true," Nightheart insisted.

"I believe him." Sparkpelt stepped up to stand at Nightheart's side, her fur brushing his. "I think that we can see his place in our Clan at last. And ThunderClan will be lucky to have him."

Nightheart blinked, touched that his mother was standing up for him. "Thank you," he breathed.

But not every cat agreed with Sparkpelt.

"We don't have to take him back!" Bumblestripe yowled, glaring at Nightheart. "Why should we? He didn't want us when he visited only this morning!"

Squirrelflight glanced at Bramblestar, who stepped back with a wave of his tail. "It should be your decision," he declared. "This will be your Clan."

A shiver passed through Nightheart from ears to tail-tip as Squirrelflight looked him over, her green gaze seeming to penetrate his fur as far as his very heart. A heavy weight gathered in his belly as he remembered how he and the Clan deputy had never really liked each other, and now his fate was in her paws.

"I hope this whole experience has taught you to communicate thoughtfully," she meowed. "Not to just storm off when things don't go your way. And I hope you can appreciate the many gifts your Clan and your kin have given you."

Nightheart ducked his head, his conscience pricked by her words. "I can," he admitted. "I can see ThunderClan for what it is, and I want ThunderClan to see me for who I am. I have great love for this Clan, the Clan of my ancestors, and I want to be the best warrior I can be."

Squirrelflight paused for several heartbeats before she responded. "Very well, you can rejoin us," she meowed at last. "But you have heard that many cats are not giving you a warm welcome. I hope you will prove them all wrong, and show them how badly you want to be here."

Sparkpelt and Finchlight instantly let out purrs of relief, and pressed up on either side of Nightheart, covering his ears with affectionate licks.

"Thank you, Squirrelflight. Thank you from the bottom of my heart." Nightheart stood erect and tried to hide how his legs had begun to shake. "I promise I'll do exactly that. I will make my Clan proud of me."

# CHAPTER 22

*That night, Frostpaw lay awake in* the apprentices' den, watching the moonlight as it crept through the entrance. Mistpaw and Graypaw were both curled up in their nests, their breathing gently stirring the sprigs of fern in their bedding.

At last, when the moon was high, Frostpaw stealthily rose and slid out into the open. The camp lay quiet under the wash of silver light. Minnowtail, the cat on watch, was a gray-and-white shadow across the camp. Her back was turned to Frostpaw as she kept her gaze fixed on the wider territory, alert for intruders.

Frostpaw took a deep breath, squared her shoulders, and headed out.

The night was cold, with frost furring every stone and every blade of grass. When she came to the stream, she padded alongside until she reached the log that stretched across to the opposite bank.

*No swimming tonight,* she thought, fluffing out her fur against the chill.

But as Frostpaw ventured out onto the log, she realized that clouds had drifted up to cover the moon, making it hard for her to see where she was putting her paws. Almost at once she felt herself slip on the mossy surface, and let out a cry of alarm as she toppled into the stream. For a couple of heart-beats she flailed helplessly until her head broke the surface and she could strike out for the opposite bank.

"Fox-dung!" she hissed.

Now the icy water took her breath away, but she forced her-self to splash through it to the far side. After hauling herself onto the bank, she dived into a clump of long grass, hiding herself in case any of her Clanmates had decided on a night hunting patrol.

Once she was sure she was out of sight, Frostpaw gave her-self a good shake, scattering water droplets everywhere, then tried to groom the remaining water out of her fur. But it was taking too long; she knew that every heartbeat she stayed there, close to the camp, she risked being discovered.

Frostpaw was well aware that this mission had to be a secret. If her Clanmates discovered her, there was only one way she could explain why she was sneaking out of camp. She would have to confess about her vision of Reedwhisker's death, and she wasn't ready to do that yet—not until she had discussed it with Whistlepaw. She only hoped that she would agree to help her without alerting the other medicine cats.

As she rose to her paws, ready to go on, Frostpaw thought she heard a sound behind her, close to the river she had just crossed. *Was that a paw step? Is some cat there?*

But when she turned around, she couldn't see anything but the lush vegetation on the bank of the stream. The only sound was the gentle gurgle of water running over the pebbles.

*I'm imagining things,* Frostpaw told herself. *Which cat would be swimming the stream at night if they didn't have to?*

She was shivering hard; she knew she had to start moving quickly and hope that Whistlepaw could help her warm up. Giving her pelt one last shake, she set off, creeping along the lakeshore through RiverClan territory.

The Twoleg dens of the horseplace soon loomed up in front of her, darker than the night. Her fur rose along her spine at the strange smells and the huge, menacing shadows.

As Frostpaw crept past, trying to make herself small and inconspicuous, the drumming of huge paws sounded from somewhere in the darkness. A high-pitched bellowing noise came from high above her head.

Frostpaw didn't wait to find out what made the sounds. *A horse? It must be huge!* Her heart pounding, she fled, her muscles bunching and stretching as she forced out every last scrap of speed. She didn't stop until she reached the small Thunderpath that stretched down to the lake and another of the weird Twoleg halfbridges.

Pausing at the edge of the hard black stuff, Frostpaw gazed around cautiously for monsters. She picked up a trace of their acrid scent, but she couldn't hear any growling, or see their fearsome glowing eyes cutting through the darkness.

*It seems okay. . . .* But Frostpaw knew that Twolegs and monsters were unpredictable. Just when a cat thought it was safe to move, they would pop up out of nowhere. *Like that horse.*

Trying to push away her fears, Frostpaw reflected that she

had never made this journey alone before. She had been this way with Mothwing, on their way to the Moonpool, and once with Curlfeather, a trip that had ended with the disastrous dog attack. Back then they had both supported her, not only on the journey, but in everything. Now she was completely alone.

*That's enough, flea-brain!* Frostpaw scolded herself. *What are you, a kit? You won't be alone once you get to the WindClan camp and find Whistlepaw. Just believe that, and pull yourself together!*

Stiffening her resolve, Frostpaw knew that she couldn't stand all night dithering beside the Thunderpath. With a last glance around, she scuttled across, and paused on the far side to catch her breath.

As she moved off again, she thought once more that she heard paw steps behind her. But when she whipped around, hoping to catch a glimpse of any cat who might be following her, the shore and the lake lay silent and empty.

*I must be imagining things.*

The swell of moorland rose up in front of her. As she began to climb, crossing the WindClan border markers, Frostpaw was acutely conscious that she was on a rival Clan's territory now. She pricked her ears, a thrill of tension running through her, and she fought the urge to flee back to RiverClan as fast as she could. The evening patrol should have passed—the markers smelled fresh—but it was still possible that Wind-Clan cats would be around somewhere.

*I can see how WindClan got its name,* Frostpaw thought as she toiled upward. The wind was so cold here on the exposed hillside, not like her home in RiverClan at all. It pressed her fur to her sides, while the stronger gusts almost carried her off her paws. And, as the wind rose, the clouds began to break up, and the moon shone out fitfully; Frostpaw realized that her pale gray pelt must be visible for fox-lengths, and there was so little cover out here on the open moor.

She tried to hurry, but she was freezing cold, still shivering from her dunking in the stream. Her added haste made her clumsy, and as she scrambled over a rocky outcrop, her paw slipped and she knocked a stone off a steep ledge. It landed on the ground below with a thud.

Immediately a cat's voice rang out. "What was that?"

Frostpaw thought her heart would stop. She pressed herself down among the rocks and peered out to see Breezepelt standing only a couple of tail-lengths below. Two or three other cats were with him, only dark shapes in the shifting light. Strong WindClan scent wafted upward.

The rocks weren't big enough to hide behind; if Breezepelt looked up, he was bound to see her. So far he hadn't spotted her, but he was so close that Frostpaw almost gave herself up, confessing that she had come to see Whistlepaw. But then she remembered that she wasn't a medicine cat anymore; she had no excuse to be on another Clan's territory.

*Splashtail said that tensions are high among the Clans just now—and he's right.*

Frostpaw could imagine all too clearly what would happen if Breezepelt's patrol caught a RiverClan warrior sneaking onto their territory in the middle of the night. They were bound to see it as a hostile act.

*How can I explain that I'm not a spy?*

She knew that she couldn't confess what she wanted to talk to Whistlepaw about. Breezepelt and the others would think she had bees in her brain, or that things in RiverClan were worse than any cat had realized.

*Did I have bees in my brain, thinking I could do this?* Frostpaw saw how mouse-brained it was to sneak onto another Clan's territory in the dead of night, alone. She could imagine exactly what her mentor, Harelight, would say. But then Frostpaw reminded herself that she had no choice. She needed help, and the only cat who could give it to her was Whistlepaw.

*I have to see this through.*

Frostpaw forced herself to take a few deep breaths as she crouched in her scanty cover, immobile so as not to alert Breezepelt. He and the rest of his patrol were clustered together, exchanging murmured words too softly for her to make out. She heard some cat sniffing the air, and cringed, expecting that her scent would give her away.

But after a few moments Breezepelt announced, "Maybe a rabbit," and the patrol headed off down the hill.

Frostpaw drew a long, shuddering breath. Breezepelt hadn't looked in her direction after all, and she guessed that the stream had washed off at least some of her scent.

As soon as she was sure they were gone, Frostpaw leaped to her paws and streaked off in the other direction, up to the moorland ridge where she hoped she would find WindClan's camp.

*I'm close—so close!*

Strong WindClan scent was flowing down from the heights; with every paw step Frostpaw took, it grew stronger. Before she reached the top of the hill, she spotted a huge hollow gouged out of the ground; boulders were scattered across the middle, and a thick barrier of gorse bushes surrounded it.

*That's the camp! Thank StarClan I've found it!*

Frostpaw began to approach more cautiously, not wanting to give her presence away until she was ready. Her heart was drumming in her chest, so hard that it hurt.

The WindClan scent grew stronger still, and another scent mingled with it. Frostpaw paused, trying to identify it. *Is that thyme?*

Then she spotted the clump of plants, still surviving in spite of the first frosts. She padded up to them and thrust her nose among the stems, sniffing the familiar scent. Gradually it calmed her, until her racing heart slowed and she could feel her muscles relaxing.

Straightening up again, Frostpaw turned eagerly toward the camp. She couldn't wait to see Whistlepaw again. It would be so good to talk—

*There it is again! Paw steps!*

Another scent, like WindClan and yet somehow different, floated up toward Frostpaw, as if another cat was approaching her from lower down the hill. She paused to look over her shoulder, but at the same moment something grabbed her from behind so that she couldn't turn her head. She let out a gasp of alarm.

"What—"

Hot pain bloomed across Frostpaw's throat, defeating all her efforts to cry out. She choked. Agony burned through her whole body as she collapsed into the clump of thyme.

*No! No* . . .

Frostpaw remembered her mother's last words: *Trust no cat.*

She struggled to turn her head to see who had attacked her, but her muscles wouldn't obey. Every scrap of strength was draining from her body. She could smell the reek of her own blood; her chest was soaked in it.

Her reeling senses picked up the same paw steps, fading now as her attacker ran away. Frostpaw felt like the whole moor was tilting, beginning to slide away, as darkness rose up like a massive wave and engulfed her.

# CHAPTER 23

❧

*The full moon bathed the Gathering* clearing in a pure silver light as Sunbeam, along with her Clanmates, pushed their way through the bushes and found places to sit around the Great Oak. Tigerstar leaped up into the branches to join the other leaders. Only ThunderClan was not present.

Looking around her, Sunbeam felt as if something was wrong, but she couldn't quite think what. *There's a cat missing....*

She was still trying to pin down what was troubling her when a powerful ThunderClan scent filled the air and the ThunderClan cats entered the clearing. But it wasn't Bramblestar who led them: It was Squirrelflight, her head raised proudly and her muscles rippling beneath her dark ginger fur as she leaped into the tree.

*But she can't be . . .* Sunbeam was deeply shocked, even more so because none of the cats around her had reacted or seemed to think that anything had changed.

Then Nightheart padded past her, and Sunbeam suddenly realized what had been wrong. *He should have been with me!*

"Nightheart!" she called, but the black tom didn't even turn his head.

Following hard on his paws was a cat Sunbeam couldn't remember ever having seen before: a beautiful pale tabby she-cat, with thick fur that the moonlight turned to dazzling silver. She sat beside Nightheart and leaned her head close to him; the two cats twined their tails together. The silver cat turned to face Sunbeam, opened a pair of astonishingly bright blue eyes, and looked her up and down disdainfully, from ears to paws and back again. Then she gave a tiny shrug and turned back to lick Nightheart's ear.

*No!* Sunbeam wanted to wail aloud, but the words choked in her throat. *Nightheart is mine!*

She sprang up, determined to shred the fur off the silver cat, not even caring that she would break the Gathering truce. But as she tried to launch herself across the clearing, her paws tangled in something soft, and she fell to the ground with a thump. She found herself in her own nest, her bedding scattered, and Pouncestep, whose nest was nearby, staring at her in surprise.

The pale sun of leaf-fall bathed the ShadowClan camp as Sunbeam stumbled out of the warriors' den. The day before, after Nightheart's departure, Dovewing had excused her from further duties, kindly suggesting she should rest. But now Sunbeam felt disoriented, as if her pelt didn't fit her anymore, and her head was filled with fog.

*Everything feels . . . wrong.*

All night her sleep had been filled with terrible dreams. In the worst of them, she had gone to the next Gathering and seen Nightheart there with a new mate—a Thunder-Clan mate. Now she looked around at her Clanmates and couldn't imagine being mates with any one of them. Her feelings for Blazefire had vanished like dew under the strong sun of greenleaf, and besides, he was her friend Lightleap's mate. Flaxfoot felt like a littermate to her, and was always explaining things to her as if she were a kit. As for Whorlpelt, he was one of Berryheart's group, and she couldn't trust him. There was no tom in the whole Clan who could ever mean as much to her as Nightheart did.

*What will the rest of my life be like?* she asked herself. *Will I always be alone?*

Sunbeam padded over to the fresh-kill pile, aware of her Clanmates casting sympathetic looks at her, or even worse, whispering together and then falling silent as she looked at them. Trying to ignore them all, she chose a sparrow, crouching down to take a halfhearted bite. A moment later Berryheart came to sit beside her and pulled out a vole for herself.

"Are you feeling better?" she asked Sunbeam. "A little sleep must have helped you see things more clearly." When Sunbeam didn't respond, she added, "To be honest, I never thought Nightheart was good enough for you, and not just because he was from another Clan. Now you can find a mate who really deserves you—a strong ShadowClan warrior!"

*Are you for real?* Sunbeam thought drearily, staring at her mother. *You want me to start looking for another mate now?* "I don't want a ShadowClan warrior," she snapped.

Berryheart's eyes stretched wide with shock; clearly she

didn't understand her daughter's feelings. "ShadowClan war-riors are the strongest cats by the lake," she asserted. "In fact, I already have some ideas. Maybe you just need to be more open-minded."

Sunbeam winced. With time and rest, her feelings about her mother's opinions had returned to their previous state. She certainly wasn't ready for a ShadowClan mate, and she wished her mother would stop interfering. The brief sympathy between them after Nightheart left had vanished; Sunbeam hadn't expected their relationship to sour again so soon.

"Sunbeam!" To her relief, Lightleap was standing over her, looking from her to her mother as if she understood exactly what Berryheart must be doing. "We were just wondering where you were. Come and eat with us!"

"Sure," Sunbeam agreed, startled but grateful for the excuse. "Sorry, Berryheart," she apologized. "Maybe we can talk later."

She had a brief glimpse of her mother's offended expres-sion before she picked up her barely touched prey and headed across the clearing to join Lightleap and Blazefire. However, once she settled down, Sunbeam immediately started to have regrets. Lightleap and Blazefire were both silent, watching her with almost comically sympathetic expressions. It felt as if they were waiting for her to fall apart.

*Weird . . . The last time I felt like this was when Blazefire broke up with me.* Sunbeam tried to remember what she had felt then, but she couldn't, except that she had been very unhappy. She knew now that her feelings for Blazefire had been no more than a crush. She should have realized that she and Blazefire had next to nothing in common, while Nightheart actually understood her and made her want to be better. And now Blazefire was giving her too much sympathy about losing him. *Life is so strange. . . .*

"You can talk to me, you know," Sunbeam mewed, taking a bite of the sparrow and forcing herself to swallow.

"So . . . how *are* you?" Blazefire asked, his eyes full of concern.

"I've been better," Sunbeam replied. "But maybe we could talk about something else. Anything else? Please?"

Lightleap and Blazefire exchanged a glance, as if Sunbeam had asked for something completely impossible.

"Er . . . okay," Lightleap began. "I'll tell you about when Blazefire and I were on the dawn patrol yesterday. Afterward we went to the warriors' den to take a nap. Blazefire was snoring so loud you would think they could hear him in WindClan! No other cat could get to sleep. So Snaketooth and Pouncestep and I made a plan. They leaped on him, and I yowled, 'Badgers! Badgers in the camp!' You've never seen a cat jump so high!"

Blazefire batted at her with one forepaw. "I'll get you back for that," he mewed affectionately. "Just you wait!"

Sunbeam could see how well Blazefire and Lightleap belonged together. They both had the same bee-brained sense of humor, so they were well suited—just as she felt she was with Nightheart. She couldn't quite laugh at Lightleap's story, but she felt better than she had since Nightheart left.

At that moment, Tigerstar emerged from his den and swarmed up the tree beside it until he could pad out onto the lowest overhanging branch. "Let all cats old enough to catch their own prey join here beneath the Pinebranch for a Clan meeting!" he yowled.

As the Clan assembled, a cold worm of dread stirred in Sunbeam's belly. *Is this about Nightheart? Maybe Tigerstar is going to change the rules about accepting cats from other Clans, because of what Nightheart did.*

Then Sunbeam realized that this didn't have to be about Nightheart. Tigerstar might have an announcement to make about RiverClan, and a possible attack from the other Clans. She felt her heart beginning to thump until she remembered that Bramblestar was still leader of ThunderClan, which meant that the Clans would stay peaceful, for now.

Tigerstar stood tall on his branch, gazing down at his Clan. When they had all found places for themselves, he began to speak.

"Cloverfoot has warned me that a group of cats in River-Clan has begun to plot against us, and against our presence in their territory."

Sunbeam couldn't help glancing at her mother, but Berry-heart was calmly grooming her ears, giving no sign that she knew what the Clan leader was talking about.

*That must be the group that Berryheart and her followers met with,* Sunbeam thought. *The ones led by Splashtail. I wonder if Tigerstar knows that his own warriors are plotting with them.*

"I don't want conflict," Tigerstar went on, "but I feel I

must protect Cloverfoot and the other ShadowClan warriors who are sent there to keep the peace. And it doesn't look as if we can pull out of RiverClan anytime soon." He paused, letting his gaze travel over his Clan in the clearing below. "So I have no choice but to send more ShadowClan warriors to live in RiverClan—full-time. They will sleep in the warriors' den in the RiverClan camp, keep their eyes and ears open, and report anything suspicious back to me."

*RiverClan won't like it,* Sunbeam thought. Either the River-Clan cats would attack the ShadowClan warriors living among them, or the increased ShadowClan presence would change Harestar's or Bramblestar's mind about joining SkyClan in an attack. Either way, Sunbeam knew it couldn't end well.

She shot a glare at her mother. *See what your meddling has done? You wanted to avoid fighting, but you've more likely caused it!*

Berryheart wouldn't meet her gaze; she was looking upset, as if the same thoughts were going through her mind too.

Meanwhile, murmurs of surprise broke out among the listening cats as they glanced at each other, clearly wondering what these new duties would mean.

"The cats I have chosen for this task," Tigerstar went on, "are Flaxfoot, Whorlpelt, Lightleap, and Sunbeam."

Her leader cast a sympathetic glance at Sunbeam as he named her. Sunbeam wondered if he had given her this task on purpose, to take her mind off Nightheart. Maybe Lightleap had even suggested it.

Lightleap was flexing her claws excitedly, her eyes gleaming at the honor of being chosen to return to RiverClan. But the thought of going back to live in their camp made Sunbeam's belly roil.

*We don't belong there.*

Knowing that the RiverClan cats were angry and plotting resistance made it even worse. Until now, the RiverClan cats had been aiming for a peaceful solution. But Sunbeam knew that having more ShadowClan cats in their camp was likely to push them to a breaking point. *My paws are leading me into danger,* she thought. *Yet I agree with the RiverClan cats that ShadowClan shouldn't be in their camp at all. Great StarClan, what a mess!*

She still wondered if she and Nightheart had been right not to tell Tigerstar about what they had overheard Berryheart planning. *What's more likely to keep the peace: telling the Clan leader, or not telling him?* Not telling him, she supposed, but her conscience wasn't easy about it.

*Whatever I decide will be wrong,* she thought with a sigh. *A storm is coming—I can feel it in my fur.*

# CHAPTER 24

*The sun had risen high over* the stone hollow by the time Nightheart and his dawn hunting patrol returned to the camp. Prey had been running well; Nightheart had caught a pigeon and two mice using techniques Sunbeam had taught him. He was feeling pretty good about himself.

"Wow, you *did* learn something in ShadowClan!" Cinderheart exclaimed, looking impressed.

"Yeah, you'll have to teach us those moves." Sorrelstripe added.

Now Nightheart dropped his prey on the fresh-kill pile and chose a mouse for himself. Glancing around, he spotted Bayshine and Finchlight sharing a vole near the bottom of the tumbled rocks, at the edge of a group of senior warriors and elders. He padded over to join them.

"Hi," he began. "Are you—"

Finchlight waved her tail at him. "Shh! We're trying to listen."

With a nod of understanding, Nightheart settled down beside his sister and began to eat his mouse.

In the center of the group, Lionblaze was holding forth,

his head set determinedly and his chest puffed out as if he was certain he was right. "This isn't how things are done," he insisted. "Leaders are meant to lead until the end of their nine lives. Abruptly changing leaders like this, without waiting for the change to happen naturally, will weaken ThunderClan. Don't think the other Clans won't take advantage of us!"

"That's not necessarily true," Birchfall objected mildly. "Bramblestar is stepping down because he feels that he *isn't* the best leader for ThunderClan anymore. So won't having Squirrelflight as leader make us stronger?"

"Just like it made ShadowClan stronger when Rowanstar did the same?" Poppyfrost hissed.

"I've heard stories about Pinestar," Thornclaw put in. "How he gave up the leadership to become a kittypet, long before any of us were kitted. That was outrageous! They say it took ThunderClan a long time to find its paws again after that. . . ."

"This isn't the same." Bramblestar's voice cut through the discussion; Nightheart looked around to see him jumping down from the tumbled rocks, closely followed by Squirrelflight.

The Clan leader padded up to Thornclaw, looking him directly in the face; the golden-brown tabby elder stared back at him, clearly unwilling to take back his words. "I have no plans to become a kittypet," Bramblestar pointed out. "I'll be right here, in the elders' den, ready to give advice to Squirrelflight. But only if she wants it," he added, casting a fond glance over his shoulder at his mate and deputy.

Squirrelflight let out a purr.

Nightheart realized it was moons since he had seen the Clan leader and his deputy so united. It was clear that Bramblestar and Squirrelflight had really talked over the future before they came to a decision. And now they had come to an agreement about how to run the Clan.

*And I for one am glad they did,* Nightheart thought.

"Tonight Squirrelflight and I will go to the Moonpool to talk to StarClan," Bramblestar announced. "We'll see what the spirits of our ancestors have to say about our plans, and we'll act according to their advice. We would never dream of going against StarClan's wishes; all we want is to make ThunderClan as strong as it can be."

"Does that mean we'll be going to war with ShadowClan?" Stormcloud asked. "To make them leave RiverClan? I know Leafstar would like that, and Squirrelflight seemed in favor of it at the last Gathering."

"That will be Squirrelflight's decision to make," Bramblestar replied. "I will support her, whatever she decides."

Stormcloud's question, and the Clan leader's reply, made Nightheart's belly twist in apprehension. He had avoided having to fight his Clanmates, but if they attacked Shadow-Clan, he would find himself forced into battle against the cat he loved.

*How can I do that?* he asked himself, and could find no answer.

He still missed Sunbeam with every breath: her sweet scent and her silky fur, but more than that, her cleverness and courage. It was hard to accept that she wasn't still sleeping beside him. How could he unsheathe his claws against her, or her kin?

*This must be why StarClan didn't allow cats to change Clans for love in the first place,* he mused. *There's such a chance that it will end badly— like for me and Sunbeam.*

"What will you tell the other Clans?" Lionblaze asked.

Before Bramblestar could reply, the meeting was interrupted by Lilyheart, who emerged from the thorn tunnel and bounded across the camp to stand in front of the Clan leader.

"Is there a problem, Lilyheart?" Bramblestar asked.

Lilyheart took a moment to catch her breath. "I was on border patrol and I intercepted this ShadowClan warrior, Sunbeam. She wanted to come to our camp and speak to Nightheart."

While the tabby she-cat was speaking, Nightheart's gaze flew to the camp entrance. His heart soared as he spotted Sunbeam standing at the end of the tunnel, nervously glancing around her. At last she saw him, and her eyes lit up with joy.

Every cat turned to stare at Nightheart. Their indrawn breath sounded as loud as wind in the trees.

Nightheart could not bring himself to care what any cat thought. He leaped to his paws and eagerly took a pace toward Sunbeam. Lilyheart, his former mentor, was giving him an amused, knowing look, her head tilted to one side.

"Okay, Nightheart," Bramblestar meowed, his eyes glimmering with laughter. "Go and see what it's all about."

Nightheart didn't need telling twice. He raced across the camp to Sunbeam's side and led her out into the forest. The discussion started up again as soon as they headed into the thorn tunnel, but as he left the camp behind, Nightheart couldn't make out the words.

He paused in a glade where the ground was covered by brilliant red and gold leaves. Facing Sunbeam, taking her in from her nose to the tip of her tail, he meowed, "I can't believe you're here!"

At the same moment Sunbeam blurted out, "I can't believe I'm here!"

Both cats let our *mrrows* of laughter. Then Nightheart dipped his head toward Sunbeam. "Tell me what's going on," he asked.

"I know this is crazy," Sunbeam began, her voice shaking. "Maybe it's the craziest thing I've ever done. But I love you, and I've realized that you mean more to me than my Clan. I've never thought about a life outside ShadowClan, but now, to be with you, maybe it's time I did."

Nightheart drew in a painful breath. "Really?"

Sunbeam nodded. "I don't know much about Thunder-Clan," she mewed, "but I'm willing to learn. And I'll work as hard as I possibly can to prove myself and to pass my tasks, just so that we can be together."

Nightheart could hardly believe that he was hearing the words he had never dared to long for. At first his heart was so full that he couldn't speak; he buried his nose in Sunbeam's shoulder fur, drinking in her sweet scent, and twined his tail with hers.

"Oh, Sunbeam, I want us to be together so much," he whispered at last.

"Do you think Bramblestar will accept me?" Sunbeam asked. She drew back, and Nightheart could see the anxiety in her eyes.

"Any Clan leader would have bees in their brain if they didn't want a brilliant warrior like you," he replied. "But I have to tell you—there's a good chance that ThunderClan will attack ShadowClan soon. Leafstar wants our support to get ShadowClan out of RiverClan, and if Squirrelflight becomes leader, she's made it pretty clear that she's willing to give it."

Sunbeam frowned, puzzled. "Squirrelflight, leader? Is Bramblestar okay?"

"Bramblestar plans to go to the Moonpool tonight and give the rest of his nine lives back to StarClan. And if everything goes as planned, Squirrelstar will lead ThunderClan by sunrise."

A chill shook Nightheart as he understood fully what the future might hold. It was wonderful that Sunbeam had come to find him, that she was prepared to leave the Clan of her birth to be with him, but now he knew that it wouldn't be as easy as that. He could see sudden panic in Sunbeam's eyes, too. She hadn't seen this coming.

"Could you take part in a battle against ShadowClan?" he asked her. "Your own former Clanmates?"

Sunbeam stared at him, stunned. "I don't know," she admitted in a small voice.

Nightheart's happiness that Sunbeam had come to him in ThunderClan was beginning to fade, driven out by rising anxiety. He tried to tell himself that their love for each other would carry them through all the trouble ahead, but he had believed that when he went to join ShadowClan.

*This is bigger than our feelings,* he realized. *Changes are coming, and any cat could be swept away like leaves in the wind. Oh, StarClan,* Nightheart prayed, *please watch over us and guide our paws!*

## THE BROKEN CODE
- Lost Stars
- The Silent Thaw
- Veil of Shadows
- Darkness Within
- The Place of No Stars
- A Light in the Mist

## A STARLESS CLAN
- River
- Sky
- Shadow

## GRAPHIC NOVELS
- Graystripe's Adventure
- Ravenpaw's Path
- SkyClan and the Stranger
- A Shadow in RiverClan
- Winds of Change
- Exile from ShadowClan

## GUIDES
- Secrets of the Clans
- Cats of the Clans
- Code of the Clans
- Battles of the Clans
- Enter the Clans
- The Ultimate Guide

## NOVELLAS
- The Untold Stories
- Tales from the Clans
- Shadows of the Clans
- Legends of the Clans
- Path of a Warrior
- A Warrior's Spirit
- A Warrior's Choice

## SUPER EDITIONS
- Firestar's Quest
- Bluestar's Prophecy
- SkyClan's Destiny
- Crookedstar's Promise
- Yellowfang's Secret
- Tallstar's Revenge
- Bramblestar's Storm
- Moth Flight's Vision
- Hawkwing's Journey
- Tigerheart's Shadow
- Crowfeather's Trial
- Squirrelflight's Hope
- Graystripe's Vow
- Leopardstar's Honor
- Onestar's Confession

**HARPER**
*An Imprint of HarperCollinsPublishers*

warriorcats.com